Looking for Leticia

Alan Johns

Burninghouse

To Rosalyn

The barbecue

I went to a barbecue today. I don't know why I went, I think
I just needed to get out; I've been spending too long inside
recently. Anyway, yesterday I invested in some khaki shorts
for the occasion (and because I'd be able to make use of
them throughout the summer and, if I avoided putting on
the pounds, in summers to follow), and I also got a four-pack
to bring.

When I turned up the barbecue had got going. I wasn't
surprised; I'd intended to be a tad late. Smoke was billowing
over the fence and I could hear people chattering. I made my
entrance inconspicuously; in fact, I doubt anybody noticed me
at all. In all honesty, I practically tiptoed in, although there was
an old fellow, sitting on a wall in a kind of stupor, perhaps he
raised an eyebrow to me. He certainly raised an eyebrow, no
doubt about that. No idea why though. In any case, I did the
same in response. And then I emerged. Couple of kids running
about with a bat and ball. Groups of adults spread about. Doing
the barbecue, in a sort of splendid isolation, was Ted. Some
people have that air about them; untouchable. Nothing much
would ever go wrong for Ted. The smell of freshly cut grass.
The grass had just been mown. Now where was that guy I
vaguely knew?

Couple of hours later and I'd not managed to have a
conversation. I'd spent most of my time investigating the

hedgerow. It's an interesting matter, feigning interest in some-thing. Take me and the hedgerow for instance. There were certain points during my 'inspection' when I felt something akin to 'interest' in the arrangement of the leaves or some other thing. Then it passed. It passed quite quickly but none-theless, for that fleeting moment, I'd been interested in the hedgerow.

Remember that guy I vaguely knew? I tried to start a conversation with him coming out the toilet. I said, 'Oh hello, how are . . .' but he walked straight on past and down the stairs. I suppose you shouldn't accost a person outside a toilet.

It was a hot day. One woman described it as 'glorious.' Of course it was glorious; Ted could choose days like he could choose shirts. I was drawn to that shirt of his; somehow conservative and wild at the same time. I don't know how he pulls it off. That print, the print of his shirt, should, by rights, look absurd. Not on Ted . . . Funky Ted.

I've heard more than once that barbecues are one of the more hopeful places for singletons. Don't go to the bars or clubs, go to the family occasions, mill about, strike up a conversation. Well, it wasn't working for me. Although I must admit, this wasn't a family occasion, or rather it was, but not for me. I was no relation of anybody there.

I burn easily and I'd forgotten my sun cream, so I found myself hanging about under a big tree not so very far removed from Ted and the barbecue. He'd not moved from that spot. That Ted, he must have an iron bladder. And he knew how to cook. Slowly. He took about an hour over a grill full of sausages. But you *could* tell the difference. His sausages, I'd only managed to lay my hands on one but bloody hell I've never been so excited by a sausage. One man said, 'I've never tasted a sausage as good as this.' He'd said this to Ted's wife,

but I don't think he was placating the woman by compli-
menting her husband. No. You could see it in his eyes; the
sausage had made that man's day.

So I was under the tree, circling the tree actually, so slowly
nobody would suspect I was making circles. I'd been there
nine minutes and made one and three quarter circles.

'Excuse me.'

I froze:

I spun around:

Ted was looking directly at me:

'You mind giving me some help over here, mate?'

I think I nodded, I tried my best in any case, and set off,
on unsure footing, for Ted.

'I need some help with the cooking.'

I was dumbstruck.

'I've been looking about me for an assistant. It'd been a
fruitless search. Then I noticed you. I sized you up. You got
what it takes.'

Still dumbstruck.

'What a bunch, eh? What. A. *Bunch.* Look at them. They're
. . . all over my garden. They're . . . You know what they
remind me of? They're *crawling.* What crawls?' He flipped a
burger. 'Babies. That's what.' He looked me straight in the
eye. 'I recognise you.' He flipped a burger. 'Where you
from?'

I forgot where I was from. 'Various places . . .'

'Citizen of the world. You speak Portuguese?'

'No. I'm afraid not.'

'I used to speak Portuguese once. Of the Brazilian
variety.'

'Oh.' I laughed too loudly. 'Did you forget it?'

'Yes. I forgot it. And it's a source of great agony to me.
Forgetting a whole language. Christ!'

'I'm sorry . . .'

'It's not your fault.' He took a swig from his beer can. 'Is it?'

'No.'

'I was in a coma, see? Woke up in a pretty good mood. Only been under eight days, didn't wake up a wrinkly old man or nothing, and I thought I'd retained everything. Then, couple of weeks later the phone rings, I answer it: gibberish. The bloke on the other end was talking gibberish, or, as it turned out, Portuguese. He was my Brazilian mate I'd known him *seven* years, but . . . Well anyway, we've fallen out of touch. He don't speak English and me, I don't speak Portuguese.'

'You could learn again.' What had I just said?

'You having a laugh, mate?'

'Yes. No. No'

He stared at me. 'Want a beer?'

'Please.'

'You look like a man who likes his beer. You like your beer?' He handed me a beer.

'Sure.'

'Yeah. Sure you do. Sure you do. What do you think of my wife?'

I went into a panic; hopefully it didn't show. 'She's, she, she seems very nice.'

'She certainly thinks a lot of you.'

'She does?'

'Wants you round for dinner. What do you say, fella? Want to come round for dinner?'

'Well, um . . .'

'My wife would appreciate it muchly. As would I.' He gave me an intense look.

'Yes,' I said, in a daze.

'Yes?'

'Yes, I'll come. I want to come.'

'Bravo, there's a good chap. Here, hold these for me, squire.' He handed me the tongs. 'I'll go tell her now. She'll be delighted.'

He stood there for a moment and looked me up and down. 'Absolutely delighted.' He laughed, and then he was off.

I couldn't quite comprehend the situation and, rocked as I was, when I heard his wife howl with delight and saw her give me the double thumbs up, it all seemed quite unreal.

Ted then bundled the delighted and delirious woman up in his arms and rushed into the house with her. I realised that I had been left in charge of the barbecue.

I got a lot more attention while attending to the barbecue. Everybody seemed quite interested in me, probably because Ted had entrusted me with the cooking. My hands were shaking so much I couldn't flip any of the burgers and I was sweating to a worrying degree. My shirt was stuck to my back and there were sweat circles under my arms. Luckily they didn't show up too badly since I was wearing a cream coloured shirt. The smoke kept getting carried this way and that, and every so often it would blow in my face. I really was on edge, and every time I dared to look up it seemed as though the guests were all closing in on me with their empty plates, but the burgers were getting blacker and blacker on one side and still raw on the other. I just could not flip them! One burger I'd almost got over but then it disintegrated. I was getting in a bit of a panic. Every so often I'd hear Ted's wife scream with delight from inside the house. I was getting dazed and confused and all that smoke was making my eyes sting. Then, a man advanced towards the barbecue. I rubbed my eyes; he was the guy I vaguely knew, the one from outside the toilet. He had a great big smile on his face and he reached out his hand and clasped my shoulder. 'I can't believe it.' He hitched up his belt. (I never wear a belt with shorts, that's one of the things I like about my khaki shorts, the elastic waist band). 'I can't believe it. I thought I recognised you.'

'Hello,' I said.

'Having a spot of trouble with the old barbecue, mate?'

I shrugged. What could I say?

'Let me give you a hand.' He took the tongs from me and started flipping burgers. 'Look how black they are,' I heard one man say. 'They're inedible,' said another one of the guests. 'I'm *hun*gry.' A little girl burst into tears. I was pretty ashamed; I'd let Ted down.

'First time cooking outdoors?'

'Huh?' I tuned back into the guy I vaguely knew. 'Oh, I don't remember.'

'Well,' he said. 'Ted obviously saw something he liked, eh? That's good enough for me. Still, two hands are better than one and all that.' He flipped a burger. 'How you been then?'

'Yeah. OK.'

'Hot summer.'

'I bought some khaki shorts yesterday.' What did that mean? I felt very light headed.

'Oh yeah? Got them on have you? They're not bad, them.' He was looking at my shorts, then his eyes glazed over. After a few seconds he looked me straight in the eye. His face seemed more intense somehow and I noticed that he had a, well, a glass eye I suppose. 'Listen,' he said. 'We're old mates, yeah?'

I had met him once and I didn't know his name. 'Yeah,' I said.

'I was thinking.' He looked down at his shoes; they were dazzlingly white, so much so that an ant crawling across his left shoe seemed to take on some sort of special significance. 'I was thinking about maybe we could . . .' He cleared his throat. The barbecue sizzled. 'I heard, I mean I heard you were invited to . . . Ted's wife invited you to dinner didn't she?' He was looking right at me, trembling, in spite of the heat.

'Yes,' I said.

He was trembling, his slightly podgy body set against the backdrop of barbecue smoke, and beyond him were the other guests, who I felt sure were watching us; none of them seemed to be moving and it was absolutely silent.

'We haven't arranged a time yet,' I said.

He didn't respond.

I said, 'It depends when she's free I suppose.' The barbecue was hissing and spitting. 'I mean I'm free all week.'

'So am I,' he said. 'If I'm needed.'

'Right,' I said. 'I think maybe the burgers need . . .'

His mouth twitched. Ted's wife screamed with joy, a sort of delirious ecstasy in her voice. The air was still.

'Some blokes have all the luck,' he said.

'Yeah . . .' I suddenly felt cold, the sun had stopped burning my neck. I looked up at the sky; clouds had gathered. I shivered. A few seconds passed. The guy I vaguely knew was still looking at me and I was feeling pretty uncomfortable now. Black smoke drifted from the barbecue, the burgers were really burning now. What would Ted think? I was in charge of the barbecue after all. The whole afternoon was taking a difficult turn.

'What the fuck is going on here?' Ted stormed into view. 'My burgers have gone to pot. Bloody hell.'

I wanted to explain myself but no words came out. Ted's

7

face was as red as beetroot. He snatched the tongs from the hand of the guy I vaguely knew and flipped a few burgers; they were beyond saving. He flung the tongs to the ground and stood looking at the barbecue, hands on hips. I could hear him breathing in and out. The burgers sizzled on the grill. Ted seemed to stand there for an age. His whole body heaved from his deep breathing. I felt sure that the guests were watching all this unfold, and my stomach was twisted in a knot and sweat was pouring down my forehead and into my eyes. Then Ted turned to me. He waited for me to raise my eyes to him. I could feel my heart racing.

'Who is this clown?' Ted indicated the guy I vaguely knew.

'He was helping with the barbecue,' I said.

'Yeah but what's the bugger's name?'

'I don't know.'

'I'm an old mate of his,' the man I vaguely knew said. He looked pale and nauseous as Ted stood there for a moment, as if processing this information.

Then Ted turned to him. 'You what? An old mate? What are you on about? He don't even know your name! How many mates you got don't know your name? Difficult one to remember is it? Some kind of long, complicated double barrelled affair or something?'

'It's –'

'You've ruined my barbecue, mate. Look at it. It's a mess. What you going to do about it?'

'I could . . . I could go and buy you some more burgers?'

'Them burgers were imported, mate. You know where from? You know where I got them from?'

The guy I vaguely knew shook his head. I felt somehow responsible for his plight.

Ted said, 'Well that's your mission then, son. Find out where I got them. Then go there and bring me back some more.'

'But, the barbecue will be over by the time –'

'You arguing with me?'

'No.'

'Off you go then! Bloody hell!'

The man walked off, the crowd parting to let him out of the garden, his white trainers contrasting sharply with the lush green grass. It was artfully cut, that grass. I bet Ted knew what he was doing with a lawnmower. I felt a hand clapping me on the back.

'You see that?' Ted said. 'Not enough that he's ruined my barbecue, he's having a go at me as well. What's the world coming to, eh?'

I laughed. Ted and I stood facing the guests who were dispersing and getting back into their groups.

'Look at these people,' Ted said. 'I can't fucking *stand* them. Neither can the wife. That's why she's inside. They come here . . . Parasites.'

'Why do you invite them?' I asked.

He stared at me. 'I've got a daughter,' he said. 'Bit younger than you. Love her to death. I'm so fucking proud of her you wouldn't believe it. She should be about come to think of it. When you come round. You'll meet her when you come round for dinner.'

'I'm looking forward to it,' I said. I really was, too.

'I bet you are, you saucy devil.'

'No, I mean –'

'I know what you bloody mean! I was young once. I'll tell you one thing what I didn't do when I was young though, I didn't waste my Saturdays at bloody barbecues. You not got anywhere better to be?'

'Nowhere special.'

'You're a closed book, mate,' he said. 'I like that about you. There's too many dickheads going around they think everybody wants to hear about how they *feel* and blah, blah, blah. Gets on my tits it does.' He sighed and put his arm around me. 'You reckon these pigs have had enough time at the trough?'

'Well, I mean there's no food left.'

'Yep,' Ted said. 'They can fuck off I reckon. Actually, the weather's about to turn. Look up there, mate.'

I looked up and saw that the clouds had got very dark indeed.

'Changes in a flash, don't it?' Ted said. 'I blame global warming. Causes extreme weather conditions.' It started to rain. 'And there we go. Listen, I've got to go and do something for the wife. You mind putting the barbecue stuff away and sending these clowns packing?'

Before I could answer, Ted said, 'OK, cheers, pal,' and jogged off to the house and I was alone by the barbecue. I felt ill-suited to the task of sending people home; I didn't know anybody there. But what could I do?

I cupped my hands to my mouth. 'Guys.' I couldn't get any power into my voice. 'Guys, I think it's about time to be headed home. That's about it, guys.'

I looked down at the floor but I could hear the voices of the other guests. 'Who the fuck is he?' 'Who does he think he is?' 'Wanker.'

Then the rain got harder and all the guests ran in. I went and took cover under the tree. I was looking forward to having dinner at Ted's house. And I was especially looking forward to meeting his daughter.

Putting the barbecue stuff away proved a difficult task. The rain just got harder and harder and I was standing there under the tree with no idea *where* to put the stuff. I scanned the garden for a shed or some other storage unit, but there was nothing in view. It was a big garden though, and my view was not panoramic. I thought back to earlier, when I was on my wanders, had I seen a storage unit of some sort? I might have done but my observational skills leave a lot to be desired. I'd have to venture out from under the tree and scout around but the rain really was hard. Pretty much torrential. Making puddles where the grass couldn't absorb it all at once and the pond was about to overflow. Perhaps I should wait for it to stop. This kind of shower never lasts for long. Then I heard a clap of thunder. That was that. With thunder comes lightning and I was standing under a tree.

I ran out from under the tree and looked around me. By the time I'd done that I was already soaked. I ran down to the bottom of the garden where the hedgerow was. Looked left. Looked right. And there it was, the storage unit. I couldn't believe my luck. How had I missed it though? I must have spent hours by that hedgerow. But there was the storage unit. It did have a layer of moss over it I suppose, sort of blended into the background. I dashed back to the barbecue and my clothes were heavy with water and my hair plastered over my face. Damn it. I have no idea how to disassemble a barbecue. I was pretty sure that barbecues did disassemble though. I had a go, pulling at various parts of the thing, mostly the legs, but nothing happened and I could hardly see with all the rain pouring down my face and into my eyes. I picked the thing up as one piece and carried it over to the storage unit, the door of which was open, and dumped it in there. I was just about to leave the storage unit when I realised I was out of the rain in there. Perhaps I should hang about, and I like that smell in here, the smell of woodcuttings. Ted must be a man with great practical skills. I wondered did he construct the storage unit? I shivered. It was pouring outside but I was so wet already it hardly mattered if I went back out there. So off I went to fetch the bag of charcoal.

Walking to the house, the rain eased off but I was soaked through. I squeezed the bottom of my T shirt and wrung an incredible amount of water out of the material. I couldn't go inside like this. I'd just have to head home. Unfortunately I didn't have an umbrella. It had been such a lovely morning that I walked out of the house admiring the clear blue sky, wearing my new khaki shorts, and the last thing on my mind was that it would rain. I took one last look at the garden before heading off down the side of the house, and it was with a wistful pang that I did so; the garden had been so lively and busy so little time ago and I had been part of that, and now it was empty and you'd scarcely have known anything had happened. Particularly since I'd put the barbecue stuff away.

On my way down the side passage I came to an open door. It led into a room with a washing machine and dryer in, but my shoes were covered in mud and I was dripping wet so there was no chance of me going in, not even into a relatively functional room like that. I did want to talk to Ted though. We hadn't finalised dinner arrangements after all. And I wasn't certain that he had my telephone number. I called 'hello' a few times but there was no sign anybody was about. Oh well. I can always come back and post my number through the door. Just in case they don't have it. Satisfied with my fall back plan, and with the rain having all but cleared and the sun out again, I felt happy and set off for a walk home in the sun and the chance to toss the details of a lively day, and the potential of a delightful dinner, around in my head. However, it was not to be because just as I emerged from the side passage a man parked at the far end of the driveway got out of his car and walked over to me.

'Hello.'

'Hello,' I said.

'Jesus Christ,' he said. 'You're soaked.'

'Yeah.'

'Why didn't you run for cover, you lunatic?'

'I was putting the barbecue away.'

He looked at me and chuckled. 'Doug.' He offered me his hand

I shook it and he held on for a long time; we were still shaking hands a good while after I'd told him my name was Sam.

Finally he let go. 'Got any plans, Sam?'

'You mean right now?'

'Yep, right now.'

'I was going to go home and change clothes.'

'My wife and I wondered if you fancied some supper. You know, French bread and all that jazz. What do you say, eh?'

I wasn't doing anything else, that was true, and the barbecue had whetted my appetite for a bit of chit chat and general socialising. But my clothes were soaked. 'It's just my clothes. They're soaked.'

'You're not wrong. Hmmm. I'll tell you what, how about this, what we'll do is we'll stop by your place, you run in and change, and then we head off to mine for a well earned bite to eat. Sound OK? You don't live too far away do you?'

'No,' I said. 'Not really.' He was very enthusiastic and friendly, infectiously so; I felt like bursting out into happy laughter standing there with him. But I did wonder was he a little drunk? 'I wouldn't want to put you out, or your family.'

'Oh nonsense!' He punched me on the arm. 'It's settled

then. Now you're a tall chap so we'll have you in front, yes? We'll put Celina in the back. Suits me, sitting there fiddling with my radio settings, I'll be glad to have rid of her for a while, much as I love her of course.'

Before I could protest he was off and he had a word with his wife and she was out of the car, but she seemed happy enough, waving at me before she got in the back. So I set off for their car, my feet squelching in my shoes.

What a lovely family. Doug's wife was charming, so much so that I was almost overwhelmed. And their little boy. He was delightful and lively and very clever for his age I thought, anxious to show off his maths skills. The car journey went quickly, the radio unnecessary because Doug and Celina were constantly talking, a lovely couple, with little James occasionally chipping in. And they didn't live too far away from me at all, if this goes well, perhaps I can be a regular visitor. We pulled into Doug's driveway.

'Everybody out,' he said.

We bundled out of the car and I stood in the driveway and admired the incredible evening sky, now with shades of purple. I realised that Celina was standing next to me. I could hear her breathing but she said nothing.

'It's a magnificent sky,' I said.

She didn't reply and I looked at her. The woman was crying. Looking at the sky and crying. What a woman. What a sensitive woman. What a sensitive, wonderful woman. I was filled with emotion, then James was hugging at my leg and I laughed and walked all the way to the house with him attached to my leg.

Just as soon as I was shown into the kitchen they all went off somewhere or other and I was left alone. It was a big kitchen with a breakfast table in it, and all the food was already laid out, covered with cling film. Perhaps they'd called ahead about supper, but who took the call? Who else was in the house? I felt a bit uncomfortable, alone in a house belonging to people who an hour or so ago I'd never met, and with the possibility of there being another resident about who I might run into and who would wonder what on earth I was doing there. With this on my mind I paced up and down the kitchen. Even the sight of the evening sky through the window couldn't hold my attention for long. Added to this restlessness, I was absolutely starving. And the food was right there. After a while I'd convinced myself that nobody would know if anything was missing. The food wasn't carefully arranged or anything. But what if I was caught in the act? And so, the next twenty minutes dragged by as I paced around, hungry and restless and wondering where everybody went.

Then, with twenty two minutes gone, I sensed that somebody was in the doorway. I stopped pacing and turned. There was somebody at the doorway. A young woman, maybe only eighteen or nineteen, with a mesmerizing face, who was sitting in a wheelchair and gazing at me. Or rather through me. Her eyes seemed to have no focus. It crossed my mind that perhaps she was a simpleton or something, but it didn't seem to fit. In any event, I didn't know what to say to her, and the longer it went on, the more uncomfortable I became. Then, just I was about to say hello, Celina appeared in the doorway and placed her hand on the girl's shoulder.

'I see you two have met,' Celina said. I offered only a timid smile, and Celina crouched down beside the girl. 'Have you said hello to Sam, Alice?'

Alice said nothing, and as Celina crouched there in silence, I thought that she would start crying again.

But she didn't, and stood up. 'The food. Sam, you haven't touched it. You should have just gone ahead. You didn't have to wait around. Oh, I am sorry. But do help yourself, for God's sake do help yourself.' She started stripping the cling film off everything and by the end she had a big ball of the stuff in her hand, and she flung it in the bin. I waited until I was sure that she had finished, then stepped toward the food.

Celina blocked my path. 'You just go and sit down. I'll fix you something.' She paused, distracted. 'Is there anything here you don't like?'

'Everything looks great.' I somehow felt that Alice would find this remark contemptible, but I didn't look at her to find out.

'Why don't you sit down and relax then? I'll bring your food over.'

I went and sat down at the table. Alice's silence was definitely on Celina's mind. No doubt she was a woman of great sensitivity. The way she'd reacted to that sky. I wish I could react to nature like that. But of course that might have it's flipside, feeling everything so deeply. While I was thinking about this, much to my surprise, Alice wheeled her way up to the table, right next to me. We sat there in silence while Celina prepared the food. There was tension in the air and I'd actually lost my appetite.

Celina brought my supper over to the table. 'I just threw a bit of everything together. I hope it's OK.'

'Looks delicious,' I said.

Alice sniggered and I felt a hot flush as the blood rushed to my face.

Celina was crying now, and for some reason I, too, felt the pressure of tears against the back of my eyes, but I managed to hold them back, squeezing my hands into fists and concentrating hard on the task.

'Where is Doug?' Celina said. 'This is absolutely ridiculous. It's just so rude. You start, Sam. Please. I'll go and get him.' She left the kitchen.

And then, silence. Just Alice and me. My face and ears burned and tension squeezed my muscles and I ached all over and was having trouble breathing. Calm down, I told myself. Calm down. But Alice sitting there so close had an intense affect on me and I just couldn't shake it off.

Then she said, 'You going to eat that, or what?'

I gained some relief from the fact that she'd finally spoken, and nodded, then put some slices of cheese onto my French bread and took a bite. My motions were slow and deliberate, my muscles still feeling delicate from all the tension. I chewed at the same deliberate pace; the bread was soft and fresh but in the circumstances I wasn't really able to enjoy it.

'Who are you?'

I swallowed my food. 'I'm Sam.'

'Yeah, I know *that* but, like, who *are* you?'

'I don't know,' I said. 'I mean, what do you want me to say?'

'Why are you here?'

'Your . . . Doug and Celina invited me.'

'So that's what they do now, huh? Just, like, invite total strangers round and stuff? I mean I'm *vulnerable*, Sam. I'm, like, completely defenceless. And then they leave me in the kitchen with you. It's wrong on so many levels.'

'I suppose they're trusting people,' I said.

'I am disabled, Sam. They can't afford to be trusting.' She took a little sausage from my plate and ate it. 'And *please* don't go around being, like, this admirer or something. Of Doug and Celina. I mean look at this food. It's just shit out of a packet.'

I didn't say anything.

17

'Are you shy?' she said.

'I don't know. I mean, a little bit maybe.'

She hovered her hand in front of me. 'Feel my hand.'

I touched the top of her hand.

'Cold, huh?'

'Yes.'

Perhaps it was because she was so direct, but I felt an unusual degree of intimacy between us. It was like each of us had taken on a sort of emotional transparency as regards the other. Or maybe it was just that I'd touched her.

'Other times I'm absolutely boiling,' she said. 'That's usually when I'm in bed and I'm freezing and shivering but my skin is burning up. That happens to me loads. Most nights I guess. And then Celina she comes in with her thermometer and I throw it back in her face and I'm like, "Go. Away." What can a thermometer tell her? Huh? It tells her about I'm sick. Of *course* I'm sick. Do I look healthy to you, huh?'

'She just cares I suppose.'

'Are you one of those people that never says anything bad about anyone? Because those people usually just have all that stuff bottled up. That's why you get serial killers and stuff.'

I was pretty upset by this remark but she changed the subject as though it was nothing. 'I used to play tennis and have these legs I was so proud of,' she said. 'I used to love my legs. Now they're just pale sticks.'

'Will you ever get better?' I asked.

She looked at me and laughed. 'You're a nice guy,' she said. 'Would you do anything I wanted you to do?'

'Anything at all?'

'Yeah. Like, I say, "I'm going to ask you to do something for me but you have to say yes or no before you know what it is. And after that, like, you can't go back on your decision. Would you say yes?'

'I mean, if I didn't know what it was, I mean, I suppose I'd say no. Anybody would.'

She looked at me like I was a pile of shit. 'Loser.'

What had I done? I mean I'd obviously have been lying saying anything else. My face flushed red.

Doug came in, in a bit of a fluster. 'I'm really sorry, Sam. Work stuff and the guy on the other end, he's one of those you just can't get him off the line. Celina gave me a bit of a talking to. She'll be down in a minute.' He caught his breath. 'Aha. I see you've met Alice. But the question is *which* Alice? Eh? Moody little tyke that she is. Depends what side of the bed she gets out of. I must admit, some days I just stay out of her way. Probably for the best, eh, sweetie?'

Alice stared at him for a moment. Then she started rocking her wheelchair left and right.

'Now, Alice. Now come on.' Doug looked anxious.

She rocked the chair harder, and it leaned over further on each side. Her teeth were gritted and her cheeks red. What on earth was she doing? If she rocked much harder she'd topple over. Should I intervene? Doug kept touching his face and running his hand over his head, nervous but staying back. She was rocking the chair violently now. She teetered over onto her left wheel, then her right, nearly falling both times. Then, just as Celina walked in, the wheelchair toppled and hit the floor with a crash, and Alice was knocked out of the seat with the impact of the fall. She was motionless.

Celina turned to Doug. 'What did you say to her?'

'Nothing. That's how it is with her. Sam will tell you, won't you, Sam? I didn't say anything, right?'

I didn't feel it was my place to answer, and sort of shrugged. Then Alice started moving, sliding across the floor. It seemed that she still had some power in her arms. She got a few metres, then stopped and caught her breath.

Celina was in anguish, it was obvious. But she was trying her best to hold herself together. What a sensitive woman. I really felt for her.

'Alice, *why?*' she said. 'You know how easily you bruise. When I think about the bruises you had last time.'

'I like bruises,' Alice said.

Celina took a deep breath, she looked so fragile. 'You like bruises.' She paused. 'You like bruises. I'm doing my best, Alice. I'm doing my best to establish psychological safety fences for you like the psychiatrist was saying about. But you have to . . . I mean, now you're saying you like bruising yourself, and then what? Where does it lead? You cut a vein and . . . Alice, please. We love you so much. Alice?' She looked down at Alice who wouldn't meet her eyes. 'Alice. Alice! Answer me! I'm talking to you!' Celina burst into tears and put her face against Doug's chest. I thought that perhaps this was the moment for me to go, but as much as this was no place for me to be, with Celina in tears it was no time to say goodbye either. So I sat there, waiting for my chance.

Celina lifted her face from Doug's chest. 'Alice, I love you. I do love you so much. It's completely ridiculous how much I love you. I wish you knew that. I do wish you knew that.'

'I know you do, Mum. It's just that I'm dying.' Alice's tone was flat.

Doug cleared his throat. 'I thought we'd banned that word.'

'*You* banned that word.'

There was a pause which seemed somehow to release some of the tension in the air. I looked at Alice on the floor and felt once again that connection I'd established with her. I'd love to see her again. I didn't live far away after all. How long did she have left?

'Let's get you up.' Doug bent down to Alice.

'No,' Alice said. 'I want Sam to do it.'

Doug thought for a moment. 'Fair enough, fair enough. Sam, it's your honour, mate.' Doug righted the chair.

I had an attack of nerves. 'What do I do?'

'Just pick her up and bung her in the chair.'

'. . . OK.' As I crouched down I was worried about the logistics of the thing, but how to do it came pretty naturally to me; I placed one arm under her legs, the other under her back, then sort of turned her, and that was that, mission accomplished; she was in the chair.

Alice yawned. 'I'm going for a nap.'

'OK, sweetie,' Doug said.

'I get tired a lot,' Alice told me.

'Oh right.'

'Will Sam be coming back?'

'Would you like him to?' Celina asked.

'Yeah, sure.' Alice wheeled herself away.

A few moments passed, then Celina let out a huge sigh. 'My goodness I don't know how much more of this I can take.'

Doug rubbed his wife's back. Then, just as I was about to tell them I should get going, he said, 'Sam, mate, now might be a good time for us to have a chat.' He walked over to the breakfast table, shepherding Celina along with him, and they both sat down opposite me. A while passed before anybody said anything, then Doug asked, 'Why do you think we invited you here?'

'I don't know.' I felt disappointed by the fact of his having asked the question. Did there have to be a *why*? I was just happy being invited.

'We have an ulterior motive I'm afraid,' Celina said.

'Not that you're not a great guy,' Doug said. 'You are.'

21

'And Alice has taken a real shine to you,' Celina said. 'I mean, I would absolutely love to have you back over again.'

'We both would,' Doug paused. 'Nonetheless, as Celina mentioned, we have got an ulterior motive. I'm sorry, mate, but we're at the end of our tether and that's the truth of it. And we *would* love to have you over again. It would be spot on if we could arrange that. And next time we'll have something proper for you. Cooked even.' He chuckled, then his face went serious almost immediately. 'Look, it's about Ted, OK. I mean, I heard you talking to him and from what I understand you've got an invite, dinner round his place.'

'Well, sort of . . .'

'Help us.' He seemed sort of desperate. Celina was looking down at her hands.

'I'll do what I can,' I said.

'Show him the photos,' Celina said. 'You know, the ones from our holiday.'

'Good idea, love.' Doug stood up. 'Back in a tic.'

He went out of the room. Celina put her hand on mine. 'I know how this must seem to you, Sam. But it's amazing what stress can do, that's all I can say. And when you've been under as much stress as we have for as long as we have, you end up praying for a miracle. And then you come along, and maybe we've got our miracle after all.'

'I hope I can help.' And I really did. There was something wonderful about their emotional openness, all of them. It was something I needed in my life.

Doug returned with a photo album. 'These what I'm going to show you, they're from when we went to South America with Ted and his family.' He flipped through the pages. 'Here we go.' He opened the album up on the table. There were pictures of Doug, Celina, Ted and his wife pictured in various combinations. Little James was in one picture, even littler. Doug turned the page. Somebody new appeared in a couple of the photos. It took me a few moments to realise that it was Alice. She was a couple of years younger, but most of all she was healthy, tanned, and not in a wheelchair. And she did indeed have lovely legs. It really was a shock how different she was. And she was as happy as the rest of them. They all seemed pretty happy. Doug turned the page again. A new person appeared. Something came over me when I saw her. I couldn't say what, but whatever it was affected me deeply. My stomach felt weightless, as though I was falling and I was buzzing all over, and I felt this nameless emotion consuming me physically and, well, spiritually I suppose.

'Who is that?' I said, pointing to the person.

'That's Ted's daughter,' Doug said.

'But . . .'

'I know, I know.'

'But she's black.'

'I know.'

'Is she, is she adopted?'

'Nope,' he said. 'Don't think so.'

'Her mother?'

'Ted's wife,' Doug said. 'Just one of those one in a million things I suppose. It never got mentioned to be honest.'

'She's such a lovely girl,' Celina said. 'She and Alice used to get on like a house on fire. Even if Leticia is that few years older. Alice would love to see her. She hasn't said anything but I know she would.'

'That's when she got ill,' Doug said. 'Somewhere in South America. Caught some virus. Doctors can't tell us what she's got. Some sort of mystery illness. She wasn't bitten or anything. Only thing we know for sure, she's getting weaker by the day. She's not joking about when she says she's dying. At the rate she's going it won't take long either. Months maybe. The doctors agree about that, they just can't do anything.'

'We tried alternative medicine, too.'

'Fuck of a lot of good that did.' Doug said. 'Do you remember? Just gave her a rash. That's all she needs, isn't it? On top of everything else. Load of old bollocks that is.' He looked down at the photos. Doug didn't seem the sort to lose his temper, perhaps he was a little embarrassed now. I really wanted to help him and Celina, but it wasn't clear what they wanted from me.

'Um, well, if there's anything I can do to help you then . . .'

Doug closed the photo album. 'You've seen us. We're under strain. There's a lot of love in this family. A *lot* of love. There really is.' He took hold of Celina's hand. 'But we're under strain. It's since South America. Alice got ill but then there was other stuff. Stuff between . . . Stuff between me and Ted, OK. And since then we've been ostracized. I mean we were at the barbecue and all the rest of it, but the fact is, since South America to all intents and purposes we've been ostracized. Ted won't talk to us. Won't take my calls. And we just feel, it's hard to explain, we just feel that if we could just have the chance to sit down with Ted, sort all this stuff out. We just feel like if we were able to, you know, reconnect with Ted and his lot, things might get better for us again. I don't suppose that makes much sense to you but that doesn't really matter. All that matters is you agree to this one thing. This one thing which is just put a good word in for us. That's all. When you go round for dinner, just tell him what you've seen, OK? That we love each other, Celina and me. What we've got on our plate with Alice. How much we'd love to see Leticia.'

'Such a beautiful girl,' Celina said.

'Yeah,' Doug said. 'Yeah, of course. Would you help us, Sam? Would you? I mean I'm right, aren't I? All that stuff about us being a loving family. We really need this, mate.'

'We need to reconcile or . . .' Celina's voice cut out.

'We need this. If we could just see him again. I mean you saw the photos. Didn't that look like a proper holiday? A proper good holiday. All the sights and that. Those were the days. If it could just be like that again. Or even just go round for dinner once in a while.'

'Then everything might be alright.' Celina's eyes were tearing.

I wasn't sure I fully understood, but I wanted to help any way that I could. Perhaps my understanding was somewhat impaired by the fact that I couldn't get Ted's daughter, Leticia, *Leticia*, I love that name, I couldn't get her out of my head, and my eyes were burning a hole in the photo album. I was desperate to fling it open and take another look at her. I tried to focus. It seemed that some incident with Ted had affected Doug and Celina badly, and that South America was important. So I told them what Ted had said to me about knowing Portuguese, and going into a coma, forgetting the whole language and losing touch with his Brazilian friend.

'This is what I need to talk to him about,' Doug said. 'Some of it anyway. I don't know if he really thinks that's the truth or not.'

'What is the truth?'

'Don't worry about that,' he said. 'You're already doing too much. I don't want to drag you any deeper into this.'

'It's OK,' I said. 'I'm interested.'

'Really, Sam,' Celina said. 'I think Doug's right about this. And it is not often I say that, that's for sure.'

They both smiled.

'Watch it,' Doug said.

There was a pause. I did want to know the truth, but it was clear they didn't want me to know. It must be private. I glanced at the photo album again. I wondered if there was any way I could take a picture of Leticia home. Any viable excuse I could give. I couldn't think of one.

'So, will you help us, Sam?' Celina said.

'Any way I can,' I said. 'If you just, I mean, I'm not exactly sure what I can do.'

'What I said,' Doug said. 'All about us, Alice. Put a good word in basically. Recommend that he might like to contact us and imply that we would be amenable to any such contact.'

'OK,' I said. 'But I don't know when dinner is. In fact, I'm not even sure if Ted has my phone number. I was going to post it through his door tomorrow, just to be sure.'

'Great idea,' Doug said. 'Except don't wait 'til tomorrow. Let's do it tonight.' He got out of his seat. 'I'll give you a lift over there.'

'It makes sense,' Celina said. 'Then you won't have to worry about it tomorrow.'

I could tell Celina was very keen for me to take Doug's offer. And it did make sense. But something in the back of my mind was telling me that I was being rushed, that I'd rather do it in my own time. I'd planned on a walk tomorrow anyway. But I ended up buckling under the pressure and then I was out of the house and in Doug's car before I was able to come up with some reason for why I needed to take a picture of Leticia with me.

Doug and I scarcely said a word to one another in the car. It wasn't uncomfortable though. We just listened to the radio. And I sat back and relaxed, tired after all that had gone on but pleasantly so. I was holding an envelope in my hand which had my phone number in; Celina had ran off to give me an envelope while Doug was getting the car out. I really was out of the house before I knew it. I would have liked to have said goodbye to Alice. But then she had gone to bed I suppose. I love car journeys when the road is clear and the car is in constant motion, especially at night. I like to close my eyes and feel the reverberations of the car against the road going through my body. There's something about driving at night. I don't drive though, but that suits me. Otherwise I'd have to keep my eyes open and I wouldn't be able to soak everything up.

I opened my eyes and recognized the road that we were on. The next road we turned onto was Ted's and Doug stopped outside the house, not going up the driveway.

'I think it's best I don't go any further, mate,' he said. 'It's alright, I'll wait for you here.'

'OK.' I got out of the car and walked up the driveway. The light was on in the front room and I realised that whoever was in there may well see me walking towards the house. The idea of getting seen disturbed me somehow. I'd only left the barbecue a couple of hours ago after all. I quickened my pace and got to the door and opened the letterbox as quietly as I could, and posted the envelope. Then, just as I turned to go back to the car, I heard the door open. I froze for a moment, then realised I had no choice but to turn around.

Ted was standing in the doorway. 'Hello, mate. What are you doing back so soon?'

Before I could answer, the sound of Doug's car screeching away filled the air.

'Was he with you?' Ted asked.

'No.'

Ted looked up and down the road. 'Bastards.' He paused.

'Lovely night, eh? It's fucking boiling inside, but out here, just right. I was thinking of going for a walk as it goes. Breath of fresh air. You up for it?'

'Um, OK.'

Ted turned back and shouted into the house, 'Babe, I'm off for a walk.'

His wife said something I didn't make out.

'You'll be fine. They ain't come by now, they ain't coming.'

She said something else.

'Yeah, babe, no problem.' He closed the door behind him. 'Women, eh?'

I chuckled.

'You got a girlfriend, Sam?'

'No.'

'Get one,' he said. 'People got this impression of me, reckon I'm some big womaniser. Truth about me, I met Ellie I was twenty years old. She was the third woman I'd fucked. And the last. I'm proud of that. It arouses me, too. Fires my loins.' We were walking down the road now. It was a clear night and you could see the stars. 'What a night, eh?'

'It's great,' I said.

'I love the outdoors. Get claustrophobic I'm indoors too long.' He sighed, and went quiet for a few moments. 'Hassles at work,' he said. 'Stressful job I've got. That's what we was talking about before you came round, me and Ellie.'

'What do you do?'

'I'm in business.'

We spent the next ten minutes strolling along in the quiet. I felt under no pressure to say anything. Ted was a man with whom you could share a comfortable silence. I just enjoyed the freshness of the air and tried to find patterns in the arrangement of the stars.

Then Ted said, 'Ellie's got herself worried about something.'

'Is it anything serious?'

'She thinks it is. Her basic problem is ignorance. I don't mean that unkindly but she rushes to conclusions. Don't think things out that woman. Don't wait to assemble all the facts. And I'll have her saying to me, "well, what are the facts?" I tell her I don't know all the facts yet. Gets her even more wound up. Vicious circle.'

I had to admire Ted. Whatever his problems were, it was obvious he'd always deal with them in a calm and considered manner. He'd just go out for a walk for instance, like he had tonight.

We walked along quietly for a few more minutes, then Ted said, 'I'm glad you popped over as it goes. Ellie realised earlier, we don't have your number.'

'That's why I came round,' I said. 'I posted an envelope through your door. It's got my number on it.'

'Good thinking, mate.' He was quiet for a few moments. 'Why didn't you just knock?'

'It was late,' I said. 'I didn't want to impose.'

'Fuck that,' he said. 'Don't confuse timidity with politeness. One lesson I've learned, don't be a pleaser. You want respect, show you've got it for yourself. Fight your corner.'

It reminded me of something Alice had said, about not showing so much admiration for Doug and Celina. Coming from her I found it a little embarrassing. Coming from Ted I took it to heart. His advice had *gravitas*. I would try and find the steel within myself.

Ted stopped at the end of the road. 'You want to turn back the way we came or this way takes us round in a circle. It's about half as far again.'

I thought about it. 'Let's go round in a circle.' My tone was clear and definite.

'Right you are.'

We continued on our walk.

When Ted asked me to come in, I almost declined. We'd had a very pleasant walk and I wanted to leave on a high note. I was worried that if we went into the house the easiness between us would fade and I would leave under a cloud; maybe they wouldn't even invite me to dinner. In the end though, I thought it would be rude to refuse. I could hardly tell Ted my real reason for not wanting to come in and I couldn't think of anything else to say.

I needn't have worried though. Within minutes of us sitting down in the front room Ted was fast asleep. There was no sign of his wife. I looked around the room. On a table in the corner was a small framed portrait photo of Leticia. I walked over and picked it up. Again the nameless emotion came over me and a shudder even went through me. Perhaps if Ted hadn't convinced me that I needed more steel, more resolve, I would never have done what I did next. What I did next was put the photo in my back pocket and walk out of the house and all the way home with it.

Two Policemen Come Round

I woke up in a sweat. I really felt bad, like my dream was a monster stretching its hand out into the waking world and groping for me. The whiff of a threat. The mornings haven't been good to me lately. I tend to spend them lying in bed feeling somewhat feverish. Not that it affects my mood that much; if anything I'm rather joyful in the morning. Sometimes if I don't have to get up I'll be lying there in my bed having a laugh about this, that or the other. If anybody were to walk in on me they'd probably think I was mad as a hatter. But I live alone so there's no danger of that. I always keep a pair of flip flops beside my bed since the floor is a bit dusty and the dust sticks to my feet, and I'm not keen on the feeling of granules rubbing against my body. I actually suffer from what you might say was a rash or some sort of nervous aggravation. It only comes out at night. When I'm lying there I'll be scratching myself all over and once I've scratched one bit another bit will start itching. It really keeps me awake some nights. Hours I'll spend scratching. Anyway, the granules get onto my feet and my feet get into my bed and the trouble starts from there.

I slipped into my flip flops and stood up to my full height, shoulders back, head erect. I cast my eyes down at my body. I'm in decent shape. I'm no bodybuilder but there's not much fat on me. I'm OK. I headed for the shower. I took a lot of pleasure in massaging my head when applying the shampoo. I love massaging my head, it really gets me going and ready for the day ahead. Not that I had anything planned but I wasn't going to just sit about either. In fact, I was going to go for a walk, nowhere in particular, I just had a walk planned. The sun was out, or at least it had been yesterday, so why not? I had nothing else to do. And anyway, I had some thinking to catch up on. Ted and his wife had invited me to dinner. I mean they hadn't phoned me to confirm yet. Of course not. But I'd have to be ready when the invitation came. I'd have to be mentally and physically prepared. I'd need a present for one thing.

I was really looking forward to the dinner. I usually eat on my own and I find it reduces my enjoyment of the food, which is a bit of a shame. Once upon a time I used to be a great fan of food, but that was a long time ago, food hadn't really done much for me for as long as I could remember. If I had some company, it might make all the difference. Plus, I'd heard Ted's wife was something special in the kitchen, really good. Almost comparable to Ted himself on the barbecue. If that was true, I was in for a treat and a half.

I dried myself off thoroughly. This was important because recently I've found that things stick to me if I walk around naked and wet for too long. I'll find fluff and all the rest of it attached to my skin. Then it takes forever to get off. So I take the preventative approach, which works for me.

I picked up my khaki shorts and smelt them, the scent of barbecue smoke was still quite strong, but I reasoned that that would fade away in the fresh air and put them on. Then, just as I was about to put my socks on, I remembered about Ted's daughter. The whole of yesterday rushed back to me. I mean I'd been in a good mood since I'd woken up (what a day, if only every day could be so, I don't know, vibrant) but now I was really buzzing, an avalanche of vivid images all falling on me at once. So much had happened. And wow. Leticia. I had a tremendous feeling of lightness, like gravity couldn't hold me down. Gravity, you're no match for me! I shook my fist and had a chuckle. Then: Oh shit. An unpleasant feeling of realisation descended on me. I stood there chewing my knuckles. Maybe I'd dreamt it? No, I really had stolen a family photo from Ted's living room.

There was a knock at the door. Bloody hell, it's Ted, come about the photo. I looked around my room, like I was expecting to find a secret exit or something. How about the window? You're on the top floor. More knocking. Ignore it, he'll go away. Come to think of it, how does he know where I live? A third knock, much harder this time. 'Open up.'

I stood there, completely still. My mind had gone blank.

'This is the police. Open up.'

Huh? In a bit of a daze, my legs unsteady, I walked over to the door and opened up. Two men walked straight in, one in a police uniform, the other in a suit.

The one in a suit gazed around the room. 'DCI Campbell.' He showed me his ID, not looking at me. 'That's Ben.' He indicated the uniformed officer. 'We're investigating a missing person's case, possible links with organized crime slash homicide slash people trafficking. You wouldn't know anything about that, would you?'

'No.'

'Would you mind if Ben took a look around, he won't be long, just a look around, a quick look around.' The DCI spoke quickly and looked in ill health.

'OK,' I said.

Ben went to have a look around.

The DCI took out a handkerchief and wiped his face. 'It's

a furnace in here, I mean, Christ, man, it's hot, how do you live in here with it being so hot?'

'I'm used to it I suppose,' I said. 'I mean it's hot outside.'

'It's a fucking furnace in here though.' The DCI fell into my armchair, took his jacket off and flung it to the floor, and sat there with his eyes closed and pinching the bridge of his nose. I just sort of stood there, in limbo. The DCI didn't look at all well. I wondered should I offer him an aspirin or something? But really he looked in need of prescription drugs.

Ben came in. 'Sir.'

The DCI didn't move.

'Sir.'

The DCI came to with a jolt. 'What? What?'

'I found this, sir.' He handed something to DCI Campbell. It was the picture of Leticia. Oh shit. My body went weak and floppy and I stumbled back against the wall. What have I done?

DCI Campbell stared at the photo. He stood up, then held the small of his back and winced with pain, before taking a few steps towards me. He coughed. 'Where did you get this?'

I couldn't get any words out. I was in a real haze.

'I said where did you get this because the reason is I want to know where did you get this?'

'I . . . Ted's house.'

'Yeah. You've been keeping some interesting company recently, we were keeping our eye on you yesterday, very interesting it was. You had yourself quite a Saturday afternoon'

'I just . . . went to a barbecue.' I took a few deep breaths. 'I took the picture from Ted's house last night. I don't know, I just, she had some sort of . . . I liked the picture.' Taking the picture seemed absolutely nuts to me now. What was I thinking?

'This girl's missing,' Ben said.

'Ben.' The DCI coughed. 'I'm burning up. Would you fish around in the freezer, see if you can find any ice cream because I'm burning up.'

'You got any ice cream?' Ben asked me.

'Yes,' I said. 'In the freezer.'

'Really? I was going to look in the oven.'

'Just go will you?' the DCI said.

Ben disappeared.

The DCI beckoned me closer; I took a step towards him. He cupped his hand to my ear and said in a whisper, 'That guy, he's paid off, he's taking bribes, and they've paid him and he's with them now. Whoever you are, I don't know you are, whoever you are and whatever you're doing with that photo it's not worth it, you back away because the reason is I'm advising you back away.' He went over to his jacket, put the photo in one pocket and got a bottle of pills out of another pocket and tried to open the lid but his hands shook and he dropped the bottle. 'Fuck it!' He picked the bottle up, steadied himself, opened it, and poured some pills into his mouth.

Ben came back in with a tub of ice cream and a spoon. 'I couldn't find any bowls. Christ, sir, you've got to take some leave. You've not been the same since you came back from that South America trip of yours.' South America rung a bell but I was too confused to remember why.

'Yeah, yeah. I'll be alright.' He took the ice cream tub off Ben, pulled the lid off and let it drop to the floor. He ate a few spoonfuls. 'That's better, that's better. I love ice cream.' He ate some more. 'Come on, Ben. He doesn't know anything.'

'You sure?'

'You what?'

Ben looked at the floor.

'Right,' DCI Campbell said. 'We're off, but we might be back but we're off now.'

'OK.'

'We might be back.'

'OK.'

And then, along with Ben, DCI Campbell left, the tub of ice cream in his hands and the photo of Leticia in his pocket.

I sat in the armchair where DCI Campbell had sat. The curtains were closed but not quite pulled together and in the ray of light that shone across the room I could see particles of dust floating around. The dust didn't worry me though. Dust gets everywhere. I'm a relatively neat person. I didn't sneeze an undue amount when I was in my flat.

I'd woken up with a lot of energy for the day ahead, but now I was in a strange mood that however else it affected me, left me completely incapable of getting out of my chair. The idea of getting up seemed like an incredible effort. Just yesterday morning I had got to the point where I really needed to get out for a bit of socializing and human contact. And, really, the following twenty four hours had exceeded all my expectations. I seemed to have met so many people who had let me into their lives. Hopefully I'd get the chance to see them again. But right now I was zapped. I vaguely needed the toilet but wasn't about to let that get me out of my chair. And I was sort of enjoying the shadowy gloom from the curtains being closed and having it be a mystery what the weather was like outside.

It was safe in my chair, that was the main thing. The

world, which recently seemed sort of empty, which I'd wandered through like I was in a zoo, looking but not joining in, now seemed pretty scary, and I had no idea what would jump out. The policemen coming round was pretty odd, there was no doubt about that. I had a vague, almost subconscious thought that they were waiting for me outside my door. And what did they mean about Leticia being a missing person? And the whole thing about Ben taking bribes (he did have something, I don't know, was sinister the word? about him), and DCI Campbell telling me to back away. Back away from what? And Leticia wasn't missing. She was Ted's daughter. I was going to meet her. The police must have come to the wrong address, coming here. They must have been thinking of a missing person that maybe looked a bit like Leticia.

I should never have taken that photo though. If Ted notices the photo is missing. Or if the policemen go round to Ted's house and tell him about me and the photo. Oh shit. They could do that. I can't go to dinner now. The thing I have to do is to just stay out of Ted's way. Hope he doesn't phone me and ask me why did I steal a photo of his daughter. But I want him to phone me. He has to phone me and then I'll go round to dinner and Leticia will be there. I thought about Leticia being there and it made me smile. I wonder if the policeman would have given me her photo back if I'd asked him. I'd love to have a look at that photo. My head nodded forward and a little while later I drifted off to sleep.

I woke up with a jolt. Knocking at the door. I stood up; my bladder was really burning. More knocking; I flinched. My mouth was dry and frothy and I had a nasty headache.

'Sam, you in there, mate? It's Doug.'

Doug? I went and answered the door. Doug was leaning

against the wall. 'Jesus Christ, Sam. How many stairs you have to walk up to get here, eh?'

'Sixty seven I think.' I smiled. It was great to see Doug again. He had such a friendly face. I liked Doug, I really did.

'What, you've counted them have you?'

'I wanted to know.'

'You're a funny chap, Sam. Anyway, you need a lift installing. Tell the landlord. Still, if nothing else it keeps you fit, eh?'

'I don't know,' I said. 'I read somewhere about it's bad for your knees.'

Doug wiped his face with his arm. 'Well, I've certainly worked up a sweat.'

Obviously my mind wasn't fully in gear because there was a pause before I said, 'Come in, Doug. Come in.'

'Cheers.' He followed me in. 'So, this is where you do your scheming?'

Did Doug know something about the photo? 'Scheming?'

But he had wandered across the room and now he was opening the curtains. Light flooded in and I squinted.

'Yeah,' he said. 'What else would you be doing but scheming, this cave you've made for yourself? You're living like a bat in here. You are aware that it's gone one o clock?'

'I fell asleep.'

'So did I,' he said. 'But then I got up. That's how it's usually done.'

I chuckled and the pain in my bladder regained my attention; I almost winced.

'I really need the toilet,' I said. 'Would you like a drink or something?'

'What's this? You're going to the toilet and would I like a drink?'

'Sorry?' I was confused and in pain.

Doug chuckled and slapped me on the back. 'You're not with it today, are you? I wouldn't say no to a glass of water.'

Coming back from the kitchen, my bladder was about to burst. I was hopping around as I gave Doug his water. Then I rushed off and felt an astonishing amount of relief. It just kept on and on and as I stood there, on auto-pilot, my head rested against the wall, I started thinking clearer. Well, Doug's here and he seems just as friendly as yesterday. It's weird, I've had three people in my flat already this morning, but before today I don't think anyone has ever been round. Not that I can remember. It's nice that Doug's here. I thought about Alice and that I'd like to see her again and the thought made me smile. At last, the stream stopped. I washed my hands and splashed my face and left the toilet. Then I drank two glasses of water, one after the other, and went into the living room, feeling rejuvenated.

Doug was strolling about, hands in pockets. 'You've certainly gone for the minimalist look in here, haven't you? Most places, first time you're in them there's things to pick up and have a look at. Not here. Not even a photo or something.'

'I don't like clutter.'

'So I see.' He continued strolling. 'So how'd it go with Ted last night?'

'Fine,' I said. And it had. And then I stole Leticia's photo.

'Sorry I drove off like that. Like I say, Ted and I have some stuff needs sorting out. Hopefully we'll be able to do that.' He went quiet, still walking about. 'Did, um, did you get the chance to find out when you'd be going round for dinner?'

'No,' I said. 'Ted was in the middle of something.' Just tell the truth, Sam.

'Oh, well, never mind. He's got your number. I'm sure he'll be in touch.' He stood still and the thought came to me, What if he saw Ted and me on our walk? 'Actually, that's why I'm here,' Doug said. 'I wondered if you'd been shopping.'

'Shopping?'

'You know, for the dinner. I mean, obviously you'll have to take some sort of present along with you.'

'Yeah, I was –'

'And then there's what are you going to wear? I mean, not for Ted's benefit so much, but I know his wife likes her guests looking smart. And not forgetting Leticia. She's always well turned out from what I remember. Had you thought about what you're going to wear?'

Leticia. But Leticia's a missing person. But she can't be. There was a lot I should probably have told Doug. Then again, maybe it would all turn out OK anyway.

'I don't know,' I said. 'Like what I'm wearing now I suppose.'

He looked me up and down. 'Thank God I came over. No, no, no. We'll sort you out with something, don't worry. You're not busy are you?'

'No, not really.'

'Great,' he said. 'Do you fancy it? Bit of shopping. Down Oxford Street maybe? I know it's a drag and all that, but it's got to be done and better that you have someone to suffer with, eh?'

'Yeah, yeah, I mean if you don't mind.'

'Happy to. You ready now or you want me to disappear, come back in fifteen?'

'No, no, just give me a minute.' I had been planning on a walk today but this was much better. I really enjoyed Doug's company. Still, with me having stolen Leticia's photo and maybe sabotaged my relations with Ted, it was possible there wouldn't be a dinner, and that from Doug's point of view the shopping trip was pointless. I felt a bit dishonest, vulnerable to the accusation that I was withholding information so that he'd spend time with me. I wasn't though. It wasn't that at all.

. . . Leticia's photo. Maybe I'll see Leticia. I know London's a big place, if she's here, but maybe I'll see her. Who knows. Maybe I'll see her. My heart leapt and I tingled all over.

Oxford Street is no fun in the summer with all the tourists, particularly when it's so hot. Plus, Doug had me trying on all sorts of suits. I protested as best I could that a suit was overdoing it. I mean, I'd never really been to a dinner party but I was sure that I shouldn't turn up in a suit. Eventually, though, I relented. He seemed so sure. 'We want you looking your smartest, mate.' Right now I was in the changing room of some menswear department or other. I had a suit hanging up in front of me, the third suit I'd tried on in here; I'd been OK with the other two but Doug had rejected them. So far today I'd tried on thirteen suits. I looked at this, the fourteenth suit, and started sobbing. No tears, just dry heaves. Enough was enough. My legs and arms felt dead, drained of energy. I was hot and bothered and my face was bright red in the mirror. Bloody Doug. At first I thought that he just wanted to help, but then I began to detect a kind of frantic desperation in him that the dinner go well. He'd said to me, 'I know I can't be there, Sam, but I'll do what I can beforehand. This'll all work out.' He'd said it as though trying to convince himself.

I reached a tired arm out to take the shirt off the hanger. I can't do it, I can't. I collapsed on the bench and sunk my face into my hands. I started sobbing again. Just this one last suit. If he doesn't like it then I'll be honest with him, I can't take it anymore. When he'd said he hadn't liked the ninth suit I'd tried on, which really was a nice suit, 'I just can't put my finger on why, Sam, it's just not, you know', I'd wanted to scream at him that enough was enough and what did he want from me? But I calmed down and felt a bit ashamed really, Doug was a good guy, and from then on I just went along with him. But this was the end of the line for me.

With all the energy I had I pulled myself off of the bench and tried the suit on. I was sweating all over and nauseous from the heat and the trousers were too tight, and in this state I burst out of the changing room and told Doug, 'I really like this one. I really think this is the one I should get.' He circled me, inspecting the suit. I didn't know what to do with myself I was so uncomfortable. It seemed to be even hotter out here with bright lights overhead; I was wilting. Doug went and stood in front of me, at a bit of a distance. 'Yep,' he said. 'I reckon we've got ourselves a winner here. Not too tight are they, the trousers?' He stuck his finger down my waistband.

'No, no, no.' I pulled myself away from him. 'They're fine.'

'Righty ho,' he said. 'Good timing, this. I'm a bit peckish. You fancy something to eat?'

I nodded; I hadn't eaten all day.

'I'll wait for you here then.'

I nodded again, and managed to turn away from him just before I started to cry.

Hot. Hot, clammy day. The pavement was overcrowded. Everybody pushing for space. I was sweating and I'd forgotten my sun cream and could feel my skin cooking. That's not good, I'm back at work tomorrow. Maybe people will think

I've been somewhere exotic for my holiday. I doubt it though. I couldn't really think, I was so exhausted, and carrying the suit as well. I walked with my head down, except for two occasions when I looked up at the crowd and spotted someone and thought, if only for a fraction of a second, is that her?, and a jolt of excitement went through me. But then I realised it wasn't her and my nerves were left jangling and I felt even more unwell than before.

In the restaurant, I cooled down and calmed down. There was air conditioning and once I'd had a big glass of water I felt better. Now, Doug and I were sitting eating sushi.

'That's a good suit, that,' he said. 'I know I put you through it a bit today, Sam, I'm just anxious everything goes as well as it can. I'm doing this for my family. I care about them, I really do. Let's just hope you pull through for us at the dinner, eh? No pressure of course.' He chuckled.

I smiled, not looking at him. His whole family's fate seemed to depend on this dinner. His eyes flickered when he spoke about it. He was a man under pressure. I'd really messed up.

After a moment he said, 'Alice was asking after you.'

'Oh?'

'Yep. I told her I was popping round to see you. She said to ask you would you come over and see her sometime? You must have made quite an impression on her. She doesn't take to new people in the normal way of things.' He swallowed the last of his sushi. 'So shall I tell her you'll be popping in?'

'Definitely,' I said. 'I'd like to see her again.'

'Excellent. I'll let her know. Evenings are good. She tends to sleep in the daytime.'

I felt a bit better. I'd felt a connection with Alice, a fizz in the air. I hardly ever get that. Still, the photo situation. I looked at Doug's fingers, wide and avuncular; he was a good man. Who steals photos? I mean seriously, Sam. An image passed across my mind of me stretching my arm through people's windows and stealing their photos while they sat unknowing, happy, a loving family, a roaring fire. Meanwhile I'd be scampering off down the street cackling to myself.

Doug got the bill and when I took my wallet out he said, 'No, no, no. This is on me. Everything you're doing for us. I know it might not seem like much, but it means a lot to us. So thank you. I want you to know that we appreciate it.'

I smiled. Shit. He was looking at me, a desperate intensity in his eyes. What a lovely family. The air was thick with love in their house, it really was. And Celina. What a sensitive woman. 'It's no problem,' I said. 'Happy to do anything I can.'

It's just a photo though. I was brushing my teeth. He's probably got loads of them. He's not going to notice that one gone. I gargled, left the bathroom. Even if he does, the last thing he'll think is that anybody stole it. Why would someone do that? And out of all the people there, why would I be under suspicion any more than anyone else? There were loads of people at the barbecue. I slipped my feet out of my flip flops and got into bed. The trouble is the police. They might tell him where they found the photo. Just think of him finding out. I'll look like a nutter. I hid my face under the duvet, embarrassed.

. . . The police though, that's the weird thing. I mean, Ted said she'd be at the dinner. She'd be at the dinner i.e. she's not a missing person. It must be a case of mistaken identity.

I lay there in the silence and didn't like it. One thing I don't like about living on my own is the silence, but I can usually handle it at night time, that's when it seems most apt. But, now, lying there, it was like there was a hole going through me, sucking air right though me. I could feel the air whooshing through my middle, and my whole body was affected and I couldn't get comfortable. Then I heard the tap dripping. That tap is my nemesis. You have to make a particular effort to turn it all the way off or it drips. But given my restlessness, it wasn't such a bad distraction. I went and turned it all the way off, then got into bed and made myself lie still for a while. It's all the excitement and noise that's gone on this weekend, I told myself, that's why you feel like this. But silence is good. It helps you sleep. I turned onto my side and closed my eyes. I visualised Leticia, and after a bit of effort she was walking and talking and I imagined the clothes she was wearing and she and I were talking and laughing, and I felt warm inside and fell asleep smiling.

Going to see Alice

Back at work. I'd had the last two weeks off; accumulated leave, take it or lose it; and had just finished sorting through my emails. I had a dull task to do now. A file sat on my desk and I was supposed to check that the database record of the file was accurate. There were ten other files piled up next to me and more on the racking by the back wall. I worked for a large insurance company. My job was not stressful but was perhaps beneath what I was qualified to do. But I had no compunction to do anything else. My job was just something I did because I needed money and then went home. I didn't want a career. If one came along then I suppose . . . But, it wasn't important. I knew there was room for improvement in my life, but it never seemed that my job affected me one way or another.

It was dull work though, particularly this task, and I was having trouble concentrating. I just needed to get back into it. Looking back on my holiday, I suppose I wasted most of it. I spent a lot of time hanging around my flat, not doing very much. It was only on the final weekend that I decided enough was enough and off I went to the barbecue. And look how that had worked out. Now I could hardly imagine life before the barbecue. So much had changed. So many possibilities had opened up. Of course there'd been some problems too, but it was all pretty exciting. Which was why work seemed particularly uninspiring perhaps. I had other things to be doing. Or at least, I had plans to make. When would I visit Alice? What would I say to her? And Leticia. Ted could phone at any moment and I could go to dinner and *Leticia could be there.* I sat there jigging my leg up and down, the file open in a random place. I was sure work wasn't usually this *actively* dull. Never inspiring, but usually I could get into a sort of routine and the hours would pass and the days would draw to a close. Not today. I just couldn't get back into it. I needed an incentive, something to excite me. That's it, I'll visit Alice. If I work hard all day then afterwards I'll go and visit Alice. Good. The decision felt right. I'd come to terms with myself. My concentration returned and I began altering data fields. Then, after about ten minutes, I heard two of my co-workers coming towards me, talking and laughing. I realised that nobody had asked me about my holiday. In fact, thinking about it, I hadn't talked to anyone all morning. How had that happened? It was pretty much par for the course for me at work, but the barbecue seemed to have put a different spin on things. Should I say hello? They were getting close now. My heart rate quickened. I'd have to interrupt them. I mean, they're not looking over here. I decided against it and they walked past me. One thing at a time. Concentrate on work, and then off to visit Alice. I got back to work. The two who had just walked past got the attention of the woman sitting next to me, something about the crossword. I knew the answer but stayed out of it and filled in some data fields (best not to spoil their fun). My co-workers were bandying around answers, all wrong. Then one of them got an answer that seemed to fit and there were high fives all around. I sat there feeling very much on the periphery of things. Even the realisation that the answer was wrong caused uproarious laughter and back slapping. I felt frustrated for some reason, and smacked my fists down on my desk, making a bit of a show of it. Apparently the three of them remained oblivious of me. It's a shame, they were nice people and I'd have liked to have joined in with them.

Thinking about going to see Alice got me through the day, but when I got home something seemed to change. I was tired after work. It's tiring doing a repetitive task all day and I had been off for two weeks. I kept yawning and my feet ached and sitting there in front of the TV, dinner on my lap, I decided to put the visit off. I would go tomorrow. Probably best to leave it anyway. It's only been, what, two days since I last saw her? My decision made, I sat there watching TV. It was a boring evening and I couldn't relax. I kept fidgeting and couldn't get comfortable, my chair seemed to have lumps and hard patches on it. I decided to go to bed. I dragged myself out of the chair and went to bed but it was quite early and I couldn't get to sleep. I hope Ted phones. Wouldn't he have phoned by now though, if he was going to? His wife seemed delighted about me coming over. I'd have thought she'd have wanted me round sooner rather than later. Maybe the police went round and told them about the photo and that was that. I felt sad. The police's visit and stealing the photo and the barbecue were beginning to fade in my mind. I tried to summon up images of the events but they'd lost focus. The weekend was drifting away from me and my life was returning to normal. Back to work and back to normal. There was a dull feeling in my stomach, and a sense of hopelessness spread out from there and consumed my whole body, right out to my fingers and toes which seemed to ache with their own futility, or my futility in operating them, or something. Still, I tried thinking about Leticia but I couldn't imagine clothes for her or get her talking. It seemed impossible that I'd ever meet her or have a conversation with her. She slipped away from my mind, I couldn't keep hold of her. I didn't want to either; the hopelessness she evoked was too crushing. At some point I drifted off into a restless sleep.

The next morning was better. Things never seem so bad in the daytime. My manager came straight up to me and instructed me to reorganise the files on the shelving by the back wall into alphabetical order. And I was just about to tell her OK and ask how her calculations for weather based premiums were going when somebody called her and off she went. Oh well, I had my question prepared. I'd ask her next time our paths crossed.

Time flew. It was a physical task which made a change, and I spent half the time sitting on the floor surrounded by files. I had a practical problem to solve. I thought I looked pretty good, sitting there in amongst the files, applying my mind, coming up with solutions. Busy and involved. Nobody seemed to notice me or anything, but still, I was there for all to see, should they look. Coming up with solutions. It occurred to me that I could tackle bigger problems than this one. Come up with more important solutions. Perhaps I *should* see about a promotion of some sort.

I'd deliberately left my phone on my desk so that I couldn't check it every five minutes. It had now been one hour and forty three minutes since I'd last checked so it was all the more possible that Ted had phoned. I checked; Ted had not phoned. Oh well, I wasn't really expecting that he would. I sat down at my desk. The woman next to me, Angela, was doing the crossword.

I turned to her and said, 'Are you doing anything for lunch?'

She didn't say anything and for a moment I thought she hadn't heard me. Then she said, 'Bank stuff, stand in a queue for an hour. How come?'

'Oh, no reason.'

'OK.' She paused. 'You know, tomorrow, there's a couple of us, off down the pub. If you fancy it?'

'Yeah, great,' I said. 'Count me in.'

'OK.'

There was a pause, which grew uncomfortable. I wasn't sure if I'd 'started a conversation' and she was anticipating further comments. Then she looked at her watch. 'Right. Best be off, miss the queue you get there early.' And then she was off.

'Bye,' I said. She'd left her computer unlocked. Obviously she was in a hurry.

It must be those stairs. That's why I've got no energy when I get home. Sixty seven stairs. It kills you after a whole day's work. I can't go and see Alice now. Tomorrow . . . tomorrow . . .

'Don't laugh, I'm serious!' I hadn't laughed but now Angela did and the next thing I knew her hand was on my thigh. She gave it a squeeze. We were in the pub and I was feeling a bit hemmed in, Angela on the one side and the wall on the other. (There were two guys on the opposite side of the table, but only one of them had spoken to me, and then only to say, 'What you having, mate?') I forced a smile. She was a bit overbearing was Angela but she had this sort of frantic vulnerability about her that pulled at something inside me and made me want to hug and kiss her. But as time had gone on I'd felt more and more restless in her company. I really should go and see Alice.

I'd missed a call! I sat down at my desk, tingling with excitement. Memories of the weekend came flooding back to me. My recollections were clear and vibrant. I could reach back and feel some of what I'd felt then. And Leticia. I remembered Leticia. I was so excited I didn't even think to compose what I was going to say before calling back. The phone started ringing. My heartbeat got quicker.

A bleep. 'You're through to Detective Chief Inspector Riley Campbell's phone. Leave a message after the tone.' The tone followed. I hung up. Maybe I should have left a message, let him know I called. It's alright, I'll call him back later. I stood up for no particular reason and walked out of the office and down the stairs and went outside. I asked one of the smokers out there for a cigarette. The smoke blew into my eyes, but it tasted pretty good. He was probably phoning to tell me it was a mistake, him coming round. It wasn't Leticia who was missing. It was somebody else. I dropped the stub and went back to my desk. I wondered was it obvious I'd gone out to smoke? I smelt my clothes; no aroma. The rest of the afternoon I couldn't get anything done. My concentration was zero and I kept shifting in my seat and jigging my legs and staring out the window. Every time I tried to type something my fingers felt like lead, and when I tried to apply my mind to the task at hand, my brain clouded over. As the afternoon wore on, things just got worse. The air seemed thick and it was as though the walls were pulsating, pushing in on me. I felt nauseous and with ten minutes left of the afternoon I was squirming in my skin. At two minutes to five I leapt out of my chair, shuddered, and ran out of the office, down the stairs and out of the building. Once outside, I took a deep breath and recovered as best I could. I looked back at the building thinking there was no way I could ever go back in there.

It was just work. It had never really affected me one way or the other. What was happening to me?

Those bloody stairs! What other explanation was there? This hot weather we're having, it's exhausting, and just thinking about those stairs is enough to make your legs feel like lead. By the time I got up them I was in no mood for going out again. I just wanted to grab something to eat and relax. I went to the toilet then came out and stood in the middle of my living room. It wasn't clean in there. There were specks of this and that on the carpet. And, to my surprise, I'd left last night's dirty dinner plate out. I never do that. I'm letting things slip, I really am. Then I realised: Wednesday nights I usually clean. Oh well, I'll do it tomorrow. I sat down in my chair. I can't clean tomorrow, I'm visiting Alice tomorrow. I've really got to go tomorrow, I really have. Otherwise it'll be Friday and she'll have weekend commitments. I yawned. What I'll do, I'll visit her straight from work. Avoid those stairs. Then I'll come back and do the cleaning. I stared into space for a bit. If DCI Campbell was phoning to tell me the whole thing was a case of mistaken identity, then maybe he'd realised the mistake before going to see Ted, and Ted had never seen the photo. Which meant Ted just hadn't got round to phoning me yet. He did seem to be having work related problems if Saturday evening was anything to go by; I wouldn't be surprised if he phoned me tomorrow, fixed up a date. I felt a swelling of positive energy inside me, and imagined meeting Leticia. Ted and his wife would go off somewhere after dinner, leave us alone. I'd make her laugh. I might even make a cheeky remark or two. 'I can't *believe* you,' she'd say. She'd tell her friends about me, 'Did I tell you what he said?' and I'd be sitting right there, a big grin on my face. It was such a jolly thought I started chuckling out loud. My good mood faded pretty quickly though, and I was left with a hollow feeling that sapped the dregs of energy I had left. I was pretty hungry but I couldn't be bothered cooking anything. I'll just have some cereal, I decided. Then I fell asleep in my chair.

I woke up feeling like shit. I had a sickly feeling in my stomach and my mouth was dry and frothy. I checked my watch; the time was five past nine. I really should have gone and seen Alice this evening. I'll go tomorrow. I'll make sure I go tomorrow. I sat still for a number of minutes, afraid that if I moved, the fact that I needed to eat and drink and go to the toilet would be pushed to the fore and force me to get up. Then I heard footsteps outside my flat and sat up straight. Somebody knocked on the door. I stood up. They knocked again. I went over and answered it.

Doug was standing on the other side. He looked agitated. He walked in without saying anything and put his hand up. 'Just let me catch my breath.' He didn't seem particularly out of breath. 'Those fucking stairs, Sam. I'm sweating buckets.' He was sweating a moderate amount. He put his hand down and looked straight at me for a long time. It got a bit uncomfortable and I looked away.

'What's going on?' he said.

I didn't know what he meant.

'It's Wednesday,' he said. 'Have you heard anything?'

'What do you mean?'

'From Ted! Wake up, Sam! Jesus Christ.'

'Oh,' I said. 'No.'

Having absorbed this answer, he just stood there, lost in thought it seemed.

'I thought he phoned today,' I said. 'But it wasn't him.'

He didn't respond. I suppose it wasn't a particularly helpful comment.

After a pause, he said, 'Celina's going mad over at our place, she practically shoved me out the door. I've had nothing to eat tonight.'

I said, 'It's only been a few days.'

'It was a firm invitation, right? I mean, I was listening but I want to be sure. It wasn't some woolly maybe we'll have you round some time was it?'

'No,' I said. 'It was pretty firm.'

'Then why the bloody hell is it taking so long? What's he waiting for?' Doug sort of threw the question out into the air rather than asking me directly and it seemed to hang there for quite a long time. Then he said, 'You sure he didn't see me on Sunday?'

'I don't think so.'

'I hope not,' he said. 'If he did then we're fucked. I know Ted and if he saw me we're fucked.'

My mouth seemed to race ahead of my mind. 'He might have done.'

'Eh?'

I heard myself say, 'He thought he saw someone in the car but then he said, "Oh no, it can't be him." And he seemed OK after that. I don't know though.'

'Bollocks. Bollocks! I knew I shouldn't have driven so close to the house.' The poor man was in turmoil, but I actually felt OK. I'd certainly surprised myself but my little lie had relived the pressure a bit and who knows, maybe Ted had seen Doug. The whole thing might have nothing to do with the photo. Quick thinking really. I was pretty pleased with myself and went over to Doug and slapped him on the back. 'It'll be OK,' I said, then belatedly added, 'mate.' I was sure it would be OK, too.

He put his face in his hands and stood there, motionless, for some time. Then he looked up at me. 'What do I do?' I didn't have time to answer before he repeated, 'What do I do?' He laughed, a strange sort of laugh, so contrary to the pained expression on his face which laid bare what he was going through inside. He had such an honest face and I felt an instant rush of sympathy for him. He said, 'I'll tell you what, Celina is going to give me all sorts of hell when I get in. She'll "do her nut." I dread to think, I really do. God, if she knew I'd driven up to the house.' He sighed. 'I've got a family, Sam. They're all I care about really. Maybe I'm not fit to have a family. I keep slipping up, I'm a bungler is what I am.'

He seemed so sad, and if it hadn't been for my recent injection of good cheer, I might have blurted everything out about the photo. Instead I said, 'It probably won't help much, but I'd like to see Alice. I mean, if she'd like to see me. I've been meaning to all week, I've just been, you know, busy.'

'Alice?' He paused. 'Oh, what you mean now? Yeah, sure, I'll give you a lift no problem. Come on then. No use hanging about here.'

He hadn't been as enthusiastic about my offer as I'd hoped and I left in a kind of limbo. I hope Alice wants to see me, I thought as I closed the door. I felt like I didn't know where I stood in relation to anybody. I took the key out of the lock and realised that I'd left not having eaten or drunk or gone to the toilet.

As we drove up the hill that turned into Doug's road, Doug turned the radio off. 'Listen,' he said. 'Obviously don't mention to Celina about me driving up to Ted's house the other night, that goes without saying. But the other thing you could do for me, indicate . . . No, I guess not indicate, you're just going to have to tell her; tell Celina Ted's called you up and he's said not to worry, he hasn't forgotten about you, he's just sorting some stuff out and then he'll set a date for you coming round.' He drove into the driveway. 'It would help me out, it really would. She's on my back, you don't know what she gets like.'

'But what if he doesn't invite me round?'

'We'll cross that bridge when we come to it, OK?' He looked at me; we weren't getting out of the car until I agreed.

'OK,' I said.

'Good,' he said. 'That's settled then.'

We got out of the car and walked up to the driveway to the house and Doug opened the door. As soon as he closed the door behind us there was the sound of feet and then Celina rushed towards us, frying pan in one hand, dish towel in the other. She stopped in front of us. 'Sam' She hugged me. 'You didn't have to come over. Did Doug say you had to come over?'

'No, no,' I said. 'I came to visit Alice.'

'Alice? Oh Alice! Yes, she'll be absolutely delighted.'

We all stood there for a few moments, saying nothing.

Then Doug told Celina, 'Sam's got some good news.'

Celina glanced at me, then looked at Doug, an irritated expression on her face.

'No, seriously,' he said. 'Tell her, Sam.' He nudged my shoulder.

'Oh yeah.' And I told her what Doug had asked me to tell her, with a sense of unease, finding it tough to look at her. I'd said and done a number of things lately that had left me confused about who had reason to be angry with me and why. I was in a bit of a mess really.

It didn't help that I could almost see Celina suppressing her excitement as I spoke. When I'd finished, she said, 'Well that's good news. We'd be grateful if you'd keep us up to date, Sam. Now, come on, let's get you to Alice.'

Doug patted me on the back. 'Yeah, let us know how it goes. I think I might go to bed now, I'm shattered. It's the wind, have you noticed? Really takes it out of you. So, if I don't see you again tonight I'll no doubt be talking to you soon.'

'Yeah,' I said. 'Sure.'

In the moments that followed, the three of us just stood there. No words were exchanged, but I felt as though some form of communication was going on between Doug and Celina. Then Celina said, 'Right, I'll take you upstairs.'

As we reached the top of the stairs, Celina said, 'After that incident with the wheelchair on Saturday she had a few good days. She even bordered on polite on a couple of occasions. But today she's been just awful. She told her brother she was contagious and started chasing him round and making him cry. So just . . . I'm sure she'll be fine with you. Sometimes I think it's me. I used to get on so well with my daughter, Sam.' We came to a stop. 'This is her door.'

'Thanks.'

She smiled and went back down the stairs. I took a deep breath. I had imagined that when I did finally come round to see Alice I would be well received, but the evidence suggested nobody was as excited by my visit as I thought, Alice included no doubt. Doug had probably mentioned visiting Alice as some kind of off hand remark. This could go very badly. I knocked on the door. After a moment, Alice said, 'Yeah.'

'It's Sam. I just came round to uh . . .' What was I doing here?

After what seemed like a long time she said, 'Well come in then.'

I opened the door and went in. Alice was sitting up in bed; her bed was opposite the door and she watched me as I entered. There was no sign of what she might have been doing before I knocked on her door.

'Hi.'

'Back already, huh?' She had a mocking look on her face.

'Yeah.'

There were a few moments of quiet, during which I realised that I desperately needed the toilet.

'Are you going to sit down, or what?'

I looked around for a chair.

'Under the desk. See it?'

'Oh yeah.' I put the chair down beside her bed and sat down. I pressed my thighs together and swallowed hard.

'Is there something wrong with you? You look like you're in pain or something.'

'I am,' I stood up. 'Whereabouts is the toilet?'

She laughed. 'You are such a weirdo. I'm *so* pleased my parents, like, let you into my room with me and I'm bed ridden.' She dissolved into a fit of giggles and when she recovered her cheeks were flushed. Meanwhile, I was dancing on the spot. 'Turn right and it's at the end of the hall.'

'Thanks.' I dashed out and went to the toilet. Afterwards, I could think more clearly. She seems to be mildly delirious. I dried my hands. I mean her face went really red after that giggling fit. I suppose she doesn't get many visitors. It's a shame though, it would be better if she wasn't so hyper and we could just have a chat. I went out into the hall and heard Celina downstairs, saying, 'You told him to say that. I wasn't born yesterday, Douglas.'

'Don't call me Douglas,' came Doug's voice.

Celina said, 'As if a man like Ted would phone up and be

like "Oh, and just to put your *mind* at rest." I felt sorry for Sam, standing there saying that.'

'I'll talk to you when you've calmed down.' A door shutting. Shit, that was my fault. I think. I'm really losing the plot. I can't think about this now. I went back into Alice's room. She watched me as I came in.

'Feeling better?'

'Yeah.' I sat down.

'I didn't mean to call you a weirdo,' she said.

'Huh?'

'Just then. I called you a weirdo. Sorry if I hurt your feelings or something. It's just Doug and Celina they completely crack me up. They're, like, tip toeing around me all day, like I'm so delicate, but then they happily let you in my room and who are you? I mean, think about it, you could rape me. I'd be totally defenceless.'

'I suppose so. I wouldn't.'

'Thanks!'

She'd calmed down now and there was that fizz in the air. I could feel it. Two people having a good time together. What a wonderful thing. I looked her right in the eyes and she looked right back. I felt myself filling up with joy, right up to my chest and throat until there was nowhere else for it to go and I laughed out loud.

'Hey,' she said. 'Come sit on the bed.'

'OK.' I went and sat on the edge of the bed. The physical closeness made me feel even happier. I felt like humming or whistling, and I was just about to fill the fizzing air with a little ditty when she said:

'Not *there*, Sam. You'll be turning around the whole time. All I can see is your back. Sit on the end of the bed so you're, like, facing me.'

I went and sat on the end of the bed, cross legged, facing

her. Just in front of me, under the duvet, were her feet. We smiled at each other, Alice and I.

'Will you come back and visit me?' she asked.

'Definitely.'

'Cool.'

'How are you?'

'I'm sick, Sam.'

'Yeah I know but . . .'

'I would describe my quality of life as poor.'

'OK.' I could feel myself clamming up.

'Listen, Sam. If you're going to, like, come round and stuff, don't take shit from me, yeah? Stand up for yourself. Otherwise I will have, like, zero respect for you.'

'OK.'

'I like people who defend themselves. I've always been like that.'

'Can you move your feet?'

'Huh?'

'Can you move your feet? I mean, are they paralysed?'

'No. Neither are my legs. It's just I've got no muscles. I can move my toes though. See?'

'Oh yeah.'

'Don't you think it's weird though? Sometimes I, like, look down at my toes and it's weird thinking they're attached to me. They seem too far away or something.'

'They're even farther away for me; I'm tall.'

'Yeah . . .' She paused. 'I want to see your toes.'

I didn't know what to do.

'Come on, take your shoe and sock off. I want to see your toes.'

I took my right shoe and sock off; she looked at my toes and giggled.

I said, 'I thought my toes were pretty normal.'

She wrapped her forefinger around my big toe. 'Ew, it's *sticky*.'

'It's been in my sock.'

'Don't you wash your feet, Sam?'

'Of course I do.'

'Between you toes?'

'*Yes.*'

She gave me a look of mock suspicion and I chuckled, I couldn't help it, I was in a delightful mood. Then she said, 'My toes are freezing. My feet are like blocks of ice or something.'

'Oh . . .'

'Even when I wear these thick socks I have and I hate wearing socks to bed.' Her expression darkened somewhat and I detected a threat to my high spirits. She said, 'Did Celina say anything about me?'

'When?'

'Tonight. About my mood. She's always saying about my mood.'

'She said you were having a bad day.'

'I can't believe how much complete shit her and Doug talk. Talking to them it's like, "Oh, oh, and we had this sweet little daughter and just the cutest little thing, but then she got *sick*, so now you don't know how she's going to be. But what can you do? She's sick. Obviously her behaviour will be, like, erratic and stuff." It's such a load of shit though. It really annoys me.'

I hesitated before saying, 'It must get to you sometimes though, being sick.'

'Loads of things get to me. I wasn't some princess or something before I got sick. I was *exactly* the same. It just suits them pretending I was this perfect little thing. They're such, they're such . . . *revisionists*. It's like on this documentary I was watching about Chinese history. I watch loads of TV, Sam. Sometimes I read but I have this tiny attention span so most of the time I just, like, watch TV. But OK so this programme was saying about how with communism and everything the government just, like, used history to make themselves seem great and stuff. They just erased stuff and changed stuff they didn't like. And these people having to swallow this complete shit, the Chinese people. It's exactly the same for me. Oh she's disabled. It's so difficult for her. Just so they don't get the blame for me. And they've got this thing about South America. Like South America is to blame for me being ill. It's complete shit. It's, like, the reason I'm sick is I have zero immunity. They really annoy me.'

'I met a guy the other day though. He'd just got back from South America and he was sick.'

'So what?'

'Well, I just meant . . .'

'Some guy gets sick in South America so that must be where, like, everybody gets sick?'

I shrugged.

'That's the sort of thing Doug and Celina would say.'

'Sorry.' I looked down at the foot shaped lump on the duvet.

'*Please* stop apologizing all the time.'

'I don't apologize all the time.'

'Yes you do.'

I didn't reply. She was getting prickly; the atmosphere between us had changed. I tried the direct approach she seemed to respond to. 'Are you dying?'

'Yep. How come?'

'I like talking to you.' I flushed red, not looking at her. I was afraid she would start making fun of me, I wouldn't have been able to stand that. I felt very fragile and for a second I thought I might start crying.

'Oh, *Sam*.' She stretched her arms towards me but didn't touch me.

I glanced up.

'I *hate* it here, Sam. Doug and Celina and all their shit.'

'They care about you,' I said.

'They annoy me and I can't take it anymore. I want to move in with you.'

'Eh?'

'Doug and Celina are completely unbearable. It's my only option.'

'You'd be on your own all day.' The idea appealed to me though.

'What, you go to work?'

I nodded.

'What do you do?'

'Insurance. Admin stuff.'

'Admin stuff?'

'Yeah.'

'Couldn't you do something different?'

I shrugged.

'Quit,' she said. 'You can claim some carer's allowance or something.'

Having someone in my flat all day. Have a chat in the evenings. It's not such a bad idea. I could feel myself getting excited about it.

'What do you think?' she said.

'Wouldn't your parents miss you? And your brother.'

'The less my brother gets to know me the better. Since I'm dying anyway. And Doug and Celina just annoy me. OK so it's like, Celina comes up to me today, this look on her face, sort of like she's got good news but doesn't want to look too excited. "There's just a chance we might be able to get Leticia round," Leticia is this girl we used to know, and I'm sitting there, I'm thinking, "yeah? So what?" And she's like, "You'd like that wouldn't you?" She goes, "I just want you to know, it has nothing to do with you, that Leticia stopped coming round. It was our fault." I don't even like the girl. Where did they get this idea I want to see her again? It's just shit like that. They come out with it and I just want to tell them to fuck off. If I don't move out I'm going to go crazy and they'll know their daughter died hating them.' There was a pause. 'What's wrong?'

'Nothing.'

A few moments passed in silence. Then she said, 'Is it Leticia?'

'Uh . . .' I was still off kilter from the mention of her name.

'I'm a good reader of people. Your face goes funny when I talk about her.'

'No it doesn't.'

'You're *such* a bad liar. How do you even know about her?'

I didn't know what to say.

'Did Doug and Celina say something?'

'Not, not really.'

There was a pause; I tried to get myself together again.

'Oh no! They showed you the *photos* didn't they? That's so embarrassing. It's like, "look how happy we were." God.'

I kept quiet, hoping she'd drop it.

'You haven't, like, fallen in love with a photo, have you, Sam?'

'No.'

'You have! You saw her photo and obviously you were like, "oh she's so beautiful." That's hilarious.'

'Why don't you shut up?' My throat was constricted with anger. I tried to calm down; I don't like being angry.

'Have I touched a nerve?'

I was tense all over.

She said, 'It's OK if you do. I guess she's cute. I guess she's, like –'

'AAAAAAAAAARGH!' I thumped the wall ten, twenty times with my fists. It was a thin wall and very satisfying to pound away at. When I finished I was breathing heavily and feeling rather thrilled. It was quite an outburst, I couldn't remember ever having done that sort of thing with another person in the room. Embarrassment would have set in but Alice seemed quite entertained. 'Wow.'

'Sorry.'

'What did I say about keep apologizing?'

I caught my breath; I felt pretty good actually.

'So can I move in with you?'

'It's up to your parents. I can't go behind their backs. They've been really nice to me.'

'They probably want something from you.'

'Still, I'd feel more comfortable if –'

'I'm not a child, Sam. I'm nineteen years old.'

'I know but, it's just I don't want to interfere and –'

'Yeah, yeah, yeah.' She yawned without covering her mouth. 'You can go now. I'm bored.'

What had I done wrong?

She looked at me. 'Are you still here?'

I stood up, put my shoe on, stuffed my sock in my pocket, and left the room. That was sudden. I had a sense of the unfinished. Everything seemed bland on this side of the door.

Just as I was about to set off down the stairs, the doorbell rang. I moved out of view and peered down the staircase.

Doug appeared and opened the door. After a moment, a man came in.

Doug said, 'What do you want?'

'Why don't you just come with us?' I recognised the man's voice. I adjusted my position so I had a better view. It was DCI Campbell. I felt a knot in my stomach. I was sure to be found out on one count or another. I'd constructed a sort of web of deceit somehow. I hadn't meant to, I really hadn't.

Doug said, 'I haven't done anything.'

'Then you've got nothing to worry about. If you've done nothing, what are you worried about?'

'I object to this. My daughter's sick for Christ's sake.' He paused. 'I'm not involved anymore.'

'I've got a warrant for your arrest.'

'You going to cuff me?'

'I hope not.'

Then Celina appeared, looked at Doug then DCI Campbell, then just stood there. Doug went to touch her but she shrunk away from him. 'I'll be back in a couple of hours,' he told her.

DCI Campbell coughed. 'You ready?'

Then they were off. Celina just stood there as if Doug and DCI Campbell were still right there. Something pulled me towards her. I just wanted to comfort her. Such sensitivity she had. I found myself walking down the stairs and then I was standing opposite her, looking into her eyes. A tear formed and rolled down her cheek. What a sensitive woman. She stepped toward me and placed her palms on my cheeks. She kissed me on the lips then turned and walked up the stairs.

I left the house and it was only when I was halfway up the road that I wondered, did she want me to follow her upstairs?

The Photo Is Returned To Me

Ted phoned me. 'Alright, mate. You fancy dinner tonight? You ain't busy or nothing, are you?'

'No.'

'Sorted. I'll tell the wife. She'll be bouncing off the walls she will. Can't wait to see you that woman. Let's say half seven, yeah? How does that sound?'

'Great.'

'Sorted. See you then, fella.' And then he hung up before I had the chance to ask if Leticia would be there.

I sat there at my desk; the moment didn't feel as significant as I thought it would. I thought I'd have been really excited. I mean he'd actually invited me to dinner. Which meant he couldn't know about my stealing the photo. Unless he'd invited me over to confront me about it. But that didn't seem likely. Wow. Great. I got back to work.

An hour or so later it had started to sink in. I couldn't concentrate on my work. I was excited and nervous and worried that my level of nervousness did not befit an occasion of this importance. I knew it was best not to worry but I kept telling myself how important it was, the dinner. I tried to see how nervous I could make myself. Eventually I wound myself up a bit and I was sitting there with a cloud of tension drifting inside me and my muscles ached from me keep tensing them up. I tried to get rid of my nerves by thinking about practical matters. I needed a present. I leaned back in my chair and tapped my pen against my teeth. Hmm. Another practical problem. I did enjoy this, sitting around, working things out. It really passed the time. I mean it wasn't really living as such. It wasn't the stuff of life. But I felt a vague sense of satisfaction, well, contentment. Sort of. It kept the restlessness at bay.

Yes, it might be that I should get into problem solving. Make a concentrated effort to pursue a professional path that would open up problem solving opportunities. Whatever else happens, happens. But at least I could spend the majority of my time moderately involved with something. I thought about my options. All the usual. Flowers, chocolates etc. Nothing came to mind. Clothes, candles – it was my understanding that people bought one another candles, although I was unsure why. Perfume. All uninspiring. I tapped my pen against my teeth but nothing came to me. Then, in a flash, it came to me. Perfect. I could hardly believe how perfect it was. I looked around the office to see if anybody had seen my face at the moment of inspiration. Unless they had turned away quickly, it appeared that they had not. Still, a job well done. For some reason I clicked my fingers, which I never do, then rolled my chair right up to my desk and got ready to enter some data.

I couldn't do it. I was too excited to concentrate. I was squirming in my skin wanting to run out of the office and get the present. I doubted that anybody would notice if I did leave, but I just about held back. I re-focused. I made a few entries. But pretty soon my fingers started shaking and I felt a physical compulsion to leave the building. In a bit of a panic, I got up and as I did so my chair flew back into the desk behind me. In a daze, I staggered out of the office.

Once I got outside I could breathe again. I leant against the wall and closed my eyes and waited for my head to stop spinning. I saw Leticia in my mind's eye; she was smiling and I felt a burst of happiness that was almost overwhelming, too rich or something, and a wave of nausea came over me. When it passed I had an overwhelming desire for a cigarette and said to one of the smokers, 'I've left my ciggies at home. Can I borrow one?' The word 'ciggies' tickled me and I chuckled to myself. I was feeling a bit delirious really. I lit up and as soon as I inhaled I felt really, really dizzy and when the guy who'd given me the cigarette wasn't looking I dropped it and walked across the car park and into the shopping centre.

The shopping centre was pretty chilly and I shivered but my cheeks were hot. Right, where am I going? I decided that my best bet was a catalogue shop and off I went, towards the escalator that would take me to the catalogue shop downstairs.

I had space on the escalator, an old couple in front of me were the only ones on there with me, and I tried to gather myself. What is wrong with you, Sam? You're a bundle of nerves. I got another image of Leticia in my mind's eye and it felt as if my heart was being ripped out of its chest, it was beating so hard wanting to just get there, to her, before the rest of me if necessary. In a daze, I looked around me and saw, going up the up escalator, DCI Campbell. His eyes flickered in recognition. 'Wait for me at the bottom.' He coughed. It all happened very quickly. Then he went up and I went down.

I stood at the bottom of the escalator. I shivered, it seemed to be even chillier downstairs. The catalogue shop was just off to my left. I went to head towards it, then remembered I was waiting for DCI Campbell. I saw him at the top of the down escalator. He looked down at me then coughed into his hand. I started feeling uneasy. The escalator was transporting him closer. I went into a panic. DCI Campbell started walking; I ran. I don't know why but I ran. I was pretty confused, thinking, this is the wrong way for the catalogue shop. But I'm not going to the catalogue shop, I'm running from DCI Campbell. Why am I running from DCI Campbell? I circumvented a water fountain and turned a corner. Ahead of me, there were double doors which led outside. I made a dash for them, the idea that DCI Campbell was behind me filled me with a strange fear and drove me forward. Then I saw a woman with a pushchair coming out of the shop to my left, panicked that I would hit her, shifted to the right, lost my footing and fell over. It didn't hurt much but I just didn't have the energy to get up so I laid there on my back.

A passer by stopped. 'Need some help, mate?'

I indicated that I was OK and off he went. Then I heard someone cough. A couple of seconds later, DCI Campbell arrived. 'You alright?'

'Yeah.'

'Need a hand?'

I nodded, took his hand and got to my feet.

'Fancy a coffee?'

'Yeah,' I said. 'Sure.'

We wandered over to the nearest coffee shop.

DCI Campbell brought the coffees back to our table. 'Did I shit you up then?'

'Uh . . .'

'Did I shit you up, coming round your flat I was wondering did I shit you up?'

'I don't know really.' I sipped my coffee.

He sipped his coffee. 'I'm freezing in here.' He looked worse than before. He really did look *in the midst* of a fever.

'You ran away pretty sharpish.'

'I don't know what came over me.'

'Good to know you can run if you need to.'

'Yeah . . .' I hesitated. 'You arrested Doug yesterday.'

'You were there?'

'Yeah.'

'Putting yourself about, eh?' He chuckled, then started to cough. It went on for quite some time. Just when I thought he was about to stop it would get worse again. Wheezing. By the end he had blood on his napkin. He leant back in his chair and placed a finger and thumb on his temples and closed his eyes. I hoped he was OK.

'I'm fucked, Sam. Stick a fork in me and all that. I'm finished because the reason is I'm sick, you only have to look at me, just look at me to find that out. That's why I don't give a shit. Being seen with you I don't give a shit.'

Why would he care about being seen with me? I put it aside; I wanted to know about Doug, he had enough problems without being in jail too.

'Is Doug in trouble?'

'He's in a cell if that's what you mean "is he in trouble?" We'll let him out though. He's clean. So is that other mate of yours, Ted.'

'I just met him.'

'You two seem pretty tight.'

There was a pause.

I said, 'What are Ted and Doug involved in?'

'Nothing. Like I say. Used to be involved, then South America came along. Something happened out there, a shift. Everything got shook up at the top of the tree because somebody shook it all about.' He sipped his coffee. 'Oh yes. I love things going through me that are diametrically opposed to the outside tem- perature.' He paused. His hands shook holding the coffee cup. 'Used to be top of the tree did Ted. Once. Top of the tree but then he got out and that's what we think, he's out. But it don't make sense "he's out." Because he's got enemies. Hence,' he took out the photo of Leticia and laid it on the table, 'This.'

I stared at the photo. The nameless emotion came over me. 'I think I'm seeing her tonight.'

'You what?'

'I'm going to Ted's house for dinner.'

'Fucking hell you're waist deep already.'

I did feel sort of waist deep but in a more abstract way than DCI Campbell meant it.

'So she can't be a missing person,' I said.

He was drinking his coffee. 'Eh?'

'I'm seeing her tonight so she can't be a missing person.'

'You won't be seeing her tonight.'

'Ted said she'd be there.'

'Yeah?'

I thought about it. '. . . Sort of.'

'She won't be there. There's something happening with her. She's caught in a tug of war. Either one side's got her or the other side's hidden her. I don't know. Let me make something crystal for you because the reason is I want to be clear with you. Ted is a man with a past. People from that past they're coming out of the woodwork. These are not people you want to meet but you will meet them you hang about with blokes like Ted and Doug. Doug's done a lot to give himself a tough time outside the pearly gates.' He laughed, coughed. 'But you're an adult. Me, I want to be watching my own back.' He fingered the corner of the photo. 'Why'd you take the photo?'

'I just . . . liked the way she looked.'

He laughed. 'Brilliant. That's brilliant. If you're going to get yourself in danger do it for love, eh? Well, if you find her be sure to let me know. Love against the odds, the sort of thing I'd like to facilitate before I die choking on my own blood.'

I didn't know what to say.

He picked up the photo. 'She's the key. Can two white people have a black kid?'

I shrugged.

'I've heard it's possible. I doubt it though. I doubt it. Here, take it, you have it, go on, take it.'

I took the photo.

'Finished?'

I nodded.

We got up. He took two steps, stumbled, then collapsed to the floor, clattering into a chair on the way down. I just stood there, probably for less than a second but it seemed like longer. He started moving, got into a sitting position. 'Give me a hand, will you?'

I extended my hand and he took it and pulled himself up. Then he let go of my hand, wobbled and fell into me. 'Sorry, mate.' He righted himself, stood there for at least ten seconds trying to get his balance. He looked at me, a resigned smile on his face. And somehow, from that look, I got the sense that he liked me, could trust me; he seemed pretty suspicious of lots of people but I was different. I felt sort of special and had a nice glow inside.

'It's the muscles, the muscles in my legs they're withering away. You should see me, talk about chicken legs. My shorts wearing days are over.'

Muscles in his legs withering away. Like Alice. I was going to ask him what was he doing in South America? but straight away he said, 'I know I said I don't give a shit but I'm not standing here like this like a target for nothing. I'll see you around no doubt.' And then he was off, gingerly at first, but he got into his stride and was absorbed in the sunlight beyond the double doors. I looked at the photo of Leticia, said her name under my breath, then put it in my pocket and left the coffee shop.

It was by chance that my eyes happened upon the catalogue shop at just the right time. I had been drifting towards work in a Leticia induced haze. I walked in, opened a catalogue and found what I was looking for pretty quickly. Great. Ted will love it. I went up to the counter and paid for the item. Then I waited, leaning against the counter. I thought of Celina, the first time I'd thought of her that day. I touched my lips where she'd kissed me. Just as I started to get an erection two shop assistants put a big box down on the counter in front of me. I recognised immediately that I had a problem.

I said, 'Is it heavy?'

'Depends how far you're taking it.'.

'Right.' Obviously they weren't going to help me, so I shifted the box towards me so that it overlapped the edge of the counter and I could get some leverage on it. Then I used my chin to push the box down until it fell into my arms. Bloody hell it was heavy. My arms supporting the underside and my chin rested on the top I walked out of the shop. By the time I got to the escalator my muscles were already feeling it. At the top of the escalator I saw the door that led to the car park outside my office building. My biceps were pulsating and my fingers, which were curled around the far side of the box, were strained and slipping. My neck ached and my calves were hurting. I gave my best effort to speed up, not think about the pain, but pretty soon I knew that if I didn't stop I would drop the box.

I stopped and put the box down. I stretched and wiped my brow. What the hell am I going to do with the thing when I get to work? Deal with that when you get there, just . . . get there. I took a deep breath and picked up the box. Shit, I hurt all over. I dug my teeth into my bottom lip and headed for the doors, shoved them open and the sun shone in my eyes and my biceps were burning and the box was cutting into my fingers and I felt unsteady on my feet. In this state I zigzagged across the car park, almost fell inside the building, stumbled a few steps and dropped the box in front of reception. I took a few deep breaths and looked up at the receptionist. She was reading a novel not very discreetly. Perhaps she'd started off reading discreetly then got absorbed. I didn't mind, it gave me a chance to catch my breath. After a minute or two she saw me, put her book aside and said, 'What can I do for you?'

'I've got this box. I was wondering could I leave it down here? I'll pick it up at five o clock.'

'We can't look after personal things I'm afraid. Policy.'

'I'll take full responsibility for it.'

'Sorry, I can't help you. It's all to do with liability and stuff.'

Travelling up in the lift, I thought about a programme I'd seen on TV where people were shown how to get discounts from shops. It was easy as long as you were confident, outgoing, assertive. I aspired to those things and at one time or another in the past week I'd felt I had those qualities. Obviously not enough to convince the receptionist to take my box though. She would've done, I'm sure. If I'd just been more confident, outgoing and assertive. I could've been too. Just a bit more effort. To be fair though, I was worn out. I really was.

The light bleeped and the doors opened. There was a man on the other side ready to get on. I smiled at him, 'silly old me, look what I've brought into the building', but he didn't respond. And I'm sure he caught my smile. Anyway, I left the lift and he got on.

Now here was the problem. How was I supposed to walk into the office in the middle of the morning with a Gold Series Deluxe barbecue without giving away the fact that I'd just bought a Gold Series Deluxe barbecue? If one of the managers sees me I'll tell them it's for a family emergency. A present for a recently hospitalised uncle or something like that. And if they fire me, they fire me. The words 'fire me' didn't sit too comfortably though, however blasé I tried to be about them. I picked up the box and headed into the office.

People were milling about, the usual. Nobody seemed to notice me. I fixed a smile on my face, 'ho, ho, look what I've gone and done.' Nope. Nothing. Straight ahead of me, standing talking to the guy at the desk behind mine, was my boss. Shit. I picked up my pace. She turned, she saw me, my heartbeat quickened, she walked towards me, she walked straight past me. She walked straight past me.

I went over to my desk, now hardly noticing the weight of the barbecue, and put it down as if it were a box of poly-styrene foam. I sat down, just sat there, didn't think anything in particular for a while. Then I said to myself, What happened? I mean, seriously, what happened? She walked straight past me. A wave of irritation came over me. I spun my chair round and stared at the two guys sitting behind me. Eventually one of them raised his eyes: 'Alright, mate?' I threw my hands up in the air and turned back to my desk. I felt disorientated and tense. My colleagues had really got on my nerves. I realised I was about to cry and determined to compose myself.

Where's Angela? Oh yeah, she called in sick, I remember someone saying. She'd have been interested in the barbecue escapade. She was OK, Angela. She and I could be friends. I calmed down and decided to do some work. Today's task: altering data fields.

I got into a rhythm at first. I had a sheet of paper with file names listed on it and my task was to change the code in the computer record of each file to match the new code in the hardcopy. I kept setting myself targets. Do five then you can get a drink of water. I'd do five and then realise I could do five more. And so it went on. But then, after about forty minutes, something happened. I set an ambitious target of seven and the first three I got through fine. Then my arms tightened. I looked at the list of file numbers left to enter and shuddered. My fingers spread out as far as they could go and I could see each individual finger bone, then my hands went to my head, grabbed two big clumps of hair and pulled. Then my legs started jigging up and down and I felt an irresistible compulsion to get up.

As soon as I got up I realised that I would not be getting a glass of water. I would be leaving. I gazed around the room and heard the clicking of keys and the sound of voices. I didn't try to fight it, my compulsion to leave. I just picked up my box and headed out of the office. It wasn't even lunchtime yet, half an hour until anybody was supposed to take their break. Just before I got to the double doors that led out to the lifts I turned and lifted one leg and rested the box on my knee, thus freeing my hand. Then, I gave the office the finger. At that moment, my boss looked up. From the expression on her face I knew she'd seen me. I lowered my knees and gripped the box with my hands again. Then I turned and left the office.

What had I done? I sat on the bus, restless. The morning wasn't even over and I'd already gone home for the day. Something felt very wrong. I was full of nervous energy, my legs buzzed with it and I couldn't relax. I'll do what Alice said, I told myself. I'll get myself a carer's allowance. She could come and live with me. What carer's allowance? Can you just get a carer's allowance? Will I be able to pay the rent with it? I'll have to move in with Mum. I can hardly imagine Alice wanting to move in with Mum. She probably wasn't serious anyway, Alice. I'll just get another job. Yeah, and what's my reference going to look like. I sneezed. All this nervous tension isn't good for me. I'm coming down with something.

The bus stopped. Another ten minutes to my flat. With the box. Another ten minutes with the box. I staggered off the bus. The pain returned to my arms immediately. But I just kept walking and the pain dulled. It dulled in my legs, in my ribs where the edge of the box was digging in. I staggered down the road, zigzagging and my forehead was dripping with sweat and my hair was sticking to my face. But I just kept going. My arms shook but something sustained me, I don't know what, the feeling that I was running on empty or something. Wondering how long I could keep going. I stumbled to the door of my building and dropped the box. I ached all over. I could barely stand up.

Sixty seven stairs! There was obviously no way I could carry the box up sixty seven stairs. But it was a Gold Series Deluxe barbecue, I could hardly leave it downstairs on its own either. I had no options. I sat down on the box but as soon as my backside made contact with it, the cardboard folded inwards and I shot up. I wandered outside into the sunshine and ran my hand through my hair and laughed. What am I supposed to do? For crying out loud. I could call on a neighbour, ask them to look after it. It's a bit weird, turning up, 'Can you look after this?' I mean I've never said a word to anyone in my building before. But then nobody knows their neighbours anymore.

I looked up the centre of the stairwell. It was too far. I rang the doorbell of the first floor flat. No answer. Rang again. Nope, no answer. Of course there was no answer. It was the middle of the day, people were at work. I felt a pang, I should be at work, tried to dispel it. Concentrate on dinner tonight. Dinner with Leticia. For a moment I floated out of my aching, sweaty body and joined Leticia in the clouds. But what with what I'd been through (in thirty degree heat and wearing work clothes) it wasn't long before bodily displeasure regained my attention.

I set off up the stairs. I'd try again on the second floor. When I got there something stopped me from putting the box down. The idea of picking it up again maybe. True, my arms felt like they were about to fall off but I'd also broken through the pain barrier to some extent, or got used to it, holding the box and feeling as if my body were about to fall apart. I mounted the stairs. It became clear that I had not passed through the pain barrier, it was just that the barrier had shifted. I was determined not to put the box down though. I continued up the stairs.

My arms were shaking and I was dizzy and I kept bashing into the wall. Sweat poured down my face and ran down my sides and back. My legs were wobbly and my feet didn't seem to be making solid contact with the floor. I had a sense of weightlessness, my body was this floating thing, it's pain entirely self-contained. And my mind was cut off from everything. There was just me, the box, the journey. I became aware of a harsh thirst. My legs started shaking and I thought I would throw up. My vision was blurry. It wasn't too far now. I could see the door of the flat. My every focus was on the door. One more step. A slicing pain cut across my thigh. I was on the landing. I brought my knee up, rested the box on it, and freed my hand which was shaking so much it wouldn't fit in my pocket. I waited, the corner of the box digging into my throat. My hand steadied and I fished the key out and opened the door. Inside the flat, I dropped the box, and went and sat down. I was soaked. I looked at my watch: twenty to one. I really should have stayed at work.

After five minutes sitting in my armchair my body had enough energy to feel restless again. I shifted around in the chair. It didn't feel right, being at home. I should be at work. Seven hours until dinner. Seven hours until Leticia. A shudder went through my whole body and my thighs pressed together and my feet crossed as if trying to keep a lid on all the nervous energy inside me. I didn't know what to do with myself. Seven hours waiting around. It will be unbearable. Thinking about it got me in a panic and my breathing got heavy. Then it came to me; I'd go to Doug's house. Not to see anyone particular. Just to pop in. After all, I was a family friend.

It simply has to rain. And when it does rain, it's going to rain big. It's been so muggy and humid all week. Walking along, feeling the thickness in the air, I was acutely aware of how much pressure the weather system was under. Anything under that much pressure has to burst sooner or later. Still, the sky was clear blue. I checked nobody was looking and flexed my bicep and gave it a squeeze. Not bad. I expected it to be bulging for some reason, having carried that barbecue. I suppose the effect wouldn't show up immediately.

Before I was really ready to be, I was at Doug's door. Not at all sure why I was there, I rang the doorbell. Standing there waiting, the sun burned the back of my neck. I'd forgotten my sun cream again. Still, for one reason or another, I appeared to be oblivious to the sun this summer.

The door opened and I squinted looking into the house; Celina was on the other side of the door.

'Hi,' I said.

'Sam. Come in.'

I went inside and it took a few moments for my eyes to adjust to the light. When they had, I looked at Celina. She had her hair tied back and she looked tired. She was wearing quite short denim shorts; she has nice legs actually. I looked up so she didn't think I was staring at them.

'It's lovely to see you.'

'I just thought I'd come around to . . .' I tailed off.

Celina smiled at me and put her hand on my shoulder. I didn't know how to react. She really stirred up my emotions did Celina.

Her hand moved across my shoulder and I felt her fingers against the back of my neck. Then she pressed her body against me, her head rested on my shoulder. I could feel her calf against mine. 'Oh, Sam.'

I didn't say anything.

'It's so lovely to see you.'

'Yeah.'

She giggled in my ear.

'I just came round to, to see how you all were.'

'Oh, Sam.' She took a step back and looked at me. Then she took my hand. 'Come on.'

I wasn't watching where we were going and then I looked around and saw that we were in her and Doug's room. She closed the door. 'I'm so happy you're here. I was having a terrible day. You came at exactly the right time.'

'Great.' I glanced at the closed door.

Celina whispered, 'Mustn't wake Alice.'

'Oh, of course.'

There was a pause.

She pointed to the bed. 'Sit down.'

I sat down.

She looked at herself in the full length mirror on the far wall, running her finger down the lines in her face. She turned around. 'Would you like me to suck your cock?'

I immediately lost my capacity for thought and speech and just sat there with, I suppose, a blank expression on my face.

She walked over to me and knelt between my legs.

'Celina . . .'

'Shush.'

'I just . . .'

She unzipped my shorts. I had an erection which I was pretty grateful for, the situation having reached this point. And then she sucked my cock. Occasionally she'd move her tongue across the tip of my penis, but there wasn't much of that; she was pretty workmanlike. I watched the movement of her head and there was no danger of my losing my erection and I felt as though I'd be ready to ejaculate quite soon, so in that sense I was 'aroused.' However, my overall feeling was an unpleasant one. Maybe if she'd taken her clothes off, or kissed me, or I'd licked her neck and then into her ear and rolled my tongue around or something, maybe that would have made things better. As it was, my penis was hard, but I felt absolutely nothing in the pit of my stomach. I ejaculated into her mouth.

I zipped myself up and she placed her palms on my knees and pushed herself to her feet. I just sat there and waited for her to say something. She looked serious; I felt pretty sure she'd be short with me when she did say something. My best option was to make as quick and quiet an exit as possible.

Finally, she said, 'Doug's still being held by the police. They can hold him as long as they like for all I care.' She paused. 'We used to have such a happy marriage, Sam. Then South America came along and . . . It was such a stupid thing to have done. And things get twisted, of course they do. And in a sense, what's the point of blame? But certain people make suggestions. It's difficult. I don't suppose I'm making a lot of sense to you, am I?'

'I don't know.'

'You're a lovely guy,' she said. 'One of the few I've met who I think could handle Alice. You'd make a good couple, I do think that. A case of opposites attract I think. Of course she's not a long term prospect, is she? What with . . .' She tailed off.

'I don't think we're that opposite.'

'No?'

'No.' I fiddled with my hands. 'Was it all about Alice? What happened in South America. I mean is that the thing that went wrong?'

'Alice got ill, Sam. That's made things harder for us. But even if she hadn't been ill, this family would still be in a mess.' She came and sat next to me; my erection returned. I wanted to kiss her gently and push her back on the bed and just kiss her and stroke her and hold her. She said, 'Love drills deep, Sam. You meet someone. Love drills deep. That feeling. I don't know anything about you. Maybe you know what I'm talking about but that feeling, it's the ultimate proof of, like, an after-life. You know? The way it can make you feel. Right here, in your tummy. It's absolutely just unbelievable. Literally unbelievable if you think all we are is we're just dust and water and what have you. No way, this is something completely different. It's a spiritual feeling. You know? Which, Doug is the only man who's made me feel like that. I mean he's not a *good* man.

He's done some stuff. He's stopped all that now but before, I mean, he has. I do know that. I don't want to know. But I do know. I know some of it. I can sweep all of it aside, Sam. Absolutely none of it do I even, like, give a shit about. I *should* do. Morally speaking. But when you are in love. When you are so in love. But some things stomp on all that. I mean . . . I'll just tell you. I might as well tell you what happened. What does it matter now? We both know Ted's not inviting you to dinner. Dimwit Doug left his car in blatant view, didn't he? It doesn't matter anymore. It's all finished. You were our last chance, Sam. It's all finished now. What do I care anymore? What happened is . . .' She looked at me. 'I'd like to suck your cock again, Sam. And maybe you could do some stuff to me too next time.' She laughed, it was a sad laugh. 'I think I need an affair. I don't know how else to cope anymore.'

The poor woman. But I had some good news. 'Celina,' I said. It felt a bit strange using her name. I usually avoid using people's names when I talk to them. 'I'm going to dinner,' I said. 'I'm going round tonight. Ted phoned me this morning. So I'll do everything I can, I promise, and hopefully, you know, hopefully everything will end up all right.'

A look of confusion formed on her face. Then it was unclear. I think I detected anger. And panic. It certainly wasn't the reaction I'd expected. She stood up, sat down, stood up. She was trembling. I was anxious to leave.

'You mean . . .' She paused, her voice was shaking too much. 'You mean I knelt there sucking your cock and . . . Oh God this is unbearable.' She was in despair. 'You have to leave now, Sam. You have to leave right now. And then you have to never come back here. Do you understand? Never. Not to see Alice. Or Doug. Do you understand?'

I didn't say anything. I really wanted to see Doug and Alice again.

'Do you fucking . . . What's wrong with you? You think it's feasible, what we've done, you come here and it's like nothing happened?' Her angry expression cracked and vulnerability rushed to her face. 'I have this one final chance, Sam. This one final chance. If you can just, at the dinner, if you can just do what we discussed, then I can start putting this family together again.'

'You still want me to go to the dinner?'

'Yes!' She seemed frightened by the sound of her own voice, looked around her. 'Yes,' she said in a hushed tone. 'Please, Sam. I've put my whole life into this family.'

'OK,' I said.

'And you won't come back here?'

I didn't say anything.

'Sam!' She covered her face with her hands. She looked up. 'Sam *please.*'

'OK.' The two letters got stuck at the back of my throat.

'Good. Now you have to leave. Go, quickly, before Alice wakes up.' She pushed me out of the room and closed the door. I was standing out in the hall, my head whirling a bit. Then Alice's door opened. She came out. She just sat there, staring at me. My mind clouded over, but I knew I'd done something to upset her. She spat at me. It didn't reach me and then she started coughing and she didn't stop for a long time. Her face went completely red. About a million things went through my mind at once. Most of all the noise of the coughing and the fact of Celina so close. It was those two things that pressed on me in the end. I went into a panic and ran out of the house. The sun was really bright on the way home, and the back of my neck was starting to flake.

Shit. I was sitting in my armchair. My web of deceit had

expanded somewhat. It really had spun out of control. I couldn't really comprehend it and I tried focusing on Ted's dinner instead. But that felt doomed to failure for some reason, and I had a vision of Ted literally hurling me out of his house.

I thought about Leticia, but I was certain she wouldn't be there. Missing person or not, I'd never meet her. Leticia. Leticia. Leticia. I started masturbating but I couldn't keep her face in my mind. I could go and get her photo? No, that's awful. I stopped, felt pretty rotten about myself. Then I realised. When I was with Celina, with her mouth warm and her tongue on me, when I was with Celina I should have thought about Leticia. I can't believe I didn't think of it. I was boiling up inside. I smashed my flat up.

I laid there in the debris. Mostly I'd just knocked things over and thrown things about. I'd tried to smash the TV screen but it proved too difficult so I just knocked the set over. I was pretty disgusted with myself. I visualised my insides, cavernous, with various rodents scuttling around. You're rotten, Sam. Completely rotten. What kind of man *are* you? I asked myself. Maybe it was the seriousness with which I asked the question but it set me off laughing. I lightened up a bit. I got up and surveyed the mess. I'll clear this up after I get sacked and sent home from work. I resolved to take the photo back to Ted's in order to stop any further violations of Leticia's image. I checked my watch; nearly half five. I should start getting ready. I headed for the shower.

A lovely thing happened as I was leaving my apartment. I'd resigned myself to carrying the box downstairs. I knew it would be hard but probably not as bad as going up. However, just as I was about to set off, the guy who lived opposite me, who I'd never met before, saw me struggling and offered to lend me a hand. I had a taxi waiting at the bottom so we didn't talk for long or say anything of consequence. But he was a nice chap. Perhaps I'd go around there some time. Not for any particular reason. Just to 'drop in.'

The butterflies in my stomach were really bad on the short taxi ride to Ted's. It now seemed that everything would be wonderful and they'd all be there; Ted's wife cooking all day, Leticia come especially. All of them there. Waiting for me. And I'd have to live up to expectations. The conversation couldn't flag for one moment. Hopefully there'll be drinks straight away, loosen me up a bit. And Leticia. She'd definitely be there. It was all so wonderful and scary. I chuckled sitting there in the back of the cab. A bright, bright glow shone inside me. The only blotch on my horizon, the only tiny blotch: my trousers were too tight.

My heart was really pounding as I walked up to Ted's door. Then, just before I got there, two young men walked out. They were both dressed in loose fitting, light weight, fashionable clothes – I don't usually notice clothes but because of how uncomfortable my suit trousers were, they were on my mind. One of the men was wearing sunglasses. The other guy, it wasn't until after he walked past me that I examined his face in my mind's eye, the other guy, I was pretty sure, was Ben. I stopped and turned. He was looking at me and I turned away again. I was sure I was right though. It was. It was Ben. I remembered what DCI Campbell had told me about him being 'with them.' I went up to the front door which they'd left open. I heard a car door close behind me. I rung the bell. 'Hello? Hello?' I peered inside the house but I couldn't see anyone. I went inside and as I did so I heard a car engine start. I turned around and saw a car pull away.

'Hello?' Nobody in the entrance hall. Which room do I go into? I decided on the kitchen, even if it would be a bit odd bumping into Ted's wife. After all, I'd never spoken to her before.

Just as I was about to enter the kitchen, Ted came out. He jumped and actually put his hand to his chest when he saw me. 'Fucking hell, mate. You scared me half to death you did.'

'Sorry,' I said. 'The door was open. I called out but nobody answered.'

He gazed at me, as if sizing me up. 'You're in your suit I see.'

I shrugged, embarrassed. Ted was wearing casual trousers and a short sleeved shirt.

'Listen, mate. We need to have a word. Can I get you a drink? Beer, something else. What do you fancy?'

'Beer's fine,' I said.

'Beer it is. You go to the lounge, make yourself at home. I'll be with you in a second.' He went back to the kitchen. I heard hushed voices. I went into the lounge and sat down.

Bloody Doug. He's a great guy and everything but he really got it wrong with the wear a suit thing. The waistband was really digging in. Can I actually put up with this all night? Especially when we're eating. I suppose I could undo the button if we were sitting around the table. But what if we had to get up suddenly?

I stood up. I was too uncomfortable and nervous to sit down. Wow, think about it, one of those voices in the kitchen could have been Leticia's. I remembered about the photo. I poked my head out of the door to check that nobody was coming, then took the photo out of my pocket. Looking at her I went into a sort of trance and when I came out of it I had no idea how long it had lasted. Shit, imagine if Ted or his wife or Leticia had walked in. I'd have looked like a complete nut. I put the photo back but in doing so knocked over another one. Oh, shit! My hands were shaking but I righted the photo and then Ted walked in. He handed me a beer.

'Thanks.'

'Cheers.' He raised his glass and we toasted. 'You're looking sharp, mate.'

'Yeah.' The blood rushed to my face.

'You haven't made this what I'm going to tell you any easier wearing that.' He stalked the length of the room then turned to face me. 'I owe you an apology I'm afraid, mate. We've had a spot of trouble needs dealing with today. Couple of utter tosspots came round. It's shit the wife up it has. And of course she's the one what's cooking. No excuse though. I hate rudeness. I hate rudeness and I feel I've been rude, mate.'

'It's OK,' I said.

'I'd be pissed off if I was you. Still, I'm glad you haven't done your nut. I've had enough to deal with this evening already.'

'Well,' I said. 'I suppose I'd better leave you to it.'

'You what?'

'Well I . . .'

'What do you take me for, mate? I'm not fucking slinging you out the minute you get here. Drink your fucking beer. Relax.'

I smiled. I was pretty tense and my waistband was digging in. Ted's glass was three quarters full. I took a big swig to catch up with him. Too big, and I gagged.

'What. A. Day.' He flopped down on the settee.

'I know what you mean.' What did that mean? What a comment. But Ted didn't seem to have heard. He was simmering about something. He was pretty scary like this. 'I'll tell you something,' he said. 'Them two. Coming round here. Fucking upset my wife. Cunts. They do that again I'll break their fucking necks.' He got up and for a terrifying moment I thought that he was going to break my neck, but he turned away from me and started pacing. 'I've got to think of something. Come on, Ted. Get your fucking brain in gear.'

I sipped my beer. My waistband was intolerable. Ted caught my eye. He stopped pacing and threw his hands up in the air. 'I'm sorry, mate. Look at me. Completely self-absorbed. We was all ready for you coming we was. We was all set. The wife climbing the walls. Then this shit happens. You'll come over again, won't you?'

'Sure.'

'We'll arrange it. Sooner rather than later. We'll have to. Like I say, the wife has been looking forward to this all week. Blames me she does. Bit harsh, eh?'

'Yeah.' I laughed; Ted didn't.

We were quiet for a few minutes.

'Did Leticia make it?' I said. 'Or did you tell her you'd cancelled?'

Ted's wife shouted something from the kitchen.

'Fucking long distance conversations, eh? I'll be back in a minute, yeah?' He went out.

There was a big photo of Leticia on the wall. I had the idea of taking it. I could stick it up my shirt. I was surprised how quickly my desire to take the photo overcame me. It burned inside me. I really, really wanted the photo. I moved closer, reached my hands out as if to take it off the wall. Just before it was too late, I snapped out of my trance. I was exhausted all of a sudden. Ted reappeared.

'Listen, mate, the wife's in a worse state than I thought. I'm going to have to send you packing I'm afraid. Next week though. Let's say that. Next Friday latest. We will not let another week go by we don't have dinner. Yeah? Sound alright to you?'

'Yep.'

'Great. OK, now piss off. I've got some patching up needs doing.' He led me to the door and closed it as soon as I was outside. Obviously he had a lot to think about. I started the walk home. Halfway down the road I realised that the cab had driven off with the Gold Series Deluxe barbecue inside.

I Think I Might Have Found Leticia

I enjoy brushing my teeth, I really do. I always take my time about it, and it's paid dividends too. My teeth are pretty white. You see lots of even very young people with quite yellowish teeth but mine are in a good state. I suppose you could even say I was proud of them. I was brushing and sort of unwinding. I'd been home for about an hour. I was going to call the cab company when I got home and get the barbecue back but I didn't have the energy in the end. It had been a hectic day and a bit of a letdown I suppose, dinner not having gone ahead. Still, it was better than if dinner had gone ahead and Leticia hadn't been there. At least this way there might be another chance to meet her. Possibly. I think I enjoy the brushing noise, that's part of it. It's sort of ambient, relaxing, frees your thoughts and lets you float off with your imagination. Not like silence, which can be stilting. And the rhythm. The gentle physical rhythm. I've never been gifted in a practical sense. But I do enjoy practical tasks. Which is a good thing I think. A man should enjoy using his body. I spat the toothpaste out feeling a lot better when there was a knock at the door. That's late. I suppose it's only half nine. Oh, maybe it's my neighbour, that would be good. It would be nice to have a chat with him. He seemed like a nice, normal guy. The sort of person I needed to get to know. I'd met a few people in the last week, maybe even made a few friends, but they all seemed a bit unpredictable. I needed a predictable, sturdy friend. Which is what he would be. A normal, decent chap. Almost boring in his way. I opened the door.

It was Doug. He had a day's worth of stubble on his face.

'Hi.'

'Alright.' He walked in. As he walked past me I noticed he smelt a bit, I don't know, tangy. He didn't seem too happy. In the first few moments I observed him dispassionately. Then I remembered that his wife and I had had, what, a 'sexual liaison?' Wow. Doug was unlikely to be happy.

'I've just been at the police station. That's where I've come from. I had one call. I've got one call, OK? I ought to have phoned my solicitor but nope, I phone my wife, because I love her. She hangs up. How about that, eh? I'm at a loss to explain what I've done to her, Sam.' He looked at me as though he wanted my input but what could I say? He said, 'I can't face it back there. Do you mind, mate? If I kip here tonight. Have you got space?'

For some reason I didn't particularly want him to stay the night but I said, 'Yeah, I suppose so. I'll sleep on the settee.'

'No don't do that. I'll be fine on the . . . Jesus Christ, Sam. What the hell happened? The place looks like a bomb's hit it.'

'Oh I, I was just looking for something. I guess I got a bit carried away.'

'I guess you did.'

There were a few moments of quiet.

'No, seriously,' he said. 'What we'll do, we'll put the settee to rights then I'll be fine. No worries. Honestly, mate. I could sleep on a slab of concrete I'm so tired. And I'll be out of your hair first thing tomorrow morning, OK? It's just, a bit of breathing space. You understand?'

'Sure,' I said. 'You can have my bed though. I mean it'll only take a few minutes to change the sheets. I mean I haven't got to get up in the morning or anything.'

'Sam, mate, stop. You're a good man. And you're already doing enough for me. And I appreciate it. I really do. You're a mate.' He hugged me and held me for quite some time. I felt pretty uneasy. I wondered maybe he does know about Celina and me and he's got a knife and he's about to stab me in the side. My side tingled in anticipation. Somehow or another I'd got myself involved in a 'love triangle.' I couldn't quite comprehend it. I didn't know how you were supposed to feel in such a situation. It was like something out of a film. Doug was quite smelly.

He released me. 'Shall we put this settee to rights? Otherwise I'll fall asleep standing up the way I'm feeling at the moment.'

We set the settee to rights and both settled down for the night. And I was very tired even though it wasn't even ten o clock.

Doug snores. It was five thirty. Already light outside and the birds were chirping. I'd got up about half three and gone to the toilet. Then, getting back into bed, I'd tuned in. To the snoring. And that was that. Tossing and turning. Covering my ears with the pillow. All to no avail. I'd close my eyes hoping to slip into that lovely weightlessness between consciousness and sleep, but it was no good.

Every so often he'd stop snoring. And I'd wait and wait, the tension mounting. Then, just when I dared to think, maybe, maybe, he'd start up again. Now, when he stopped, I just assumed he'd be off again in a minute. Occasionally though, my mind would relax just enough that the snoring faded into the background, and I'd think of Leticia and feel fuzzy inside. But really my image of her was never sharp enough. It lacked resolution. I regretted giving up my photo of her. I really wanted to look at her face again.

Two more hours passed and Doug kept snoring away. I might have been on bad terms with Celina and Alice but Doug liked me enough to come to me in his hour of need. That meant something. And he'd said we were mates. It all gave me a link to the family. Possibilities to see Celina and Alice again. Still, mate or not, the primary fact about him right now was his snoring. I couldn't take it anymore. I got up. And then what I did, because I had nowhere else to go, I went to work.

I was a bit nervous about work but not too bad really. I just went and sat down at my desk. What else could I do? Nobody questioned me or even seemed to notice me. One of the guys who sat behind me was there but his head was down and he didn't say hello. Angela wasn't there yet. And there was no sign of my boss. I even thought about doing some work, just to pass the time, but it never quite happened. About quarter of an hour later, Angela turned up. As soon as she'd sat down I said, 'Hi, Angela. How was your day off?' My tone was ultra pleasant. I felt a strong desire to be friendly to her.

'It didn't feel like a day off. I was running around all day.' She told me all the things she'd done yesterday. 'I'm exhausted.'

'Well you look rested.'

'Whatever you reckon.'

'You do,' I said. 'You look full of beans.'

She giggled. 'Where'd they put the old Sam. You know, the quiet one.'

'I don't know but I'm going to find out.'

We both laughed; I noticed she had bruising on her arm.

'I'm glad to be back,' she said. 'If only for the fact of I don't have to work as hard here as I do on my days off. I mean I know it's boring and everything, but we have it easy if you think about it.'

'Yeah,' I said. Then I asked her out for dinner. Just like that. And she said yes. She'd cook for me. 'Don't worry, I'll offload the kids on their grandmother.' That's good, I thought. For some reason though, I just couldn't work up a lot of enthusiasm about it. It was like a few years ago when I booked myself a holiday; I was going on my own. I had a comparable lack of enthusiasm, a feeling that the word 'holiday' promised more than I would get, to what I now anticipated from my date. I turned back to my computer thus breaking off conversation with Angela. I was more than usually aware of her presence though.

A very short while later, probably less than a minute, my boss came to my desk. 'Do you mind if I have a word, Sam?'

'Sure.'

'In my office if that's OK.'

'OK.'

We went to her office.

'Take a seat.'

I took a seat.

'Sam.' She paused. 'Sam, you're not supposed to be here today. You weren't supposed to be here yesterday either.'

'Yesterday?'

'No. You booked both days as leave, remember. You had two weeks and two days of leave. I was there when you filled in the sheet. I approved it. I told you we couldn't give you all twelve days together and you elected to take two weeks off, then work the Monday, Tuesday and Wednesday of the following week and have a long weekend. You told me you were going camping with your friend or something. Long weekend. I noted it all down.'

I remembered it all. I felt pretty embarrassed about that camping story I'd made up. She was right though. I was more surprised that she had remembered than that I'd forgotten.

'So,' she said. 'Get out of here. I don't want to see you until Monday. To be honest, you do look like you could do with a rest.'

I hesitated. 'Is that all?'

'Yep.'

I hesitated again, went to say something but didn't.

She stood up; I stood up. I felt slightly off balance. I looked at her and she averted her eyes.

'Come on,' she said. 'Off you go. Some of us are unfortunate enough to have work to do today.'

I nodded, and with that, left. I stood there in the office. My sense of balance was off. Nothing seemed solid, people seemed to leave streaks of colour trailing behind them as they walked. In a daze, I went over to my desk. I said something incoherent to Angela about why I was leaving and I'd see her later and then I left the office.

What is going on? I *know* she saw me. It's just ri*dic*ulous. I kicked a lamppost and after a few seconds my toe really started to hurt. But I nurtured the pain. I was walking along muttering to myself like a madman. The right side of my head throbbed with a sharp pain. I leaned against a wall and tried to calm myself down. My eyes were dry and I realised how wide open they'd been. Calm down, I told myself. Calm down. Gradually I got control of my breathing. Twenty minutes later I was ready to start walking again. I didn't feel good though. I felt like I'd been attacked.

Even by the evening I hadn't quite recovered. And my sensitive state wasn't helped by a fright I got when I came in. When I opened the door I saw Doug sitting in my armchair, facing me. My armchair never used to face the door. He'd tidied up the flat but in doing so he'd rearranged everything. The position of the armchair was the most noticeable change, what with him facing me like that. How long had he been sat there? He was staring at me. I turned away to close the door and when I turned back he was still staring at me.

'Hello,' I said.

'Have you got something to tell me, Sam?'

He knows about me and Celina. I froze, and it took a very long time before Doug broke the silence.

'I had a bit of a tidy up. Least I could do you having let me stay over and all the rest of it. Anyway, I'm in your bedroom; I hope you don't mind, I wasn't snooping or anything; I'm in your bedroom and what do I find on the floor? What do I find crumpled up on the floor? I've hung it up now but what do I find? A certain suit. Yes? A certain suit that you and I purchased for a special occasion. Crumpled on the floor. I think, what's this about? What's this about, Sam? When did you wear the suit?'

Rattled but relieved, I found the words to tell him about what happened with Ted and how we'd arranged dinner for next week.

'And you didn't mention about me and Celina wanting to make up?'

'He really was distracted,' I said. 'I thought it would be better next week. When he's concentrating. And when his wife and Leticia are there too.'

'Yeah, yeah. You're right of course.' He paused. 'Do you not like the suit?'

'It's a bit tight.'

He laughed. 'I told you it was too tight. I was the same when I was your age. Couldn't give a toss if it fit or not, as long as I got out of the shop unscathed. Never mind. I was thinking about it afterwards as it happens. I reckon a suit might have been overdoing it.'

He'd seemed pretty sure it was appropriate when he had me trawling round the shops. Some people are like that though, they seem completely certain of something one moment, fiercely so, the next they're blasé about whether or not they were right and the importance of their opinion. I tend to find it a bit disconcerting, such behaviour. I have trouble getting fierce even about things where my position is ingrained and unchangeable, let alone about passing fancies.

'This is good news though,' he said. 'This is really good news. I mean he invited you round. That means he never saw me that time, parked outside his house. Means I didn't fuck everything up. Great news. Enough to get me back on good terms with Celina you reckon?'

'I suppose so. Was she upset about you getting arrested?'

'Arrested? No. Doesn't mean shit. The police do that. Once you're on file they do that. I'm not squeaky clean, Sam. I got into some things. Nothing serious though. I never had the stomach for anything serious. And genuinely, my conscience got to me. I know the difference between right and wrong, Sam. I'm a good bloke. A family man.' He stopped talking, a tear ran down his cheek. 'And I appreciate people. It's rare but when you get a person, he genuinely wants to help you out, that really gets me. Gets me right here.' He put his hand on his heart. 'Makes me feel a common bond with the rest of the species.' He laughed. 'Something like that anyway.' He stood up, came over to me and shook my hand. 'Cheers, Sam. If you can help us out with this thing I'll be eternally grateful.' He looked at me with intense fondness. I felt privileged, uneasy, undeserving of his fondness, but most of all confused. What had I done for him? What could I do for him in the future? In that moment I'd completely forgot. And I wasn't much clearer now, hours later. All I can remember is agreeing to 'put in a good word' for Doug and his family with Ted. In any case, Doug seemed to confer a great deal of impor-tance on the task and on me as its facilitator. 'Right,' he said. 'I'd best be off. I've got a wife to placate.' And with that, pretty much, he was off.

Now it was evening. I'd recently finished having dinner with Angela. I'd started recovering from earlier with my boss but every so often something Angela said, or more likely the way she said it, or some twitch she had, or something about her body language, made me shudder and I had to concen-trate hard to force down my feelings from that afternoon. I didn't feel tense in Angela's company though. I felt no pres-sure to impress. She seemed impressed whatever I did, even when I just sat there, obviously distracted. I even yawned a few times. I knew I was treating her like shit but I simply felt too lethargic to do anything about it. And she really didn't seem to care or even notice. Anyway, after dinner we went over to the settee and at some point our eyes met, and she moved her head towards me, and either I did nothing or made a minute movement towards her. In any event, we ended up with our tongues in each other's mouths. Her tongue tasted like the dinner we'd just had and so, I suppose, did mine. The erection I had was just an automatic reaction. Angela was a nice person but not only did I not think her attractive, I thought her actively unattractive. In that sense it was surprising that I continued kissing her. I certainly didn't want to see her body which struck me as shapeless and unappealing. I also, for some reason, imagined that it would be blotchy. I suppose it was my sense of lethargy that stopped me from pulling away. I felt her hands running through my hair. She was making slurping sounds and managed to force me to recline. She was on top of me. Out of interest, I squeezed the flesh on the side of her body. I wanted to find out how flabby and loose she was. Slightly more than I expected as it turned out. Next, still kissing her, I tried to get it so that I had exactly a fistful of flesh in my hand – as full as possible but with no overspill. In doing so, I must have lost concentration because I realised I'd squeezed her pretty hard and she let out a yelp and pulled away from me.

'Sorry,' I said.

'So you like that sort of thing.' She smiled. Her smile seemed to accentuate her unattractiveness and I felt my face screwing up looking at her. 'Hold on a minute.' She got off me and went out of the room. I sat up and put my face in my hands. You have to leave. I didn't like what was happening to me today. I was having unpleasant feelings about people. In truth I'd have been glad to have Angela as a friend at work. When I thought about her not in the way I was now, but purely, almost not looking at her physically at all, but into her instead, I saw something, something about her that was pretty wonderful and touching and made me glow inside. What I saw, I think, was a capacity to love.

She came back in with a pair of handcuffs and a whip. I didn't know how to react so I just sat there. She came towards me. 'I bought these when I was wanting to be a dominatrix. I just sort of kept them.'

'Oh right.'

She smiled and handcuffed herself to the arm of the settee. 'Here.' She gave me the whip. It's weird, I didn't want to whip her, but as the situation unfolded I had no real feelings about anything at all. I seemed to have an inability to look forward, I couldn't see the link between her handing me the whip and me whipping her.

'Hold on a second. Sorry.' She undid the handcuffs and stripped naked. I'd thought that I might find her body a bit unpleasant, but I didn't. I did detect a slight change in atmosphere with her standing there naked but that was all. An increase in pressure perhaps. She handcuffed herself to the arm of the couch. 'Start off you could just spank me,' she said. 'Spank?' But I knew what she meant. I spanked her on the arse. 'Harder.' I spanked her harder. 'Harder.' I spanked her harder. And harder. I kept going. My palm made a satisfying smack on her buttocks and if I watched closely enough I could see a white handprint come and go on her skin. And her flesh shook and wobbled. 'The whip.' I whipped her buttocks. Then, of my own volition, I whipped her back. The surface area of the whip was quite wide and it made a really satisfying crack where the leather hit her skin. My mind started wandering and I thought about my boss and how she'd ignored me giving her the finger and I got irritated and whipped harder. I heard Angela whimpering, but it was like a background noise, it didn't fully register. I watched her skin go red when the whip hit it and the blood came up to the surface. I had the vague thought that I'd like to cut into the skin but the surface area of the whip was too wide for that. Then I wondered what would happen if I whipped black skin? Would the skin go red when you struck it or would it go white? The next thing I knew I saw Leticia tied to the settee and me whipping her. A great surge went through me; energy, desire, anger. Then revulsion, and I let out a cry and dropped the whip. The image had just popped into my head from nowhere, it really had. 'What's wrong?' "I have to go. Sorry, I'll see you, I'll see you Monday, OK?' I left her flat.

You're rotten inside, Sam. That's clear. I was walking around my flat eating straight out of a packet of cereal. I felt empty inside, but not hungry empty, more rats have gnawed my insides out empty. I had a sort of toxic, acidic feeling in my stomach. Still, eating was all I could think to do. So I was eating, but it wasn't making any difference. I can't stand this, I thought. I actually can't stand this. I'm frazzled. I have to get her out of my head. Or I have to see her right away. I thought of going round Ted's. But what would I say? It could be a sensitive issue, especially if she *is* missing. I felt the acid rising up my chest and started sobbing. I'm dying inside, I have to do something. I paced around for a few minutes more, eating my cereal. I kept repeating out loud, 'I'm dying inside, I'm dying inside.' Then, on top of the dinner I'd had at Angela's, the cereal registered, and on top of everything else I was overfull. I burped, an acidic belch. 'I can't live like this.' Then I had an idea, not a fully conscious one at this stage, but it was enough to get me sitting at the computer. I logged on and brought up an internet dating site. I'd joined the site about eight months ago on a six month membership. I'd quickly seen that I was incapable of sustaining flirtatious conversation online and had stopped using the site. I was still a member though. I suppose they keep debiting your account until you actually quit. I don't know, I never check my statements.

Anyway, I logged on feeling quite excited. Hope had made my life seem liveable again, even if in the back of my mind I knew that the idea of my search working was ludicrous. Why would Leticia be on a dating site? And even if she were . . . No, if she was, I'd find her. I entered the search details.

She could be anywhere but I'd start with London. I put in to search for people within fifty miles of London. Age? Doug and Celina had said she was older than Alice but I was pretty sure she was under thirty. I typed in 21-30. I put in a few other details. When I came to ethnicity I immediately put in black, but then I thought, is her ethnicity black? I mean she is black but her parents are white. No, she'd have put in black. Otherwise it would just confuse people, Leticia would realise that. I hit search.

At first, the odd face made my heart jump. Maybe. I'd click on the profile but it wouldn't be her. Then such faces came up fewer and fewer times. Still, there were a lot of black women within fifty miles of London. I'd been going over an hour, head rested on my hand, clicking through the pages, when I saw the photo. My mouse was about to click onto the next page and then the photo registered and my heart started pounding and I clicked on the profile. The photo wasn't in particularly good focus and the girl in the photo was standing quite far back from the camera, but it was exactly like a picture I'd seen when Doug and Celina had shown me their South America album. I was sure of it. My hands were shaking. I clicked on 'email her.' A thousand things I could write went through my head, but in the end all I did was write 'hi' and click send. A message came up: L-Hot-Chile knows you're interested. L as in Leticia? Chile as in Chile, South America? I was buzzing. All I could do now was wait. I stood up. There was nothing to do but wait. I went to bed.

Alice Moves In

I went to sleep surprisingly quickly. It was when I woke up and went to the toilet at ten to four that my problems started. As soon as I got back into bed my mind was racing. I couldn't take it, lying there with my eyes wide open, my muscles tense. I jumped out of bed and switched the computer on and checked whether I had any messages. No. Hardly surprising really. Still, it was disappointing, which put enough of a dampener on my hopes that the unsettling expectancy in my stomach faded and I could lay pretty still. I couldn't sleep though. Was I sure it was her? It looked like her but the picture was fuzzy. But that wasn't the point. The point was it was exactly like the picture from Doug and Celina's album. And how about her name, L-Hot-Chile? I have to check their album. That'll be easy enough, I'll just go over there, tell them I need to see the photos again as preparation for visiting Ted or something. They'll go for that. They'll do anything to make sure my visit to Ted's is a success. I'll go tomorrow. What's the earliest I can get there? Midday? They're not students. Ten o' clock. I reckon I could get there for ten. They've got a little kid, Saturday morning, at least one of them will be in. I looked at my watch. Half four. Five and a half hours to go. I felt tired and I knew I'd be tired when I got up but I'd pretty much given up on sleep. My mind started floating off, and I imagined finding a message in my account, *Let's meet up,* just like that, and we would, we would meet up, in blinding sunlight, in some indistinct location, a place with nothing solid, where colours were blurred, an impressionist painting, and that bright sunlight. *Hi. Hi,* she says. And lying there in bed my insides swelled with happiness and I chuckled because I was so happy.

I liked your photo.

Thanks, she says.

It's a beautiful day.

It's perfect, she says.

I'm so pleased we met today.

Yeah.

And we both laugh and I laughed lying there feeling as though I would burst with delight and I couldn't stop laughing and then the light that shone on Leticia went up to full blast and absorbed us and I reached the pinnacle of delight and then I started crying. Weeping. It was unbelievable how much joy it would give me to be with her. How much I wanted her.

No messages. I stood up. It was seventeen minutes past nine. Eighteen minutes until I could go, otherwise I'd be too early. Still, it's no good hanging around here. I paced around. I really need to get rid of all this nervous energy I've been feeling lately. I should start jogging again or something. I checked my watch; it was nineteen minutes past nine. I would leave at nine thirty. I'd check my messages at nine twenty eight and then I'd leave. My mobile phone rang. I took it out of my shorts pocket.

'Hello.'

'Sam.'

'Doug?'

'We're having a dispute over here.' His tone was not warm.

'Oh?'

'Dispute needs solving. Seems you're the one can clear things up for us.'

'Oh?'

'Yeah. Do us a favour, get your arse round here asap.'

'OK. I'll, I'll leave straight away.'

'We'll be here.' He hung up. After a short period of confusion I froze in realization. He knew. He knew about me and Celina. He knew, he knew, he knew. Bollocks. I swallowed hard. Then for some reason I felt OK again. I checked my messages. Nope. Then I left.

Doug opened the door. 'Hello.'

'Hello,' I said.

He led me through the house to the kitchen. Celina and Alice were sitting at the breakfast table. Celina glanced at me; I looked away. I was pretty nervous again. I mean, in Doug's house. And with his daughter right here, being asked about the details of a liaison I had with his wife. Alice was staring into space. She hadn't acknowledged me.

Doug said, 'Take a seat, Sam.'

I took a seat. It was a few moments before anyone said anything; I felt particularly uncomfortable in Celina's company again. Doug said, 'We've been talking to Alice, Sam. She's been talking to us. She's been telling us things.' He cleared his throat. 'According to Alice, you asked her to move in with you. What are you playing at, Sam? I mean she needs round the clock medical care.' Alice chuckled. Doug glanced at her then continued. 'She needs round the clock medical care. She's sick as a parrot. Are you in a position to provide round the clock medical care?'

'I've been thinking of leaving my job,' I heard myself say.

Doug stared at me. 'Are you joking around, mate?'

'I mean I didn't exactly ask her to move in.'

'I thought you said you did.'

'Did I?'

There was a pause. Then Alice said, in a flat tone, 'I'm moving in with Sam.'

Celina made a noise as if she were about to cry but managed to hold back.

I tried to clear things up. 'We talked about it, Alice and me. But I said it was up to you.'

'It's not up to them.'

Celina said, 'We're your parents.'

'What are you playing at, Sam?' Doug said. 'I mean seriously. She's sick. She's really sick. It's not something you just decide on the spur of the moment.'

'You've seen her,' Celina said. 'You've seen how it affects her.' Alice chuckled but Celina went on, 'She needs love, Sam. Unequivocal love. Can you give her that? For God's sake, you only met her a week ago.'

'Sam's very loving,' Alice said. 'You should know that.'

I shifted in my seat.

'You seem like a decent bloke, Sam. I've only known you a while and all the rest of it, but you've always struck me as a decent bloke. But it's difficult to see how you've not taken advantage of a sick girl here.'

'She's nineteen,' I said.

Alice smiled.

After a pause, Celina said, 'She's not leaving.'

'What, I'm, like, imprisoned, huh? Is this communist China or something?'

Celina didn't look at her. 'I know you're sick. I know you don't mean it.'

Doug put his hand on his wife's shoulder.

Alice stared at them, half smiling, in a kind of *faux*

astonishment. She said, enunciating every word, 'I am exactly the same as I always was.'

Doug and Celina didn't move.

'Can you hear me? Can anybody *hear* me? I was exactly the same. Can you hear me, you deluded bitch?'

I looked at Celina for a reaction. I thought maybe I saw her eyes flicker.

Doug said, 'I have to say, mate, you've opened a can of fucking worms here you really have.'

'Sorry. I didn't mean to,' I said. 'I thought it might be nice.' Why did I say that?

Celina said 'Nice for who?'

'I . . .'

'You're an absolute shit. Do you know that? You take advantage of people, that's what you do. Who are you anyway? Why don't you crawl back where you came from?' Her eyes were piercing and bloodshot. I really wanted to leave.

'OK, OK,' Doug said. 'Perhaps you should calm down, love. OK?'

'Why? He's a piece of shit. Aren't you? You piece of shit.'

Alice started laughing and it pierced my ears. This really was all too much.

Doug waited for her to stop, took a deep breath, and whispered in Celina's ear. Then, when he'd finished, he said, 'OK?' She didn't respond. 'OK?' After a pause, she nodded.

'I don't see the sense in making this into a big thing,' Doug said to me. 'Like I said, I don't know what you were thinking but let's just . . . I wanted your side of things. Obviously Alice won't be moving in with you.' He paused. 'That's all really.' He paused again and I wondered if that was my cue to leave. 'And I hope, you know, I hope we're still alright about the other stuff. Ted's and that.'

'Uh, yeah, sure.'

Alice went into peels of laughter but I got the impression it was forced. 'This is so pathetic. Sort your own problems out. You two are such losers. Why does everything have to be about *Ted*?'

'Why don't you grow up, Alice?' Celina's face was tired. She looked old.

'Because I'll be dead in a couple of months. What's the point?'

Celina's eyes were wide with distress. I was sure tears were pressing against the back of her eyes and for some reason, my own eyes started to sting thinking about her. What a sensitive woman.

'Sam,' Alice said. 'Wheel me out. Trust me, like, they will do whatever you want as long as they need you about this Ted shit. Pathetic but true. They have no control over this situation whatsoever. Am I right?' She looked at Celina and Doug but Celina had her eyes to the floor and Doug was staring into space. He seemed to have resigned himself to defeat. Alice had all the power here. Plus I really did want her to live with me. I really did. It would be great. I felt different around her. Sort of more alive. Everything seemed bolder. Yeah, let's try it out. For a week at least. It'll be like an extended sleepover. Give them all a bit of breathing space.

'Are you going to wheel me out, or what?'

'Yeah. Yeah. Um, I mean, Doug, Celina, if you guys want to come round. I mean, anytime. You know where I live. We'll just see how this works out. Might give you all a bit of breathing space, eh?'

They didn't respond.

I directed my next comment to Doug. 'Um, I'll let you know how I get along at Ted's, OK?'

After a pause, he nodded, not looking at me.

'Come *on.*'

'Right,' I said. 'We best be off.' I wheeled Alice out, feeling pretty guilty about my various interventions in Doug's family life lately. I liked the man, I really did.

'This might be a problem.'

'What floor do you live on?'

'The top one. There are sixty seven stairs.'

'Well you'll have to, like, carry me then.'

I looked at her. She was very thin, more so even than last week when I first met her. God, I thought, she's really ill. I wondered, was she heavier than a Gold Series Deluxe barbecue? The answer was, probably she was. But the best thing was she was much easier to carry; one arm under her knees, the other supporting her back. Not too bad at all. After twenty or so stairs I had a spurt of energy and started running. She held on tightly and hid her face and started laughing. It was great. I felt great, I really did. 'This is going to be *so* fun,' she said, and I believed her absolutely, it certainly would. Still, I wondered how would she get out of the building if there was a fire and I wasn't around? Oh well, it doesn't matter. It doesn't matter. I burst into a run again and she was giggling and my thighs burned, but in a good way, in a good way.

I left her outside my door and ran downstairs and then ran all the way up with the wheelchair. I was out of breath but full of energy. Then it was weird; I wheeled her in and wandered into the centre of the room. The curtains were closed and it was pretty gloomy although you could tell it was a sunny day outside. The computer was humming. Did I have any messages? I was itching to go and check. Alice's eyes were glazed over. 'Here we are,' I said.

'Huh? . . . Oh. Yeah.'

Hmm. What now? I didn't really know how to live with anybody. I'd lived with my parents – I really should go and see Mum – and then at university we'd shared a kitchen; my room was my own though. Where were my university friends now? It was pretty rubbish of me not keeping in touch. I meant to. I really did. But something stopped me. It never seemed like the right time or something. Shame. I'd had some good times back then. I looked at Alice. Her eyes were closed. 'Alice?' She didn't answer. I took a few steps towards her, spoke louder. 'Alice?' She didn't answer. I listened carefully. Yep, she was asleep. You could tell it from her breathing. What now? The computer! I rushed over and wiggled the mouse about and the screen faded in. The dating website was still open on my profile. *Hi, I'm an open minded sort of guy* . . . yada, yada, yada. I checked my inbox, sort of breathless with expectation. Oh my God, she's replied. She's actually replied. 'She actually replied,' I said aloud. I checked to see if Alice had stirred; she hadn't. Good job I can hear her breathe when she sleeps. Otherwise how would I know if she died? I turned back to the computer. My hand was unsteady as I clicked on the message.

Hi ya! Thanx for the message.

Just saw your profile. I think we live really close together. Do you know the Red Deer? The one with the beer garden out front?

L xxx

I did know the Red Deer. I'd never been inside of course, but I did know it. I hovered my fingers over the keyboard and began typing.

Hi,

Thanks for the reply! Yes I do know the Red Deer.

Exclamation mark necessary? Leave it. It's, you know, expected.

I've been looking for an excuse to go there.

Nope. Delete that. 'It's my favourite pub' maybe? No, what if it's shit?

How about meeting up? Red Deer or wherever you like.

Speak soon,
Sam

I pressed send. Now I just play the waiting game. Alice was still asleep. I went over to the window and looked out. The sun was out. And it was pretty hot in the flat, it really was. I decided to go out. Then, as I was slapping my sun cream on, I realised, I couldn't leave Alice alone. Could I? What if there was a fire? I was so used to coming and going as I pleased. I stood there with my hands on my hips acutely and disproportionately conscious of my loss of freedom. It wasn't as if I really used my freedom. I just go out for my walks. Alice looked pretty while she slept. I wondered should I wake her up? Then a sort of wooziness came over me. I was absolutely shattered. I sat down in my armchair and before I knew it I was sound asleep.

I woke up with a thick head. My neck ached and my eyes felt gunky and took a while to open. When I was a kid I used to get this thing where I would wake up in the morning and I couldn't open my eyes; my eyelids would be too heavy. I used to lay there wondering if I'd ever be able to open them again. That didn't happen to me anymore but I still thought about it and was thinking about it now. My neck and shoulders really ached. I felt the back of my neck and it was hot and the skin was flaking. The sun had finally got me. I stretched and looked across the room, expecting to see Alice. However, I did not see Alice. She wasn't there. I stood up, felt a bit dizzy. Then I wandered through to the kitchen and edged the bathroom door open. Not in there. (That was another thing, I'd have to get the bathroom up to scratch for a disabled person, get those bars fitted. The whole thing seemed ill thought out now. I couldn't remember seeing bars in Doug and Celina's bathroom though). My bedroom door was shut. I pushed the handle down and eased it open.

'Close the door!' Alice's voice was croaky; she was in my bed. I closed the door. I could make her shape out in the light that managed to get through the curtains but her face was in the shadows. 'When was the last time you washed these sheets, Sam?'

'I don't know. A week ago maybe.'

'They're making me itch.'

'Sorry.'

'Sam. Please, like, seriously, *please* stop apologizing. It was me who got in your bed.'

'OK. Do they smell?'

'They're kind of musty.'

'Oh.' There was a pause. 'I was thinking about I need to install those bars so you can go to the toilet.'

'You? Install bars?' She laughed.

'What?'

'You're not exactly Mr. Practical are you?'

'How do you know?'

'Some things are obvious.'

'I'll get someone round then.'

'I'll manage.' She yawned. 'So OK, I was thinking we could share this bed. Like, I usually sleep in the daytime and I *assume* you sleep at night. So we can just swap, huh?'

So how would we spend time together?

She said, 'What are you doing today anyway?'

'I was going to go for a walk.'

'Uh huh.'

I hesitated. 'Alice, I was going to say, I mean, there are sixty seven stairs you have to go down to get out of here. So basically you can't get out. Unless I get you out.'

'And?'

'Well if there was a fire or something and I wasn't here then you'd be in trouble.'

'True.'

'So we need to make sure I'm here. That we . . . come and go together I suppose.'

She didn't say anything. I think she was looking at me; it was difficult to tell in the dark.

'. . . What do you think?' I asked.

'How likely is a fire?'

'Not very.'

'Sam, I'll be dead in a month or two anyway.'

The comment hung there and had an intense effect on me.

Then she said, 'So go out whenever you want.'

I just stood there.

'What's wrong with you?'

I said, 'Isn't there somewhere you'd like to go? We could take a holiday together or something.'

'I just want to sleep. So go for your walk, OK?'

'OK.'

She seemed to still be looking at me, then she turned over on her side, her back to me. I left the room and burst into tears.

I'd never really considered the emotional effect of 'bringing death into my flat' but it turned out to be quite strong. I really needed to get out of there. I pulled back the curtain. Another glorious day. The sun was out and bright as anything. And somewhere. Somewhere under the sun, was Leticia. Where is she? I asked the sun. Then I closed the curtain and checked my messages. Nothing from L-Hot-Chile. I left the flat.

The heat. The tourists. Sweaty in London. Crowded streets. I walked past cafes and the food looked pretty appetising but I didn't want to go in and sit down and eat on my own. The streets were surging with people. I didn't know where I was. My eyes were stinging from sun cream. The tube had got too hot and I'd had to get off. I was somewhere pretty central though. There were loads of shops and people. My body was really lacking in energy and my feet ached but I just kept walking. Eventually I got to a place where all the shops were shut and the streets were empty. It was like a ghost town; I went up to one shop and apparently it only opened Monday to Friday. I was very confused and wandered around feeling like someone was playing a trick on me. I went into a shopping arcade and all the shops were shut and nobody was about. At first I was mildly intrigued, but then I got irritated and my neck started itching and I hurried back to rejoin the crowds. It was starting to get late now and the restaurants were filling up. I found myself looking in the windows, seeing if there was anyone I recognised. Then I started looking out for Leticia. But after a while I got a sinking feeling; she wasn't here. All these people and she wasn't here. I felt very lonely. Then I spotted an internet café.

L-Hot-Chile had not replied. It probably wasn't Leticia anyway. I'd never get to see that photo in Doug and Celina's album now. I wondered had Celina told Doug about our liaison? They were such an honest pair. Such an emotional, honest pair. Surely the secret couldn't stay kept for long. How would Doug react? How *does* a man react if you have an elicit liaison with his wife and the very next day take his daughter from right under his nose? He might beat me up. I'd never been beaten up before.

I left the internet café and the sun had gone in and, in fact, it was pretty overcast. Muggy still, but now rain was on the horizon. I started walking, I had even less energy now, and after a while I ended up in Chinatown. The smells were spicy and varied and good and I sat down on a bench and just sort of took them in and watched the people go past. Most of the people were Chinese, I don't know if I was surprised by that or not, but anyway, those that weren't seemed to be white. I'd pretty much given up hope of finding Leticia by now. In fact, I'd had enough. My legs were aching and I didn't want to walk anymore. But I didn't want to go home either. I never liked going back to an empty flat but it seemed worse going back to a flat you share but where the other person is asleep. Not only are you to all intents and purposes alone, you have to keep the noise down too. But there was nowhere else to go. Angela's? . . . No. In the end, I decided to do what I possibly should have done ages ago; I decided to visit Mum.

Mum wasn't in though. I phoned her and she was off playing golf. The reception was bad and she told me she was playing the last hole and would I phone back? I felt a bit rejected, standing there outside the house. It was weird because I was usually the one thinking I should visit her more often. Oh well. I looked at my watch; it was twenty past eight; dusk was settling in. I started walking towards the tube; Alice should be up by now.

I opened the door and found Alice sitting there watching TV. She didn't acknowledge my entrance. I instantly felt tense. This was getting ridiculous. She was completely unpredictable; I had no idea what mood she would be in.

'Hi,' I said.

She didn't respond.

I sat down in my armchair. 'What are you watching?'

Silence.

'I was walking for hours. Ended up going to see my mum. She wasn't in though.'

No answer. I glanced at the TV. It was an action film, lots of explosions and all the rest of it. I didn't recognise the film. I yawned and rubbed my hand over my face. Then I heard a knocking sound and saw Alice rocking her wheelchair. It was swinging from one side to another. I held my breath and waited. Her face had a real look of aggression on it. She leaned way over to the left, then way over to the right; she seemed to be suspended in that position; then the chair fell and she slid out onto the floor. She didn't look at me but her eyes were open. I looked at her for a little while, then said, 'I'm going to bed.'

I was itching all over. I'd never get to sleep! I could hardly get out of bed now though, not having 'made my move' with Alice. She'd think she'd won, forcing me into bed when I didn't want to be there. God. I was absolutely starving as well. All that walking and, despite the number of cafes I'd passed, I hadn't eaten all day. What was really getting to me, what was terrorizing me, I wanted to check my messages. If she'd been out today she might have got home a little while after I was in the internet café and left me a message. Well this is just ridiculous. I was so frustrated I could hardly breathe. My stomach rumbled. The computer was so close it was teasing me. I spread my fingers out to their full span and felt them twitching, wanting to hit that 'check messages' key. I should move flat. If I lived closer to the ground floor I'd be able to climb out the window. I bet those internet cafes are open all night; I could have headed off to one now. I looked at my watch; it was only quarter to ten. This is ridiculous. I ground my teeth and grabbed the bed sheet with my fist and pulled at it. I sobbed. I just want to check my messages. I let out a low roar; I could feel the veins in my neck popping up. I got out of bed. Alice might have fallen asleep again. I'd pretend I was getting a glass of water and sort of wander into the living room with it. I went out of the room; the lights were off and I couldn't really see into the rest of the flat. As quickly as I could, I made myself a glass of water. Then, casually as you like, I walked into the living room with it. At this point I realised I was wearing only my boxer shorts and felt a bit exposed should Alice see me. But there was nothing I could do now. It took a little while to adjust to the shadows but it seemed that Alice was still lying on the floor and her wheelchair was tipped over. I listened out for her breathing; didn't sound as though she was asleep. Dead? Should I check? The pull of the computer was too great and I checked my messages.

She'd replied!

Hi

I'm just going to the Red Deer now. I'll be there 'til about eleven. It would be great to see you there.

L xxx

Wow. It wasn't ten yet. If I hurried I could be there in half an hour. I could meet Leticia in half an hour. I heard movement behind me. Alice getting back into her chair probably. There was no way I could turn around. That would be giving in. I'd have to sit there until she'd got up. Anyway, I needed a minute to think. I'd have to shower. Should I wear my suit? Suit, to a pub? I could hear Alice breathing heavily, the wheelchair rattling about. It would be useful to have her advice about what to wear.

'Are you going out?' she said.

I didn't turn around. 'Yes.'

'You were out all day.'

'I didn't want to wake you up.'

There was a pause, then she grunted a few times. I had a look at the photo. It was. It *was* that photo from Celina and Doug's album. I was running out of time, I couldn't wait for Alice. I stood up and, just as I was about to move away from the desk, I saw Alice in her wheelchair, moving towards me at pace; it was a pretty scary thing coming through the darkness. It smacked into the chair and bashed my leg into the desk and I cried out and stumbled around holding my thigh.

I turned around and Alice was just sitting there. I think she smiled. I found it a bit frightening and a chill actually went up my spine. I went and turned the lights on. Alice was staring at me. Her expression was blank and impossible to read.

'Slap me,' she said.

'No.'

'If I run over your foot will you slap me?'

'I'd rather you didn't run over my foot.'

'That's why you'd slap me.'

'I have to go out.'

She glanced at the computer. 'You going on a date?'

'No. Sort of.'

'Leticia wouldn't be on a dating website.'

I looked at the computer. 'Have you ever seen your parent's photo album?'

'More times than I wanted to.'

'Is that picture on the screen in it?'

'Maybe. Yeah.'

I hesitated. 'I'm going for a shower.'

'Sam?'

'Yeah?'

'I want you to slap me in the face sometime.'

'I don't want to.' We looked at each other. Right into each other's eyes. It was all too much. I turned and went off for my shower.

I slowed my pace as I got closer to the Red Deer. It was thirty six minutes past ten; I had about three minutes walking time left. I'd been quick in the shower and then put on jeans and a T shirt. An easy choice really. It was Doug who had me all messed up about clothes, but really there was no issue. I felt pretty comfortable; my clothes were a bit crumpled but it was short notice and I didn't want to look like I'd made too much of an effort. It was shame I couldn't ask Alice's opinion. Still, it just wasn't an option. I couldn't even look at her.

The Red Deer came into view. My mouth went numb

and the butterflies got going in my stomach. I thought about turning back but I knew I'd never forgive myself if I did. I could see people in the beer garden. God, she might even see me before I get there. I summoned the willpower to keep on walking. Surveying the faces I almost hoped I didn't see her. Not yet anyway. I went through the beer garden; she wasn't there. Then inside. All the seats were taken and it was very hot. There were people standing up too. I looked around, trying to appear nonchalant. Then I saw a black woman over by the bar; she saw me and waved. She started coming towards me through the crowd. I ran out of the pub.

It all happened so quickly. Not Leticia though. She definitely wasn't Leticia. I stopped running and walked down the road catching my breath. My T shirt fluttered against my sweaty body; a wind had got up. I ran my hands over my face and my palms were sweaty too. I felt really ill. I was quite surprised how nauseous I was. A group out on a hen night walked past me screaming and laughing and it made me feel even worse. Wow, this is awful. I started getting dizzy and then my mouth went numb and I rushed to the nearest garden wall and threw up.

What a horrible taste in my mouth. I needed to get home a.s.a.p. and brush my teeth. The nausea had faded but I felt very delicate, like I'd crack at the slightest impact. I was close to my building now and the last thing I wanted to do was have some sort of confrontation with Alice. I stumbled along and when I got to the door, put my hand against the wall and steadied myself. Sixty seven stairs. Bloody hell. I started laughing in a rather delirious way, then zigzagged all the way up the stairs.

At the top of the stairs I slumped into the wall and got

my key out. Well, well, Alice. What sort of mood are you going to be in now? I put the key in the lock and let out a great big sigh that turned into a laugh. I was all over the place, I really was. I turned the key and let myself in.

Alice was sitting there, her wheelchair facing the door, staring at me. Exactly like Doug had done that time he'd moved my furniture around. Must be a sort of family trait. I suppose it comes from how deeply they feel everything over at their place. And when they care about something, they deal with it. They meet it head on. It's all they know. In my fragile state, my eyes were stinging with admiration. What a wonderful family. They really embraced life, they really did. And little James. Growing up, he'd throw himself head long into the emotional swirl. Good for him! . . . Good for him. I smiled.

'Something funny?'

I shook my head.

Alice stared at me and I looked away.

'So,' she said. 'How is she? How is "Leticia"?'

'It wasn't her.'

Alice's only response was to raise her eyebrows almost imperceptibly, but even that seemed to drain her of energy and she let out a deep sigh and closed her eyes and shuddered.

I went and sat down in my armchair and put my head back and closed my eyes. We sat there in silence for a few moments. It felt good to be relaxing and the atmosphere was calm; Alice didn't seem to be in one of her explosive moods.

I felt a hand on my forearm and opened my eyes.

'Are you disappointed?'

I shrugged.

'Like, how come you want to meet her so much?'

I tried to find the words but a great force of emotion shut down that part of my brain and I just looked at her, struck dumb.

'It's cute I guess.' She tapped her fingers on my arm. 'Sam's in *love*. Aren't you, Sam? Aren't you?' She took hold of my wrist and flapped my arm about.

'Please don't tease me.' I was really pleading with her. I could hardly breathe.

'It's nothing *bad*. You shouldn't be, like, ashamed, Sam. It's just you could do better. I think you could do better.'

'Please . . .' I felt like I was about to explode. There was too much pressure against my chest. I was gasping for breath.

'Are you OK?'

I tried to nod.

'Wow.'

I nodded.

'I didn't realise. You're completely in pieces with this.'

I didn't say anything.

'You know, you have a bizarre taste in women, Sam. I mean I guess Leticia is, like, pretty and stuff. It's just when you *meet* her. But, Sam. I mean, Celina. She's got a face like she just sucked this massive lemon. And she's *really* old. You're a handsome guy, Sam.'

'She's so sensitive,' I said.

'Who is?'

'Celina. Your mum.'

'She's a bitch.'

I paused. 'I'm sorry,' I said.

'Huh?'

'I'm sorry.'

She gave me a look of disdain. 'For what?'

'For, for that thing with your . . . With Celina. I just, I

didn't know what was happening. And then it happened.'

'Yeah. What did I say about keep apologizing? You have no idea how much that weak, pathetic shit gets on my nerves.'

I nearly said sorry again but stopped myself and just nodded. We were quiet for a while. OK, so it's tense, but think about if Alice hadn't been here. Coming back after L-Hot-Chile not being Leticia and there being no one to talk to and it's completely silent. The idea struck me as untenably awful.

'Sam,' Alice said. 'I have a proposition.'

I looked at her.

'I don't want you to be like, "there is no way I'm doing that" and not even thinking about it. So you have to just, like, listen to me, OK?'

'OK.'

'I know when I said earlier about you slapping me and stuff you didn't want to. I completely understand. It's like, slapping someone, especially a woman, slapping someone it has this "social baggage." Like that phrase, "a slap in the face." And you're a nice guy and obviously you don't want to, like, associate yourself with all that stuff. So fine. Don't slap me.' She looked at me, not smiling but sort of friendly. 'But OK so what I was thinking is I was thinking about we could do something completely different where there's no, like, social stigma or anything. Yeah?'

I made some kind of response, probably an expression of confusion.

'I want to run each other over with my wheelchair.'

I looked at her. 'Why?'

'Because. I'm not going to sit here and give you this, like, theory of sadomasochism. I just want to do it.'

'But it's just . . . ridiculous.' It did appeal though. For some reason it did appeal. I had this vision of the wheels going over my torso and I could almost conjure up the sensation of the weight against my ribs and it felt good. A physical, animal sort of good. I felt like saying Grrrrrrr! and banging on my chest with my fists.

'I knew you'd say that. You're so fucking predictable. Why don't you just, like, *do* something for a change?' There were a few moments of quiet, then she said, 'I'm dying, Sam. I'm like, almost dead and I want to do this.'

I hesitated.

'Sam?'

'OK.'

She laughed, out of happiness rather than humour and I felt sort of good about myself.

She said, 'Who runs over who first?'

'You're in the chair.'

'OK. OK, cool. Lie on the floor then.'

'Don't we need to clear some space? For a run up I mean.'

'Yeah. Yeah I guess you're right.'

'OK. Well if you start by the kitchen and then I'll lie here, give you as big of a run up as possible but so you don't smash into the wall on the other side.'

'Makes sense.'

'OK then.' I cleared the furniture out of the way. 'Alright?'

'Yep.' There was a pause. 'Lie down then.'

I laid down on my back and she wheeled herself over to the entrance to the kitchen and turned her chair towards me. I started getting nervous, but excited too. I was certainly excited. I was definitely right to agree to this. I mean, why not, eh? Why not? I chuckled, lying there on the carpet.

'Ready?'

'Yeah.' I turned my head so that my cheek brushed against

the carpet, and I could see the wheelchair which was about to move towards me. It started moving. Oh shit. I held my breath. The wheels were turning and the chair looked big and was moving towards me. Oh for God's sake, Sam, what are you doing? It smacked into me, started to climb up my side, pulling the fabric of my T shirt against my skin, shit that hurts, stopped for a moment that seemed longer than it could have been. Then it slid back down my side and rolled backwards across the room.

'I'll try again,' Alice said. 'I need to go faster.'

Eh? I wasn't sure I was ready for another go but before I knew it the wheelchair was coming at me, and I was thinking, oh bollocks, and it really was coming at me faster this time, then the wheels smashed against my side and the tyres pinched my skin and the chair stopped with a jolt and Alice was sent flying and fell to the floor on the other side of me. Shit. I sat up, there was a sharp pain in my side and my skin was burning where it got caught. Alice was in a heap. Still. She's dead. Living with me for less than a day and she's already dead. Then she moved. Using her forearms she pulled herself over to me. Her hair was covering her face. She stopped beside me, raised her arm and tried to push her hair away but fell sideways, unable to balance on one arm. She tried again and the same thing happened.

'Shall I do it?'

'Yeah. Go on then.'

I pushed the hair away from her face. We looked at each other for a moment then we both smiled.

'That was so amazing.'

'Yeah.'

'Did it hurt?'

'Yeah,' I said. 'It really pinched my skin.'

She burst into laughter. 'You're hilarious, Sam.'

I laughed with her. No one else could make me feel as *full of life* as Alice. We really had a connection. And what she showed on the outside was exactly what she felt on the inside. It was like being with not just another person, which is nice. Another person with all their guardedness and manners and observation of social norms. Instead it was like being with her soul. It was spiritual, it was really was. Something powerful and beautiful came over me and I almost cracked open with joy and love, love for everything. I was breathless.

'Now it's your turn.'

'Eh?'

'To sit in the chair,' she said. 'You have to run me over.'

'Right.' As I got up my legs turned to jelly and I felt dizzy. I wheeled the chair over to the entrance of the kitchen. Alice was lying on the floor waiting for me. I'll kill her. If I run her over I'll kill her. I'll actually kill her.

'Come on.'

'Alice?'

'What?'

'Do you, I mean, do you think this is such a good idea?'

'Just sit in the chair.'

'It's just if I run you over, with you being sick and everything, I mean I could really hurt you.'

'What, like break my bones you mean?'

'Maybe.'

'The one thing I don't have is brittle bones. I fall out of that chair all the time and I just bruise. And I like bruises.'

'Right.'

'So sit in the chair, Sam.'

'. . . Yeah.'

'Sam?'

'Yeah?'

'Sit. In. The. Chair.'

'Yeah. Yeah, OK. But, but what about, I don't know, not bones but other internal things. Internal organs and stuff.'

'SIT IN THE FUCKING CHAIR AND RUN ME OVER!'

Her ferocity shocked my mind into blankness and I sat in the chair and looked at her and her eyes were burning and glaring at me and I started wheeling the chair towards her, this is insane, I'll kill her, I'll be arrested for murder; an image flashed in my mind's eye of me being led to my cell and all the inmates were stamping their feet and shouting at me, 'you killed a sick little girl, we're going to smash your fucking skull in,' me trying to tell them, 'she was nineteen and she asked me to do it'; I hit her. The wheels climbed her body and then I stopped for a second, the chair balanced on her torso; as soon as I realised what had happened I frantically wheeled the chair over her. The wheels back on carpet I was still thinking about how it felt having a body under them. I was so frightened I didn't know what to do. She's dead. She has to be dead. I heard her groan. The chair was facing away from her and I tried to turn it around, gave up, and got out and knelt beside her.

'Alice?'

She had a dazed look on her face.

She looked at me, smiled, a tiny smile, then used her arms to push herself into a sitting position. I put my hand on her back to support her.

She started coughing up blood. Shit, she's choking. What do I do? 'What do I do, Alice?'

She stopped coughing for a second, then coughed again; more blood came up; then there was silence. Blood was running down her chin and the front of her nightdress was stained with the stuff.

She looked at me and smiled; her teeth were red. 'That

was so brilliant.'

I couldn't help smiling back. Then she burst into laughter and I stared at her in wonderment at first then went off into a bit of a laughing fit myself and then we both fell back on the floor, laughing. And then we just laid there, saying nothing, and every so often one of us would have a chuckle and the other would follow suit. I felt warm inside and fell asleep smiling.

Doug Gives Me A Lift To Work

When I woke up it took me a moment to orientate myself. Then I heard voices and sat up. The TV was on. The light was off and the only light in the room was coming from the TV. I stood up and brushed myself off from having been on the carpet then looked around the room. Alice was sitting watching the TV. She was wearing my graduation T shirt and a pair of my Umbro shorts. She didn't acknowledge me.

'Hi,' I said.

She shifted in her wheelchair.

'What are you watching?' I'd only said it for something to say, but in truth it wasn't something I could find out myself. I just didn't feel capable. I looked at the TV and all I saw was a mesh of colours.

'I'm trying to watch this.' She kept her eyes on the screen.

'OK.' I stretched and yawned but she didn't take any notice. I stood there for a moment, wondering what was wrong with her. Then I gave up and went and brushed my teeth and went to bed.

It's a good job we've got senses and things to occupy them because otherwise, unless we really were in paradise, we'd end up thinking ourselves into insanity. It's bad enough just being in bed in the dark and quiet. I'd fallen asleep happy earlier but now Alice was distant again and I'd retained none of that warmth I'd felt. And L-Hot-Chile. If it had, if it *had* been Leticia. I kicked my legs up and down and groaned. I hope Ted calls soon, I really do.

I woke up at ten past seven and went to the toilet. When I went back to my room a few minutes later, Alice was in my bed.

'What do you *want*?'

I didn't know what to say.

'I need to get some sleep, Sam. I'm tired, OK?'

'I'll just, I just need to get some clothes.' I collected my khaki shorts from the floor, took a T shirt out of my drawer and left the room. As I left I heard Alice mutter 'wimp.'

Well this is just unbearable. What am I supposed to do with myself? At least I've got work tomorrow. Get me out of the flat. I was pacing around my flat, clutching my mobile phone. Come on, Ted. Just phone! Next week, he said. Definitely next week. But next week could mean Friday night and Friday night is . . . almost a week away. I was so restless I was almost in tears. For some reason, maybe because I was at a loss for anything to do, I logged on to the internet and checked for messages from L-Hot-Chile. There were none. I clicked on her profile, wanting to take another look at that photo. However, her profile did not come up. Instead I was informed that L-Hot-Chile had blocked my access to her profile. I stood up and went over to the window and drew back the curtains. Sunlight flooded into the room. I could go for a run. Why don't I do that? I've definitely got nervous energy to burn off. I decided that I would go for a run and proceeded towards the door of my flat. However, by the time I got there it was clear that I wouldn't be going for a run. I just wouldn't. Running takes concentration. Sort of physical concentration. And I was mentally and physically distracted. I went into the kitchen and started opening all the cupboards looking for food. After a while Alice shouted at me to 'shut up.'

Once I'd finished off an entire box of cereal I sat down in my armchair and closed my eyes. The feeling of fullness in my stomach distracted from the restlessness and I felt tired from eating too much. After ten minutes or so though, my fingers started tensing and gripped the arms of the chair. Then my feet started tapping on the floor and I was squirming in my skin and I leapt out of my chair. I looked at my watch; it was thirty four minutes past nine. The day's only just begun. Unbearable. Completely unbearable. I walked over to the wall and banged my head and stood there concentrating on the pain in my head for as long as possible. But eventually the pain went away and I didn't particularly want to bang my head on the wall again. Then it came to me. I'll go and visit my neighbour. But it's not even ten yet and it's a Sunday morning. Who cares? What else am I supposed to do? I bounded out of my flat.

My neighbour answered the door almost immediately. He was wearing a black suit. He was surprised to see me. 'Oh hello, Sam. What can I do for you?'.

I froze for a moment. 'I was just . . . popping around.'

'You were? Well I'd have been glad to have you. Only thing is I'm just off out. Funeral.' He looked me in the eye.

'Oh,' I said. 'I'm sorry.'

'It was so sudden. Just like that.' He clicked his fingers. 'Electrical fault they say. House went up in flames.'

'That's terrible . . .'

'My brother. Twins we were.' His eyes glazed over. He struck me as a solitary sort of guy, and I imagined that half his life probably disappeared with his twin brother. I wanted to give him a hug, but I didn't feel I knew him well enough.

I said, 'I'll go with you if you like.'

It took him a while to register what I meant then his eyes lit up and a big grin spread across his face. 'That would be great. That's unbelievably kind of you.' He took my hand and shook it. 'Unbelievably kind.'

'I'll just go and get changed.'.

'OK,' he said. And I could still feel him smiling widely as I turned my back and went into my flat.

I only had one suit (the dress code at work is 'smart casual') and none of my trousers went with my suit jacket, so I crept into my room; Alice was asleep, breathing heavily; and picked up the suit from the floor and took it into the bathroom. It certainly was crumpled but I don't know, it wasn't un-wear-able. I put it on and stood there in front of the mirror. I wasn't bad looking. Leticia wouldn't reject me out of hand. But when I get my chance, I can't slip up. I can't slip up. I left my flat and went to meet my neighbour. He raised no issues with my suit and was just as happy as he was before. My trousers though, the waistband was really digging in.

The service was lovely and my neighbour's brother had some very nice things said about him. But my neighbour seemed to know nobody there, which was very odd considering it was his brother's funeral. But he knew no one at all. So much so that when, during the burial he finally broke down, it was me that he turned to, flinging his arm around my neck and bursting into tears, his shoulders heaving and wailing from the pit of his stomach. I've never had anyone close to me die, but as I stood there tears rolled down my cheek and I was struck by the beauty and fragility the world. Then there was the sound of rumbling thunder. I looked up at the sky. The weather system had finally cracked.

At the top of the stairs, my neighbour shook my hand and gave me a hug. He was quiet, and still. Perhaps a tears rolled down his cheek, I don't know. But he held me for five minutes or so then, without a word, turned and went into his flat and I went into mine. I was emotionally exhausted, but it was still early evening and Alice was in bed so I changed out of my suit and slumped in front of the TV taking in not very much.

It got to half eleven and Alice still wasn't up so I got out of my armchair and went into my room. It was dark in there and I couldn't hear her breathing. I tuned in closer but heard nothing.

'Alice?'

'Sam.'

'Alice, are you OK?'

'I can't get up.'

'What do you mean?'

'I just can't. My body won't move.'

'Do you want me to help you?'

'Just get in.'

'Get in?'

'Just get into bed, Sam.' She paused. 'I can't move.'

'OK.' It was pitch black and I felt my way into bed.

'Did you hurt yourself?'

'My muscles don't work.' She paused. 'This has nothing to do with South America.'

I wrapped my hand around hers. Her hand was freezing cold.

'Put my arms around you.'

I put her arms around me and then I put mine around her so that we were both lying on our sides, facing each other. She was ridiculously fragile. All hard edges and bone.

'I'm dying, Sam.'

'It's OK.'

'Sam, I'm dying.'

'It's OK.'

A few minutes later she fell asleep, and a few minutes after that, so did I.

When I woke up in the morning Alice wasn't next to me anymore. I found her watching TV. She looked ashen faced and sunken cheeked. That's how she looked before, but now she seemed to have lost some vitality. She smiled at me but her smile had less life than it usually did. But she seemed in good spirits and even cooked me breakfast, and as I left she said, 'I bet you're the smartest person in that office by a mile.' I smiled and left. On the other side of the door, I rubbed my face and composed myself. I was right in the middle of an emotional swirl and I didn't know how to handle it. Anything could set me off at any time. I felt very fragile as I walked down the stairs. Until recently I never left for work feeling much of anything.

At the bottom of the stairs, I opened the door to my building and Doug was standing on the other side, holding a suitcase in each hand.

'Sam. I was just about to come up.' His expression was unreadable somehow.

'Oh right.'

'You off to work?'

'Yeah. I was just about to get the bus.'

'Oh. It's just I've brought some of Alice's stuff round. Clothes mostly. She'll need her clothes. I mean, you don't have her running around naked up there do you?' He laughed what seemed to be a fake laugh, and as soon as I laughed he stopped laughing. 'I wouldn't want you to miss your bus.'

'It's alright,' I said. 'We'll take them up now. There's no strict start time.'

'More of a window.' He stared at me.

'. . . Yeah.'

'Window of opportunity.' He chuckled. 'Ought to suit you, eh, Sam? You're an opportunist, aren't you?' He put a hand on my shoulder. 'Opportunist *par excellence*.' He squeezed my shoulder.

I was feeling pretty uneasy and all I could say was, 'Yeah.'

'Up we go then.' And then off we went, me taking one of the suitcases, and we walked back up the stairs in silence which, from my point of view at least, was not comfortable.

'Hello, love.'

Alice didn't acknowledge him, watching the television.

'Alice. I'm talking to you. I am your dad.' The 'I am your dad' was said with real emotion that broke the *faux* friendly tone he'd struck since meeting me at the bottom of the stairs.

There was a pause, during which I was praying that Alice would respond, which she then did with a cursory wave of the hand and a mumbled 'hi', not looking at him.

'Well,' Doug said, regaining his composure. 'Well I'm certainly glad Sam's here to look after you. If you ask me, you look a touch under the weather. You know, more so than usual. Still, I'm not an experienced carer like Sam, so what do I know?' He chuckled. This was really unpleasant from

Doug. Not like him at all. He must be dying on the inside. The poor man. 'Right.' He clapped his hands together. 'You ready then, Sam?'

'Well I've got to go to work,' I said. 'But you could stay here, Doug. I mean, if you two wanted to spend some time together.' It seemed like the least I could do for him, but I'd forgotten about what Alice would think and she shot me quite a look.

Doug looked at Alice then at me. He laughed. 'You're a thoughtful bloke, Sam. But no, no, no. We'll catch up some other time won't we, sweetie? Mind you, time's not on our side.' He lost it a bit again and a look of sadness came across his face. 'I'll tell you what I'll do for you, Sam. What I'll do, I'll drive you to work. Come on, you've probably missed your bus now. Chance to get in there early, start work before the phones all start going and all the rest of it. How about that?'

'I don't want to hold you up,' I said. 'It's not exactly a stressful job.'

Doug's expression hardened. 'I'm offering you a lift, mate.'

That look unnerved me. 'OK,' I said.

'Good. Let's get going then. See you later, sweetie.'

Alice didn't respond and Doug and I left the flat. Going down the stairs I really wished I was behind Doug rather than the other way around. I was very conscious of Doug right behind me. His deliberate and obviously *faux* friendliness had made me uneasy, but that look had really put me on edge. I kept quickening my pace and then he'd quicken his. Would he push me down the stairs? It's not impossible. He might. I've taken his daughter away from him and if Celina let something slip . . .

I breathed a sigh of relief at the bottom of the stairs, and walked out into blinding sunlight. Obviously the storm had been an anachronism and the blue skies would continue.

'Over here, mate.' Doug led me over to his car and we got in and he asked me where I worked, 'I'll put it into sat nav.' I told him and off we went. He didn't turn the radio on, we just sat there quietly. After twelve minutes he said, 'I know something about how things work. Economics, you know. I've never studied it but I've been in business and all that. Anyway, and I suppose this what I'm talking about is as true for life as it is for economics. Law of diminishing returns. The more you have of something, the less pleasure each individual unit gives you. Be that CDs or tins of sardines. Do you go along with that, Sam?' He looked right at me when he should have been looking at the road; there was a red light up ahead.

'Yes,' I said. 'Yes, I do.'

It took a moment before he turned back to the road and he had to break sharply and I was pushed forward and the seatbelt cut into my sore skin from when Alice hit me with her wheelchair.

'Glad to hear it.' He tapped his finger on the steering wheel. The light turned green and we started moving again. I was anxious to get to work as quickly as possible so that I could get out of the car. 'Glad to hear it because I think the rule is true and holds for almost any area of life that you care to mention. Women for instance. Or relationships. You know, married couples. But then I was thinking well maybe that's where it might not hold. With married couples. Exception that proves the rule if you like. Take my marriage to Celina. I like to think every time I fuck her it means a thousand times more to her than if some other bloke fucks her. Even if fucks from me should be suffering from diminishing returns whereas him, he's just starting out in business. What do you reckon?' He looked right at me.

Somewhere underneath the realisation booming in my head that unquestionably HE KNOWS, I felt like his economics was faulty, or his analogy was off or something. All I could say was, 'Yeah, I'm sure you're right.'

He patted my thigh then turned back to the road. 'So you reckon my marriage is safe then?'

'Yeah.'

'Cheers.' He turned the sound system on and up to full blast. It was some power ballad I didn't recognise but it was absolutely suffocating in that small space. About twenty minutes later with the CD still playing and every song having sounded the same, we stopped in the car park outside my office. Doug said something to me but the music was still on full blast and I shouted bye and he said something else and then finally I got out and was overcome with relief, although my ears were ringing. I was just about to walk over to the smokers and ask for a cigarette when I heard the music from the car again, turned around, and Doug pulled up alongside me. He said something out of the window.

'I CAN'T HEAR YOU.'

He said something out of the window.

I shrugged. 'YOU'LL HAVE TO TURN THE MUSIC DOWN.'

He turned the music off. 'Sorry, Sam. Sort of forgot myself there. Letting the music wash over me and all that. I just want to say I'll pick you up tomorrow. I'm out early anyway and it's on my way.'

'It's no trouble getting the bus.

'Won't hear of it,' he said. 'Tomorrow.' He turned the music on and drove away.

I turned and looked at my office building. It struck me as a kind of sanctuary. I walked in.

Walking towards my desk, I saw Angela and smiled. It was nice to see her again. Nice, safe Angela. But then she looked up and saw me then looked away as if she was embarrassed or something. I was surprised for a moment, then I remembered. Oh yeah. And I didn't even un-cuff her before I left. Still. It would be OK. I'll be really nice to her. I approached my desk, delighted to make my target for the day to be really nice to Angela. And soon I had her smiling and giggling and we arranged to have lunch together.

I spent most of the morning chatting to Angela and altering data fields, not at a very rapid rate, but at a reasonable pace. It was quite relaxing in its way and I felt safe here, at work. Lots of things couldn't touch me here that I was vulnerable to outside. Still, an hour before lunch I started getting restless. This was the week. This was the week Ted said we'd definitely be having dinner. Conceivably, it could be tonight. It's more likely to be Friday but it could be tonight. My fingers started feeling heavy and my leg started jigging and Angela commented that I was knocking the desk. It was so close. So close. I imagined being there at the door, knocking to go in. Leticia so close. I couldn't take it anymore and shot up out of my seat.

'Why don't we just go to lunch now?'

Angela looked at me. 'Forty minutes left yet.'

'It'll be alright.'

'Will it?'

'We'll just come back early. Nobody will notice.'

She looked around; it was pretty light on management this morning. She smiled. 'Go on then, I'll just log off.'

We had desert for lunch, a gigantic chocolate fudge brownie sundae each. I was in high spirits but Angela was starting to go quiet so I decided to apologize for Friday.

She looked at me and smiled. 'Forget it.'

'I was in a bit of a mess on Friday.'

'I know I'm ugly,' she said. 'I've got my kids at least.'

'You're not ugly.'

She sniggered and looked away, out into the shopping centre.

'How old are they, your kids?'

'Five and eight.'

'What are they like?'

'Adorable. I know I'm their mum and everything but, well, they just are.'

We ate without talking for a few moments. Then she said. 'Nobody is ever going to want to have sex with me again.'

'Of course they are.'

'I'll have to pay for it.' She laughed, then got a tissue out of her bag and dabbed her eyes.

I didn't know what to say to her. I wondered was she right? I looked at her and felt a swelling in my chest, then my phone rang: 'Private Number Calling.'

I answered it. 'Hello?'

It was a nurse from a local hospital. She asked would I take a call from a Mr. Riley Campbell? I told her that I would.

'Sam?' His voice was croaky.

'Hello . . . Inspector.'

'Chief Inspector if you're going down that road.' He had a coughing fit and I held the phone slightly away from my ear. 'Come visit us tonight will you? Because the reason is I've got some stuff to show you. You can do that?'

'Yeah. Sure. What time?'

'Make it seven.'

'OK.'

He hung up.

142

I put my phone in my pocket and looked at Angela and smiled. She smiled back. We'd both finished our sundaes.

'Shall we go and pay?' I said.

She nodded and we paid and went back to the office.

I worked late so that I could go straight from the office to the hospital. It was actually pretty relaxing later on with not many people in the office and I got into a rhythm and felt oblivious to all the stuff going on in the outside world. I phoned the flat but Alice didn't answer. I assumed she'd gone to bed. I left a message telling her I was visiting a friend in hospital. At a quarter past six I left the office and it was bright and warm outside, and it struck me that the world really asks you to explore it in the hot weather. There's no excuse not to go out and have a look around. The bus arrived and I got on.

DCI Campbell looked even worse than Alice. I suppose that's why he was in hospital. There was loose skin all around his cheeks and jowls and his hair seemed sparser. His skin had come up in blotches too.

'Hello, mate.'

'Hi.' I sat on a chair by his bed. There were other patients on the ward but the curtains had been pulled across.

'Welcome to my deathbed.' He chuckled.

I allowed a slight smile; I wasn't sure if I should.

'I shouldn't muck about because the reason is I got you over here to tell you you need to take things more seriously. That's what I wanted to say to you.' He looked at me as though I was supposed to understand.

'I don't understand.'

'I've told you about Ted and Doug. Kind of men they are, but you don't seem to be listening. Or you don't think

I'm serious. They might seem friendly but that's because for some reason they need you. You know why better than me. Soon as they don't need you no more.' He made a pistol with his thumb and forefinger and put it to his head and fired.

Despite how Doug was acting this morning (I *was* worried he might push me down the stairs I suppose), I thought that DCI Campbell might be exaggerating.

'You're not convinced.'

I shrugged.

'Are you?' he said. 'You're not convinced.'

'I suppose, I mean, I suppose not.'

'These people were, possibly still are, involved in organised crime slash homicide slash people trafficking. What kind of people do you think get involved in that stuff?'

'Doug told me he'd done stuff.'

'Oh yeah?'

'But he said he never had the stomach for anything serious.' I paused. 'He's an honest man. He's got an honest face.'

DCI Campbell started laughing then coughing and wheezing. Once he'd recovered he said, 'Let me show you something. You decide if these are serious.' He reached for an envelope on his bedside table and chucked it to me. I opened it up; there were photos inside. The first one was of an oriental woman with her face beaten black and blue. The next was of a woman's torso. There were cigarette burns all over her and her nipples had been burned off. The third one was of a very young looking girl with welts and what looked like belt marks all over her body; I remembered Angela and felt sort of weird. Then there was one with a black woman with her head in a pool of blood. I think she was dead. The next one was of a man with half his face blown off. The others were pretty much like the first five. It was pretty awful and gruesome but like the kind of stuff you see in the news except maybe a bit worse.

I looked at DCI Campbell. 'Doug did all of this?'

'Doug, Ted, others like them. This is what they're capable of. If you're asking me, you're saying can I pin any particular one of these on Ted or Doug then the answer's no but I guarantee this is what they can do. This is what they did. Girl with the welts on her, Doug was brought to trial for that one.'

I looked at the photo again and my stomach, slowly, knotted. I said, 'Me and Doug's wife, we had a, I don't know, a liaison.'

'A what?'

'A liaison.'

'You fucked her?'

'No. She . . . gave me a blow job.'

'Jesus Christ.' He stared at me. 'Jesus Christ. Why you've not got a fucking bullet in your back is beyond me.'

'What should I do?'

'Hide.' He was about to say something else but went into a coughing fit. It got really bad and I called for a nurse and then he started bleeding from the mouth and the nurse told me to leave. I walked out of the hospital with Doug on my mind. I suppose it's possible, I thought. He's got a nasty side to him. And he has committed some crimes. He said so himself. I mean, but what? He wouldn't *kill* me would he? I was pretty worried by the time I got on the bus and started thinking about how I could avoid a lift tomorrow morning.

TRE

I decided that my only option was to get up really early and leave before Doug arrived. And better safe than sorry; I set my alarm for four AM. I suppose it might get him even more annoyed if he comes around and I'm not about, but I need some thinking time, decide how serious this thing is.

Unfortunately, after my alarm went off I fell asleep again pretty much straight away and by the time I woke up again it was half six. I leapt out of bed. Shit. I rubbed my face with my hands. It's not too late though. I mean we never actually arranged a time but yesterday he was round at what, half seven? Just leave straight away. Four o' clock was unnecessary anyway. I splashed some water over my face, washed under my arms, brushed my teeth, dressed and went into the living room. Alice was asleep in front of the TV. I hesitated then kissed her on the top of the head and left.

It was a lovely day outside. The birds were chirping and the trees were swaying in the light breeze. I looked around the car park; no sign of Doug's car. Good. Just tell him I got called into work for an emergency. He doesn't know what I do. I strolled through the car park. I felt pretty good; I'd have whistled if I could. What a day. What a lovely day! Then, ahead of me, there was the sound of a car starting. An old estate reversed out of a space and stopped in front of me. I paused then, just as I was about to start walking around the car, the door opened and Doug got out. My stomach dropped.

Doug put his hands on his hips and grinned at me. His hair was sticking up all over the place. 'Sam. Alright, mate. Got an early start this morning, have you?'

'. . . Yeah. Some stuff left over from yesterday.'

He chuckled. 'Good job I got here when I did then. In actual fact, mate, believe it or not, I slept here overnight. I had a feeling you might be getting an early start.'

I just stood there. I might have had a go at running away if my feet hadn't turned to lead.

'Come on then. In we get.'

I walked slowly towards the car. We got in. Once the doors were closed and I was in and there was nothing left I could do about it, I pretty much accepted my fate. I relinquished control. Doug was going to kill me and that was that. He turned to me and grinned. Then he started the car and drove off. Doug didn't talk, just stared out into the road. He's much worse than yesterday. He looks half crazy. What if he's, what if he's killed Celina? I glanced at him then fixed my eyes on the road. He stopped at some traffic lights.

'This early, I thought the traffic would've been light,' Doug said. (There was no traffic to speak of). 'I used to hang around a bit in this area. I know another route. Gets us away from all this bloody congestion. You up for it?'

'The traffic's not too bad.' I don't know how loudly I spoke but he seemed not to hear me. I wasn't even sure if I'd managed to say the words out loud at all.

The lights changed and he turned off in a different direction. We went down a long, pretty straight road. Still a main road but it was taking us away, all the time away from my office. After about twenty minutes of driving in totally the opposite direction, I wondered did Doug think I still believed he was taking me to work? Either side of us now there were fields and trees. Suddenly, Doug took a sharp turn into a dirt track that led up to a scout hut, drove up a little way, and stopped. He turned the engine off and looked at me. Stared. His eyes were blazing and I looked away but he grabbed my jaw with his hand and turned my face towards his. His fingers pressed hard, digging into my skin. Then he pulled my face forward, pressed his other hand against the back of my head and kissed me full on the lips. He tried to put his tongue in my mouth but as soon as he'd forced his tongue between my lips he pushed my face away and hung his head and ran his hands through his hair. Then he let out a cry from deep in his gut and heaved with tears. I felt a swelling in the pit of my stomach and I didn't know whether it was out sadness or fear; I just sat there and tried to contain it. Then Doug raised his head. His face red. He grabbed my shirt and shook me, smacking me back and forth against the window. 'I ought to slice your lips off. It's the closest I'll ever get to my wife again.' He paused. 'I thought I could trust you. I thought I could trust you.' His put his face right up to mine and let out a roar: 'AAAAAAAAARGH!' He leaned back, breathing heavily. 'I thought I could trust you, Sam.'

'I never really . . . I'm sorry.' And I was sorry. I really was.

'I've been a law abiding citizen for six years now. Haven't done fuck all since James was born. Then this morning I go out and steal a car. Crashed my one. I was driving along. Blinded by tears. I was blinded by tears, Sam.' He sighed, then opened the glove compartment. He sat still for a moment. Then he put his hand in the glove compartment and got a gun out. I let out an involuntary, quivering sound when I saw the gun.

'I'm sorry, mate.' He put the gun to my head. 'I hate this shit. I don't have the stomach for it. Some blokes they get a kick out of it, go round bragging about they've done this or that. I think it's disgusting. You've got blood. Brain fragments.'

'Were you . . .' My voice cut out on me.

'Was I what?'

I took a few breaths, tried to get my voice going again. 'Were you on trial? For beating up a girl?'

'Who told you that? Celina?'

I was aware of his finger on the trigger. 'A policeman.'

'I didn't do it. I've done some stuff. I didn't do that.' He paused. 'Right. Shut up, OK? I've got to focus.' He closed his eyes. He opened his eyes. My phone rang.

'Who's that?'

'I don't know. Not that many people have my number. Could be Alice.'

'Check.'

I got my phone out of my pocket; it took a while, my hand was shaking. It was Ted. 'It's Ted.'

Doug hesitated; the phone was still ringing. 'Answer it then. Answer it!'

I answered it. 'H–hello?'

'Alright, mate. Ted. How you going?'

'Y-yeah. I'm, I'm OK.'

'You sure? You don't sound it.'

'No, no. I'm fine.'

'Good. Good.' He paused. 'Tonight. Short notice I know but fuck it. What do you reckon? The wife can't wait no more. You free? She already up and banging around in the kitchen, I told her you ain't coming for another twelve hours but she's got cloth in her ears that woman.'

I couldn't remember if he'd asked me a question. Doug still had the gun to my head.

'Sam?'

149

'Yeah.'

'You just ain't with it this morning, are you, fella? Tonight. You coming or not?'

'Uh, yeah. Yeah. OK. I mean, please. I'm looking forward to it.'

'Sorted. Come round for seven. Dinner's set for eight but we'll have a few beers, yeah?'

'OK. Great.'

'Right. See you then, mate.'

'Bye.'

He hung up.

Doug was looking at me. 'What was that about?'

'He invited me to dinner tonight.'

'Tonight?'

'Yeah.'

There was a pause, then Doug finally lowered his gun. 'Fuck it!' He smashed his fists on the steering wheel. 'Fuck it. Things are too far gone.'

I heard myself say, 'Celina loves you.'

'You what?' He stared at me.

'Nothing.'

'Right.' He ran his hand through his hair. 'Right. This is what's going to happen. You're going to go tonight. You put a good word in for us. Tell him . . . no, fuck that, *convince* him that a reconciliation would be a good idea. If you don't, I will come and find you and I will shoot you in the head. OK?'

I hesitated.

'OK?'

I nodded.

'Right. Now get the fuck out.'

I met his eyes for a moment. Then I got out of the car and he drove away.

I was pretty lucky once Doug dropped me off. I just started walking up the road and after about fifteen minutes a black cab drove by and I hailed it. I said to the driver he must be a bit out of his usual area and he told me, yeah, some bloke missed the last train home and he ended up with a pretty tasty fare. We chatted about this and that. I felt really upbeat. And free. Things were looking good. I'd managed to negotiate a pretty close encounter with death and tonight I was off to Ted's. Off to see Leticia. I sat there in the cab, chatting to the driver, a grin plastered across my face.

There is indeed a 'window' during which you're allowed to get to work. However, in spite of my early start, what with the incident with Doug I missed the window by thirty two minutes. I wasn't too concerned though. My boss didn't seem to mind what I did to be honest and I went into the office full of beans and with a spring in my step. However, before I'd even got to my desk my boss had asked for a word in her office. She asked why was I late? I told her my car had broken down. She said I should have phoned and why did I go for an early lunch yesterday? I apologized and she gave me a hard look. She seemed irritated with me. Finally she said, 'Just go away and get on with your work', which struck me as pretty rude. Still, my morale was unbreakable. I had to cheer up Angela though. Apparently she'd had a word said to her about the early lunch and it had been suggested to her that I was a bad influence and why doesn't she move to that spare desk at the other end of the office? I seemed to have really got myself in my boss's bad books. Anyway, I cheered Angela up eventually and chatted away at her all morning, occasionally altering some data fields, and then we went to lunch (at the correct time), and the afternoon flew by too.

I left the office at five. It was a beautiful day and in two hours I would be at Ted's.

It was only ten minutes before I got there, in the cab, that the butterflies really got me. I suddenly realised that this was my chance. It didn't even seem conceivable that she wouldn't be there. I laughed. It's happening. It's actually happening.

My legs really had turned to jelly walking up the path to the house. I rang on the doorbell.

Ted opened up. 'Sam. Mate. Come in. Made some wiser moves with the old wardrobe choices this time, eh? And flowers, too. These for the wife?'

'Yeah.'

We were in the house now.

'Give them here. I'll go put them in water for you. The wife will be delighted she will. She's just in the kitchen now.'

I stood in the entrance hall, waiting. Was she here? She could come out at any time. I smiled and shivered. I felt positive. You can do this, Sam. You can do this.

Ted came back. 'The wife's ecstatic. Fucking ecstatic. Pride of place they're going in. And I have to say, fella, you are in for a treat tonight. Smells like heaven in there it does. You like food don't you? From what I remember you ain't much of a cook, but you like your food, right?'

'Yep.'

'Of course you do.' He slapped me on the back. There was a pause. Ted seemed a bit, I don't know, wound up about something, an overflow of energy. Who knows? What a charismatic guy.

'Here, look what I found in the fridge. He handed me a beer. 'Into the drinking den.' We went into a room with a snooker table in it. 'You know how to play?'

'Sort of.'

'No confidence in that answer. You've given me the edge now.' He started racking them up. 'You right handed, Sam?'

'Yeah.'

'Shit. Spare cue's for a lefty. You be alright with it?' He handed me the cue.

'I, I guess so.'

He burst into laughter. 'Left handed cue! Now I know you're a novice. Mind if I break?'

I shook my head.

He broke, potted a red. 'You know the rules, right?'

I nodded.

He potted the pink, then another red, then missed the blue. 'Bugger. Your go.'

I went for the red and missed.

'Bad luck.'

I was getting sort of fidgety. Was Leticia here or not?

Ted had his go again, then I had mine. Then Ted potted a red. I couldn't take it anymore. 'So, Ted,' I said. 'Have you got a full house tonight? I mean, your wife, Leticia . . . ?'

He chalked his cue, concentrating on the tip. He lined up his next shot. 'You done much travelling, Sam?'

'I've been to a few countries. Holidays and stuff.' I was twitching all over. It was all I could do to stay in the room rather than go off looking for Leticia in the rest of the house.

'You ever been to South America? Fantastic continent it is. You ever been?'

'No.'

'Natural beauty like you've never seen. I'm telling you. Wife went wild for it. Me, I don't mind all that stuff, but I need a city. I'm a city boy, me. You know what I mean? You're a city boy yourself, yeah?'

'Yeah.'

'Yeah. Yeah.' He potted another ball. 'It's in your blood. You need the people, the crowd. Get so wide open spaces scare you you're in them too long. Nah, I need a city, me.' He paused. 'Now Rio. Now there's a city. There's a fucking city. You got the beach, you got your jungle and all that bollocks. But it is a *city*. You can feel it. Hot, close. Teeming with people. Beautiful. Nice girls, too. Single bloke like you. In your element.'

'Sounds great.' I was thinking that maybe this was a good time to bring up Doug and his family, with South America on the agenda. But I couldn't think about that. All I could think about was, is Leticia home? But I'd asked Ted and he'd ignored me. What now?'

'I love Rio.' Ted picked up his beer can and had a swig, then he smiled. 'Tell you who else loved Rio. Leticia.'

'Leticia?'

'Yeah. Fell in love with the place that girl. It's the freedom of the place. The expression. Girl like that needs to express herself. Got so much life in her.' He chuckled to himself. Some memory or other seemed to have really affected him. It certainly seemed like he was having a private moment and I wasn't involved.

'So . . . How is Leticia?'

He looked at me. 'How is she?'

'. . . Yeah.'

He was looking at me. 'I don't know.'

My heart sank; I tried to conceal the disappointment flooding through me.

'Here. I've got something for you. Back in a sec.'

I felt like I was about to fall over. He doesn't know where she is. So she is missing. I'll never see her. For a second I thought I might die. From what I don't know. Disappointment I suppose.

Ted came back. He handed me an envelope. 'Here, have a look in there.'

I opened the envelope and pulled something out. A ticket. A ticket to Rio De Janeiro. Huh?

'What's . . .'

'You fancy it? It's like paradise on Earth I'm telling you.'

'Would I, would I be going with you?'

'Nah. I've got shit back here needs sorting. Anyway, old bloke like me, I'd cramp your style wouldn't I?'

'I don't . . .' I couldn't quite comprehend this new development.

'Club class it is. Quick transfer in Madrid. None of this cheap travel shit. Only the best. Five star hotel when you get there.'

'Great . . .'

'Fucking right, it's great.'

'Yeah . . .' I stood there in a sort of daze.

Ted came over and put his hand on my shoulder. 'Listen, fella. I ain't exactly been straight with you. Leticia. You must've seen her photo when you was round here that time. Bewitched, right? She can do that. This stuff I been telling you; come over, meet her. It's bollocks. She ain't here. But I reckon she is there.' He tapped my ticket. 'In Rio. And you, you're the bloke what can find her for me.'

'Find her in Rio?'

'Yeah.'

'How?'

'Watch it, mate. You'll argue your way out of this.'

If Leticia was in Rio, then I would go to Rio. That was clear. It's just, it was all very confusing.

There was a bang at the door. Then another. Then continuous banging. 'Fucking bastards,' Ted said. 'That's fucking Tre. Excuse me, Sam.' Ted went out.

I rolled the white ball into the pocket. I'm going to Rio. Leticia's in Rio and I'm going to Rio. I felt rejuvenated. So she's not here now. But she's there. And so will I be. A new avenue. I can still meet her. I can still meet her. I heard loud voices. Then a big booming laugh. I wandered into the entrance hall and saw two men with Ted. Ted looked agitated. One of the men had thrown his head back and was laughing the booming laugh I'd heard. The other one was just standing there. They were the same guys I'd seen coming out of Ted's house that last time; the guy just standing there was Ben. The other guy stopped laughing. Ted saw me. The other guy said to him, 'Killer. That's killer, bruv. I've gone in there, I've gone in there and I've . . .' He tailed off. He must have seen Ted looking at me because he turned to me. 'What's this? Who the fuck is this cunt? You a new cunt?' He was the most unpleasant man I'd ever met.

Ted said, 'Leave it out, Tre. He ain't got fuck all to do with this.'

'I just wanted to say hello to the cunt. I've seen him and I want to say hello.' He came up to me, looked me up and down, and smiled. Then he went to head butt me but stopped just short of impact. I jerked back and he burst into laughter. 'Boo!' He walked back into the centre of the room; he'd sort of made it his own. Ben looked at me then away again.

'Well that was fun. Fun, fun, fun. What I'm here for though, I've come here and what I'm here for, I want to know where is she? Eh? Where is she, Ted?'

'I don't know, Tre, mate.' I could tell Ted was angry but for whatever reason he was holding it in.

'Yes you do.' Tre got right in his face. 'Yes you do, fuck face!' I'd never met a man so able to fill the room with nastiness. I was pretty scared but there was a sort of fascination in watching him.

Ted said, 'I want to find her myself, mate. It was me she ran away from.'

'Never should have been with you in the first place though, should she? I had plans for that bitch. She was something else, she was. Money in my pocket.' He paused. 'I've come here and I've been rebuffed. I've come here looking for something and you ain't giving it to me. I've run out of options, bruv.'

'Look, mate. Can we not just settle this? I'll give you the money I owe you.'

'It's past that now. It's gone way past that. I just want the girl. Now, Ted. You fuck. Fuck face. Slag. Ponce. Muppet. Where is she?'

'I don't know.' They were staring right at each other.

'Ben,' Tre said. 'That little lady in there. Go pull off her fingernails.'

'Tre.' Ted was close to exploding.

'What?' Tre got in his face. 'What? WHAT?'

I was getting angry. I was pretty sure Leticia was the focus of their conversation, although I had no real way of knowing. But Tre's behaviour was completely out of order and I found myself more annoyed than scared. And I wanted to help Ted out. And I would. I would.

There was a scream from the kitchen. Tre and Ted were staring at each other. A tear rolled down Ted's cheek but his expression remained the same.

A few moments passed, then there was another scream. Show some steel, Sam. Show that you're completely confident and nobody will mess with you.

Ted's wife was whimpering.

Tre, still face to face with Ted, said. 'Alright, Ben. Leave it for a minute.' He said to Ted, 'So, you going to tell me where she is?'

'What you doing this for?'

'I've been affronted. At least that's the public reason. Between you and me though, I'm in love with her.' Tre grinned.

'Sure,' Ted said.

'I'll find her,' Tre said. 'You may as well clear the way for me.'

I said, 'Are you talking about Leticia?'

Both Tre and Ted seemed to freeze. Then Tre turned to me. 'You what?'

I did my best to stay confident. 'Leticia. Are you talking about her?'

'What the fuck does it have to do with you?'

'I . . .'

'What?' He got in my face. 'What?'

I stepped back but he grabbed me by the shoulders. I realised I might not be in a position of strength. Still, I said, 'Why don't you just leave?'

'Leave?'

'. . . Yeah.'

'You hear this, Ted? This cunt wants me gone.'

'Yeah,' Ted said.

'I'll tell you what I'm going to do,' Tre said. 'I'll tell you what I'm going to do.' He turned and walked a few feet away from me. Then he turned around again. He pulled a gun out of his jeans. Shit. I pretty much knew that he'd shoot me. He came at me with the gun. I stared at him wide eyed. He smacked me on the top of the head with the gun. I blacked out.

Rio de Janeiro

I couldn't open my eyes; my eyelids were really heavy. Why won't my eyes open? I concentrated hard; I don't have the strength. This is ridiculous. Well, they have to open sometime. I don't think I was quite awake and I drifted off again. The next thing I knew there was a knocking sound at the door and I opened my eyes and had a lot to take in. Where am I? Who's at the door? What are they saying? I felt really groggy. Foreign sounding voices. I sat up, staring at the door. Eventually the voices subsided. I looked around; my eyes were sticky and I wiped away the gunk. I seemed to be in a hotel room. I tuned into a sound and it took a while to identify as the air conditioning system. Where am I? I knew who I was but I couldn't remember the last thing that had happened to me, or much of anything really. I felt quite woozy. I fell asleep.

I sat straight up in bed. Knocking on the door. I was much more with it now. But I still didn't have any short term memories. I remembered who I was, but no particular incidents, nothing of the current flow of my life. Something possibly quite sinister was going on. It's like you hear about, people getting kidnapped for their kidneys or something. I went cold, checked my side; kidneys still in place. More knocking at the door. Who is it? I leapt out of bed. More banging; I jumped. Then, quiet; I crept towards the door. Bang, bang, bang. 'Hello!' A female voice.

I hesitated. 'Who is it?'

There was a pause, then she started banging again.

'Hold on.' As I went to the door, I realised I was wearing pyjamas. I opened the door. A girl walked straight past me, then turned around and faced me.

'I leave my bag here.' She looked at me; obviously she expected a response. How old is she? She could have been fourteen, she could have been thirty.

'Where, where do you think you left it?'

'I look.'

'. . . OK.'

She walked around the room. She was awkward looking, out of proportion or something. She was certainly squeezed into her clothes. I realised I had an erection but put it down to having just woken up. Then I realised that I was wearing pyjamas and my erection was very noticeable. I looked around the room, decided to make my way to the curtain; it would be nice knowing what's outside the window anyway. But it was too late, she was looking at me. She grinned.

'I, I just woke up.'

She giggled. 'You like Brazilian woman?'

I shrugged.

'I help you with that?'

'It's OK. I usually get it in the mornings.'

'I help you, no?'

She was happy and giggly but for some reason a sense of unease was growing inside me. Possibly because I didn't know where I was. Brazil I suppose. She took a few steps towards me; I took a few steps back. I felt woozy again. The room started tilting. My vision blurred. I blinked a few times; each time my vision got more blurry. My head started spinning.

Then, just before I blacked out, I saw a silhouette engulfed in bright white light. For a tiny moment everything became clear, and I blacked out with a smile on my face.

I was aware of a weight on me. I blinked my eyes open. Where am I? Oh yeah, the hotel room. The girl was straddling my torso. Her face was right above mine and she was giggling. 'Hi.'

'. . . Hi. What are you doing?'

She put something on my lip and I flinched.

'I make you look pretty.' She giggled.

I looked at her. She was holding a lipstick.

'You look like a girl.' She burst into laughter and fell forward and my face was covered by her hair; I love the smell of hair, I really do. I must have been kidnapped or something. What for? They wouldn't blackmail Mum would they? I felt a pang for Mum. She'd be really worried. Maybe I'm being sold for something. Some kind of drag act? I had a vision of myself in drag and had a chuckle.

The girl said, 'You like?'

I kept chuckling; I was a bit delirious.

'You funny.'

'. . . Yeah.'

'I find my bag.' She put her bag down on my chest.

'Great.'

'You like pyjamas? I give you.'

'Uh, yeah. I mean I don't usually wear pyjamas.'

'I like. I go to mall.'

'Oh?'

'Uh huh.' She smiled and looked around the room. She seemed happy and relaxed and I started to relax myself.

She sighed. 'I love this room. Is . . . amazing.' She looked at me with big excited eyes and I chuckled.

'Where am I?'

She told me the name of the hotel.

'No I mean, I don't really remember much but, I mean, what country are we in?'

'You don't know?'

I shook my head. 'Brazil?'

'Yes. In Rio de Janeiro.'

There was a pause.

'When you come you asleep. I dress you. I put your pyjamas on.' She giggled.

'You dressed me?'

She nodded, smiling. I smiled back at first, but then her face became a blur and receded into my mind. Where am I? What's going on? My body started twitching and an urgent need to get out of bed came over me. 'I'm going to get up.' I said it under my breath. I leant forward but her weight pushed me back down. 'Get off.'

'Eh?'

I pushed myself up into a sitting position and she was half toppled, half skipped off of me. My legs were buzzing. I had a look around the room. The sun was shining on the other side of the thin curtain covering the window. At least the room isn't boarded up. I jumped up and ran over to the window and opened the curtains. After my eyes had adjusted to the light, I saw a busy road and beyond it a beach and blue sky. I turned around.

'Is nice weather for winter, no?'

'. . . Yeah. Who are you?'

'Nobody.'

'Yeah but, why are you . . . What do you have to do with me?'

'Someone pay me. I look after you when you asleep.'

'Asleep?'

She shrugged. 'I think drugs.'

'Who was it? Who paid you?'

'Some guy. He OK.'

'Who is he?'

'I go to England. London. He tell me I work there.'

'Can I meet him?'

She shook her head. 'I meet you.'

'I know but I'd like to ask him a few things.'

'He no like.'

'No?'

'No.' She shook her head with some vigour.

I turned and looked out the window again. At the blue sky. And everything became clear, but then faded again before I had time to see it. I closed my eyes and felt a little woozy, but kept them closed, determined to remember. I felt my knees go, stumbled, blacked out again.

I woke up. I saw the hotel room. I sat up. The curtains were open and a big shaft of light was shining into the room. I got up. The room was quiet, seemed particularly still somehow. 'Hello?' Nobody answered. The girl must have left. I went over to the window and looked out. Cars went past. What am I here for? I felt really thirsty but my legs were almost shaking with tiredness and I went and laid down on my bed. The air conditioning unit was going. Everything smelt clinical and clean. I must have been drugged. I don't feel right at all, I really don't. My mouth was dry but pretty soon I fell into a restless sleep.

I sat bolt upright, breathing heavily. I heard some voices outside my door. I jumped up and then the voices went quiet and I moved over to the window. The sea was calm, a few people splashing about in it. Then I remembered everything.

I grabbed at the memories, thought they might fly away, but then I realised that everything was in place. Yep, it all seems to be there. Why am I in Brazil? Ted? Why would he drug me? Tre? Leticia is here. Leticia is out there. My legs started buzzing. I need to get out there. But I'm wearing pyjamas. How am I supposed to go anywhere in pyjamas? Shit. I paced up and down then ripped the sheets off the bed and chucked them on the floor. What am I supposed to wear? I stomped on the sheets. Then I noticed the wardrobe. I was pretty certain it would be empty, but went over there anyway. Wow, clothes.

On top of the underwear pile, there was a note.

Sam,

I fold up clothes. I very bad at folding. I hope you like.

D xxx

She folded my clothes? Does that mean she's coming back?

My shorts were OK, but the waistband was too loose and when I leaned over the sink to brush my teeth it dug into my stomach. Not like my khaki shorts. I love those shorts. I hope they're still there when I get back. I felt almost sentimental for the absence of my khaki shorts. I spat the toothpaste out and splashed water over my face. I hope Alice is OK, alone in my flat. And I suppose Doug thinks I've 'done a runner.' Shit. For a moment I went cold thinking about it all, but really it was all too much to comprehend and I put it to the back of my mind. I looked into the mirror: One step at a time, Sam. Leave the room first. You can find her. You can find her. I told myself 'come on' and left the room.

Nobody was in the corridor outside my room or in the lift as I went down (although I heard a few voices coming from one of the rooms) so it wasn't until I was in reception and saw a couple of people in the lobby that I really felt as if I'd 'ventured out.' Seeing people getting on with their day, my heart beat a little quicker. A couple of guys in shirt sleeves entered, both laughing about something, and the hairs stood up on the back of my neck. Must be businessmen. This is a pretty nice hotel, it really is. And my room was huge. I felt a desire to go back there, crawl into bed again, but I forced myself to defeat it and started past reception.

'Sir . . . Sir?' I realised the voice might be addressing me and stopped and saw the guy behind the desk smiling at me. 'Sir. You stay in room 412?'

I didn't know. The fourth floor sounded about right. 'I don't know.'

'You are a Mr . . .' He said my name.

'Yep.'

'I have letter for you.' He bent down and when he came up put a brown A4 envelope, addressed for my attention, on the desk.

'Thanks.'

He smiled. His forehead and under his eyes glistened with sweat even though it was pretty chilly in the lobby, what with the air conditioning. 'And here your room key. But if you go out, we look after.'

I nodded.

'You go out now?'

'Uh, yeah. Yeah.'

He smiled at me, waiting. It took me a moment to get on the same wavelength as him. 'Oh. Yeah.' I pushed the key back towards him, then turned and went and sat down with my envelope. A few more people drifted through the lobby.

I shivered; it really was getting pretty chilly in there. I opened the envelope and pulled out the contents which consisted of a street map of Rio and a folded piece of A4 paper. I unfolded the paper and read it.

SAM

TO FIND HER YOU HAVE TO GET TO KNOW THE 'LOCALS' RIGHT FROM THE GIRL WHO HELPS YOU GET SETTLED. WORK YOUR WAY UP. SHE'S HERE BUT YOU NEED TO GET TO THE PEOPLE AT THE TOP FIRST TO GET TO HER.

T

Shit. How am I supposed to find the girl? This was obviously all set up then. By Ted presumably. But why couldn't he talk to the girl himself? He made the arrangements presumably. Unless T is for Tre? Who cares? Just find Leticia . . . Just find her. My mouth went numb and desire for her pounded through my body and my toes curled and my whole body tingled. It took a good ten minutes to calm down enough to get to my feet and I stood up and walked unsteadily towards the door, then I thought of something, went over to the friendly receptionist.

'Excuse me. What's the date please?'

A day and two nights, that's what, thirty six hours? Thirty six hours ago Tre smacked me with his gun. I had to cross at three separate sets of lights to get over the road, but then I crossed the pavement and I was on the beach. Luckily, the girl had left me a pair of sandals which I was wearing; getting sand in your shoes is always annoying. It was hot, about as hot as it had been in London. Isn't it supposed to be winter in the southern hemisphere? The beach wasn't that busy; there were a fair few sunbathers though. I wandered down the beach. I kept an eye out just in case Leticia was there but nobody fitted the bill. Even the couple of black women I saw weren't her; it was obvious straight away. The sea was gently lapping on the shore and I walked slowly towards the sea, a sense of apprehension growing inside me. I tried to suck it up, kept walking, but the feeling got worse and worse. I reached the wet sand. The sea washed over my feet. I looked out at the water that went on and on as far as I could see, and then up and down the beach; I felt like a tiny speck. A sense of hopelessness came over me. I faced the ocean, aware of the beach and the city that filled the horizon behind me. My eyes stung with loneliness and the sea lapped at my feet and I stood absolutely still, too scared to turn around.

After about twenty minutes, I turned and started walking back up the beach. My legs were shaky and when I saw a jogger coming down the beach I got nervous and flinched when he went past me. The sun was really hot, the skin was flaking on the back of my neck. It must be a global heat wave or something. Or maybe this is usual for winter in Rio. I realised that I was hungry. I think there's a restaurant at the hotel. But the idea of going back there made me tense up, and I decided to venture up the road past the hotel and into the city.

I walked past a group of guys having a barbecue in the street, laughing and drinking beer. I wished I could join in. I don't speak Portuguese though. Not that I'd have joined in anyway. I wonder how my neighbour's doing. Maybe I can get in touch with him, he can check on Alice. Or I could get in touch with her myself. I'll do that. I'll ask at the hotel about international calls. What if she tells Doug where I am? I tell her and she tells Doug. Would Doug follow me to Rio? The streets were bustling and I don't know if it was the heat of the sun or what but I was starting to feel pretty good. Soaking in the culture too. I even smiled back at a cheery looking chap who walked past me, but I decided I'd better not do that again, the recipient of my smile might start talking to me and I wouldn't know what they were saying. I saw a restaurant with outside seating and various burger type dishes and decided that it would do me.

I was eating the special. The waiter had offered it me as soon as I sat down, before I'd even looked at the menu. In fact, I still didn't know what was on the menu. The special seemed to be pretty much like any other burger except it had a spicy sauce on it that I couldn't place. It was OK. Burgers are always disappointing, always promise more than they deliver (apart from Ted's of course). The chips were good though. I licked my fingers and watched the people walking up and down the street and the cars crawling along, horns honking. The sun was warm and I took a sip of beer and felt a sense of elation. This is the stuff of life, right here. I chuckled. I couldn't wait to explore the city. I felt sure that I would find Leticia. I mean, Ted thought I could find her. The sun washed over me and I felt a relaxing, smooth sense of joy. Wonderful. The waiter came over. His English was pretty limited and after we'd shared a chuckle I made the international sign for the bill and off he went. I put my hand in my pocket. Shit. Empty. Where's my wallet? Is it even in the country? Shit, what do I do? I looked around. Nobody was watching me. I stood up and left the restaurant, and then I started to run and I didn't stop for a good fifteen minutes.

After a bit of a detour up a few somewhat intimidating side roads, I got back to the hotel about an hour later. (It was probably fifteen minutes direct walk but I'd got lost.) I'd have to avoid that restaurant from now on, I couldn't walk past it again. I didn't know what the Brazilian police did to thieves but I assumed they were harshly dealt with. I'm not a thief though, I'm really not. I'm just in a foreign country without any money. My eyes stung, I felt really sorry for myself.

My friend wasn't at reception and the lobby was empty so I grabbed my key off an unfriendly woman who spoke no English at all and headed off for the lift.

I went into my room and closed the door. It was a big room and all I could hear was the air conditioning unit. It was pretty chilly in there actually. I went over and had a fiddle with the unit but I suppose Alice was right, I'm no good at practical tasks. Or problem solving. Why did I ever think I could have a career in problem solving? I shivered in the cold and looked out the window but it seemed big and scary out there. I got into bed and curled up and pulled the covers over my head.

I woke up feeling like shit. My nose was cold and wet but my body was sticky with sweat. I had a feeling of paranoia, agoraphobia, a need to hide, but she was out there. My teeth chattering, I smiled thinking about finding her on the beach, under the setting sun, and my belly felt warm and fuzzy and I started chuckling but then I shivered and realised that to find her I would have to go out there. Out there into the heat and the bustle and the bodies of strangers. But I can't just lie here. How am I supposed to get any money though? Maybe the girl left you some . . . After two hours, with an enormous effort, I hauled myself out of bed. My legs were shaky and my bladder burned and I shifted slowly into the bathroom and went to the toilet. Then I went back into the main room and rooted around everywhere, pulled out drawers, checked under the bed, threw my clothes on the floor, then I happened to cast my eye over at the bedside table. Is that . . . I walked over. Yep. Wasn't mine, but it was a wallet. I opened it up and pulled out a thick wad of notes. I didn't know how much Brazilian currency was worth but like I say, it was a thick wad. I stood there, shivered. Then I left the room and went downstairs.

I'd wanted to have a chat with my friend at reception, ask him if he had any tips about Rio, but he wasn't there and the unfriendly woman caught my eye, looked at me with what seemed to be contempt. I could feel the paranoia getting going inside me again but forced myself to suck it up and turned and walked into the hotel bar. It was a shadowy place. There were two businessmen sat in the far corner and one guy in shirt sleeves sitting on his own reading the *New York Times*. I sat on one of the bar stalls.

The woman behind the bar smiled. 'What would you like?' How did she know I was English? I must be really pasty or something. And it's been such a hot summer. I ordered a beer and she poured it and gave it to me and smiled. She had really big breasts and I wanted to bury my face in them and close my eyes while she stroked my hair. She seems like a nice lady. Maybe she'd let me. The beer was a bit gassy but I drank it anyway then ordered another one. A group of guys came in roaring with laughter and sat down behind me with the guy in shirt sleeves. Shame, I had been thinking about going up to him and introducing myself. There were too many of them now.

They were American and started telling 'drinking stories' and roaring with laughter, clapping their hands together with glee and excitement and I felt really low sitting there on my own. Every so often I'd catch the barmaid's eye and she'd smile at me but that made me feel even worse for some reason. After a while, the guys behind me started talking about Rio and I tuned in.

'Man, we *have* to hit that fucking place.'

'Fucking awesome.'

'The girls there are . . . *man.*'

They burst into laughter.

'I'm not going.'

The others protested.

'You got to pay for that shit. No way. I'm not paying.'

'How else you planning on getting laid?'

'Ooooooo' from the others. I heard movement behind me; a chair screeched back and the Americans were chanting 'Fight, fight, fight, fight' and my interest was piqued and I turned around. One of the guys had the *New York Times* reader in a headlock but the *New York Times* reader pushed himself free and sat down, red faced but with a kind of aggressive smile on his face. 'Next time,' he told the other one, who said 'yeah, sure,' and sat down. Then one of the others caught my eye. 'Hey, man. How you doing?'

I hesitated. 'Yeah. Great, thanks.'

Another one said, 'Are you British?'

'Yeah.'

'Awesome. You here on your own?'

'Yeah.'

'You up for fucking some Brazilian pussy?'

'You can't ask him that, dude.'

'I'll ask him anything I want. You going to do something about it?'

'OOO, OOO, OOO, OOO!' They roared and rocked with laughter, slapping each other's backs and giving each other high fives.

'I'll go with you,' I said, but they didn't hear me.

I waited for them to quieten down. 'I'd like to go with you.'

The guy who'd seen me in the first place said, 'Awesome.' He chuckled and finished his drink. 'Men, are we ready?' He stood up. 'ARE WE READY?'

'YEAH!!!'

'ARE WE READY TO FUCK?!!!'

Laughter, high fives, two of them fell off their chairs. It was pretty clear that they were way ahead of me in the drinking stakes, too far to catch up. Still, it was nice to have some company, and if I was going to accomplish anything, I really needed to go to a brothel.

It wasn't a brothel. Well, not exactly. The downstairs was just a nightclub, but upstairs women accosted you from all angles. The Americans, who from the cab journey over when one of them attempted to climb out of the window, 'I'm going to surf the fucking roof', I'd deduced were probably on something more than alcohol, had rushed straight upstairs, except for the *New York Times* reader who I'm not sure even went in. They soon dispersed. Once I found out that sitting still upstairs implied that you were after some 'action', I wandered around, looking for the girl from the hotel but trying not to catch anybody's eye. I didn't see her. I did get a real fright though when as if out of nowhere, one of the Americans jumped out in front of me, face red as a tomato and roared 'ENGLAND!' then fell to the floor in a fit of giggles. I hurried downstairs.

Downstairs was pointless though. I watched the people dancing and talking and drinking, no hope of joining in myself. I felt pretty low. I'd drunk a bit but it made me feel sick more than anything else. Where is Leticia? I wish I had a photo. I did a final circuit of the club. I couldn't see any of the Americans and even upstairs I wasn't in much danger of getting talked to; most of the women must have found their clients for the night. I went to the toilet. There was a cleaner in there with a mop and bucket, just sitting there, waiting for a spillage. And from the sound of it, there was a couple in one of the cubicles, fucking. The cleaner and me ended up looking at one another.

'I'm lonely and scared,' I said.

He looked at me.

'Where is she?'

He said something in Portuguese, then stood up slowly, as if his body creaked in doing so, and started mopping up over by the urinals. Then there was heavy breathing in the cubical. 'Fuck yeah. Fuck yeah. OK, get ready, I'm going to split your fucking ass open.' I wondered did she understand him? Then I left the toilet and left the club.

Walking down the road, the sea dark in the night, I was swelling with a sort of desperate pity, for myself, for the world, I wasn't sure. Tears pressed against my eyes, I couldn't catch my breath. I walked as fast as I could, a sense of panic growing inside me. Then I heard someone call my name. It was distant but then got closer. 'Sam.' There was somebody standing beside me. I looked at him.

'Sam, fancy seeing you here, mate. Listen, are you alright? You don't look too hot.'

I stared at him; it took a while to register: he was the guy I vaguely knew, the one from the barbecue. I flung my arms around him and buried my head in his chest and held on as tight as I could.

We went back to the hotel bar. We didn't speak in the cab

on the way there. I couldn't. I didn't really test it but I'm pretty sure I'd lost my capacity for speech. I was buried deep inside myself, afraid even to think very much lest it evoke images of the outside world. I was only dimly aware of the guy I vaguely knew but thankful for his presence all the same. The few seconds of fresh air between getting out of the cab and going into the hotel pulled me a little way out of my hole and after I'm not sure how long in the bar but the guy I vaguely knew was halfway through one glass and had another empty one beside him, the outside world came out of its haze, although I felt pretty sensitive. I looked at the guy I vaguely knew. 'I don't know what came over me.' I was lying. I did know what had come over me. I could feel it deeply and truly. I just had no idea how to articulate it.

'I was worried about you. You were in a world of your own you were. I waved my hand in front of your face a couple of times. Eyes glazed over.'

'Yeah. Thanks for your help.'

'Hey, you'd do the same for me, right?'

'Uh, yeah, sure.'

'Exactly. We're mates after all.'

We sat there quietly for a few moments. I really needed to find out his name.

'So,' he said. 'What brings you to Rio then?'

'I . . .' I was stumped for a moment.

'Sorry,' he said. 'I shouldn't be bombarding you with questions. You're obviously not on tip top form. Just relax. Take it easy.'

'Thanks.'

'It's just me being nosy. Well, not nosy exactly. I just like to know what's been going on, I meet a mate I've not seen for a while, I like to know what's going on with him. Nothing wrong with that, is there?'

I shook my head.

'Better than banging on about myself. I like to listen. I'm a listener. Too many people today they're talk, talk, talk. Don't give a shit what the other guy's saying. You know?'

'Yeah.'

'I'm mates with someone, I want to know how he's getting on. That's what being mates means to me. Having that genuine interest. Not just sitting there nodding but, you know, actually listening.'

I nodded. I was sure I'd only met him once. Twice including the barbecue.

He grinned at me. 'Isn't it incredible, eh? Us meeting here.'

'Yeah,' I said. 'It's pretty unlikely.'

'Too right.' He sipped his drink. There was a pause. 'So what you been doing with yourself?'

I was about to answer when he said. 'Sorry, mate. There I go, off again, asking questions. I suppose you're interested to know what I've been up to.'

'Uh, yeah.'

'Last time you saw me was a few weeks back, wasn't it? Bit less than that maybe. Ted sent me off to find those burgers of his. Seems like ages ago now.'

So he actually left the country to go and look for the burgers from Ted's barbecue? I was getting confused and the room started rocking but I managed to stabilise it. 'So did you find them?'

'Well that's the thing,' he said. 'I've been all over it seems. First off, what I did, I headed up to Scotland. I don't know why. I don't think I had my head properly screwed on at that point. I guess I figured they had a lot of agriculture over there, farms and cows and stuff. Anyway, I got a flight out of Glasgow Airport, flight to Zambia. Good of a place as any, right? It's ridiculous though. I mean, Ted's a good bloke. An outstanding bloke. But he sends me to find these burgers, I've got nothing to go on, have I? I mean I get to Africa, it's not long before I'm asking shepherds about those burgers. I mean, you know, actual, proper shepherds. I mean it wasn't fruitful but I had to have a go, right? The whole thing isn't much fun, as you can imagine. Except, except for Sierra Leone. When I got there. It's got a booming . . . trade has Sierra Leone. Anything you like. I mean they're all black of course, so if you're not keen on that, but any shape, any size, any age.' He chuckled, leaned forward. 'There was one girl, she'd lost her leg from the knee down. Using it as some kind of selling point. I fucked her' – his cheery, friendly disposition combined with what he was saying made me feel uncomfortable and I started fidgeting in my chair – 'and I have to say, it's something I might try again. You know, amputees. Anyway, this is all by the by. The point is, while I was in Sierra Leone, I hear through the grapevine that there's been a changing of the guard. Ted's not the main man anymore. I've flown all the way to Africa for nothing. Doing a job for Ted and he's in no position to reward me. Wasted my time. I mean, all things considered, I'm not delighted, right? But I think oh well and I manage to hook up with the new guys. As luck would have it, the new guys, they've tasted Ted's burgers themselves, don't know how, but they have. And they loved them. Who doesn't? Now *they* want me to get the burgers and they know exactly where I can find them. Right here. Well, not *right* here. But in Brazil. I had to drive out to this tiny little village but I finally get there, have one myself, I have to say they are spot on, and put the rest in the freezer. They are spot on. Even if Ted's not done them on the bar-becue. I mean this whole find the burgers thing, it's about proving myself, I know that. Initiation isn't it? But the truth is, those burgers are bloody nice, aren't they? Everybody thinks so. Anyway, got here last night. Rio I mean. And apparently they're so pleased with me in London that I'm to have myself a holiday. Couple of weeks at least. On them. Wired me over some money to go and enjoy myself. And I have to say, it's a fucking paradise here, isn't it?'

'It seems nice.'

'Nice?'

'I've had a strange day.'

'Yeah. I can tell.' He chuckled. 'Great to see you.'

'Yeah.' I hesitated. 'So who's the new boss? The one in London?'

'Oh.' He shifted in his seat. 'I don't know. I've not met him yet. I suppose I will do when I give him his burger.'

'Yeah.'

'Yeah.'

We were quiet for a little while. I noticed that he was starting to get a bit fidgety.

'So,' he said. 'What brings you here? I mean, if you're after anything particular. I mean just ask me. I've got some connections. I'll probably be able to help you. You know, if you want to find someone or something.' He looked right at me.

But the idea of setting him on Leticia's trail made me shudder. And if he doesn't work for Ted, who does he work for? How many people are after Leticia? What do they want with her? She must be deep in hiding . . .

'What are you thinking, mate? Anything. Anything at all. Seriously, it would be my pleasure. After all, we're old mates, right?'

The girl? Ask him about her? But even her, I felt like he might put her in danger . . .

'At your service. That's all you need to know.'

'There is a girl I wouldn't mind finding.'

'Oh yeah?' He put his drink down and sat up. His eyes opened wider, his whole being focused on me.

'It's this girl I met when I first got here. This morning. She was in my hotel room.'

'Oh right . . . Oh right.' The focus drained from him. He must have thought I was talking about Leticia. Why is everybody after her? What do they want from her? I suddenly felt angry.

'Sam?'

'. . . Yeah.'

'You were saying. A girl. In your room.'

'Yeah.' I recovered myself. 'I'd like to get in touch with her again. Nothing important. I mean all I want is to know where she hangs out. I mean that would be it. You don't even need to talk to her or anything.'

'No problem. No problem, Sam. I'm all over that. Just tell me what I need to know.'

I described the girl to him.

'Consider it done.'

'Thanks. Like I say, just tell me where I can find her. That's all I need.'

'Leave it to me, mate.' He finished his drink. 'We should do this again though. Have a drink. Go out large next time. I know some great places. What do you say?'

'Uh, yeah. Yeah, sure.'

'It's a paradise this place. Well, if you know where to go it is. Keep safe, Sam. Watch you don't go wandering off into a *favela*.'

'I'll be OK.'

'I'm sure you will. But yeah, while you're here, we should meet up, have a chat about old times.' He looked at me.

'Yeah . . .' I wondered was he delusional? I suppose it's

possible. Maybe he really thinks we've had a long friendship. I mean, I'd have been happy to have him to go around with but he had a pretty unsavoury side. And I still didn't know his name.

'We've been fantastically lucky with the weather, mate. Winters can get cold out here, you know. Wind blowing in off the sea and that. Beautiful weather we've got though.'

I said, 'I was wondering if it was a worldwide thing. England's pretty hot at the moment.'

'What, like an environmental thing?'

'Sort of,' I said. 'Like there's so much pressure on the world and all it can do is heat up.'

'You mean global warming?'

'Sort of. Not exactly. I don't know.'

He laughed. 'You're a funny bloke, Sam. Right, I'll be in touch. What's your number here?'

'We can get it at the front desk.'

We went to the front desk and he got the telephone number and we shook hands and he said, 'Who'd have thought we'd end up in Brazil together, eh?' and I sort of chuckled and then he was off. I didn't want to go up to my room yet so I went back to the bar. I ordered a juice and went and sat down. It was empty in there and I just needed to relax. Maybe I would find her. If the guy I vaguely knew could get me in contact with the girl from my room, if I worked my way up, just followed the instructions, then eventually I might find Leticia. I flushed with hope. I couldn't remember what she looked like anymore, but it didn't matter. She was part of me, intertwined with my emotions and the dreams in my heart. I sipped my juice, thought about the toilet cleaner and the blank look he gave me, and then a vision popped into my head of me fucking an amputee from behind, and she had a gag over her mouth, and I started getting panicky and gripped the underside of my chair and held myself still and waited for my heartbeat to slow down. One of the Americans walked in. He didn't seem drunk, then I realised it was the *New York Times* reader.

'Hey,' he said.

'Hi.'

'Listen,' he said. 'I'm sure you're a nice guy and all that but you need to know that I am so angry right now.'

'OK.'

'I'm about to smash up this bar, so if you want to stay here, that's your call.'

'Uh, OK.'

'OK.' He stared at me but I didn't move. He shrugged. 'OK then. OK then.'

He started 'smashing up the bar.' He turned a few tables over; I heard him grunt and I heard the tables fall to the floor behind me, then a hotel security guard came in and pulled him away. He went quietly, but his eyes were blazing and he was bristling with aggression, ready for a fight, not any particular fight, just with the first person who provoked his indignation, and apparently he expected that person to come along at any time. Once he'd gone, I realised that I was exhausted. I stood up and went up to my room.

I was confused. I wasn't sure if this was a dream or not. It must be a dream. I can't be in Rio. It's not possible. It's not possible. But then I woke up and I wasn't in my flat and I didn't know if either I was still dreaming or if I was awake and I really was in Rio. The problem seemed irreconcilable and I lay there in bed in a state of feverish half sleep, trying to resolve the problem but not being able to do it and getting more and more irritable, the answer eluding me, itching all over, tossing and turning, pulling the bed sheets off the corners of the bed, so irritated I could hardly breathe. I must have spent hours in this state before I finally woke up. I sat there, sweaty, scratching myself all over. I got up and went to the toilet, realised this was the hotel room, not my flat. I really am here then. I walked back into the main room and looked at my bed, the bed sheets ripped off, a real mess. I didn't want to get back in. I ran my hands through my hair. I'll go and phone Alice. That's what I'll do. I looked at my watch. Just gone one AM. It'll be about five there. She might be awake. I threw on some clothes and went downstairs.

My friend was at reception and helped me make the call. The phone rang and for some reason I was nervous, almost hoping she wouldn't answer.

She did answer. 'Yeah?'

I hesitated.

'Who is it?'

'Alice, it's Sam.'

She didn't answer.

'Listen, Alice, I'm in Rio. In Brazil. Don't ask me how I got here, I just, I just wanted to see how you were.'

I could hear her breathing down the phone. Then she hung up. I went back to bed.

The Americans weren't at breakfast. The food was really good but I could hardly eat anything. I was restless and I kept jigging my legs and fidgeting and looking around me, but I didn't know what to do next. I just had to wait. Wait for the guy I vaguely knew to get back to me with some information. But I couldn't just wait. I really was restless. I couldn't sit still. I burst out of my chair and left the hotel.

I felt nauseous and my face was flushed and the back of my neck was burning. I really need some sun cream. But I don't know where anything is here. I don't know where anything is! I walked along the streets in a bit of a state. How am I supposed to find Leticia here if I can't find the sun cream? I jumped up and down. I was completely lost now, my legs were tired and I felt feverish and I wondered would I ever get back to the hotel? I just want to go back to the hotel. I should have held tight. I should have just waited for the guy I vaguely knew. Then I realised where I was. I was right outside the restaurant where I'd eaten yesterday. I stood facing it. A chill went through me. I ran away. Today it took me even longer (over an hour and a half) to get back to the hotel. Still, I ended up going along the same back streets I had yesterday and this time I got a fright when a man came up to me speaking Portuguese and then he put his hand in his pocket and I thought he was reaching for a weapon and I flinched and my knees went weak and I fell against the wall. He put his hand on my arm, presumably trying to help, but I flinched again and he went off. I can't say I blame him.

Back in my room, I flopped down in bed. I think I've got sun stroke. If I'm going to go out there, I need a strategy. I need to use the buses, cover more ground. I wonder if they have bus maps? I doubt it, it all seems pretty informal. I need to have a strategy. I need to have a plan. God, I feel awful. Bloody sunburn. It's really horrible. Need to have a strategy. I fell asleep.

I woke up disorientated, but quickly established that I was in the hotel room in Rio. The curtains were open but it was dark outside. Shit, did I sleep through the whole day? I checked my watch; thirty three minutes past eleven PM. I felt sort of heavy headed but I didn't think I'd be able to get back to sleep again. What then? Go to a brothel, try and find the girl? How do I know where to go? Leave that to the guy I vaguely know. What do I do then? I stared getting panicky, felt stuck in my room but ill equipped to go outside. Then I had a thought that instantly drew my enthusiasm; I would go to the beach. The beach at night. Under the stars. Listening to the sea lapping against the shore. What a lovely thought. I got changed and set off.

I took my sandals off and the sand felt lovely and cool against my feet. The air was fresh and I could hear the noise of the traffic going past in the background and it all felt like a perfect mix of nature and civilization. The air was fresh and it was a clear night and I could see the stars and I kept on down the beach and I could hear the water lapping against the shore. It seemed a longer walk to the sea than earlier; maybe the tide was out. I imagined walking along the beach like this, at night, holding hands with Leticia, and quivered with joy. If I could just find her. My mouth went numb with the intensity of my hope.

I heard voices off to my right and looked in that direction but I couldn't see anything in the dark. I'd thought I was alone but apparently not. The voices were getting closer, laughing and shouting out. I stood still, told myself it was nothing to worry about, but not too sure, starting to get nervous. Then a group of one, two, three . . . five people came out of the shadows. As they came closer I could see that one of them was female, the rest male. They were young, not children, but young and the guys were well built. They didn't seem to notice me at first and I thought they'd walk right past me, but then one of them said something and I realised he was talking to me. 'I'm sorry I . . .' They came and formed a circle around me. The girl kicked sand at my ankles and giggled. I smiled. One of the men said something. 'I'm really sorry but . . .' He pushed me in the chest. I thought he was just messing around and chuckled but then he pushed me harder. He spoke, his voice was louder, firmer this time. One of the other guys pushed me in the back. 'I . . .' The one who did the talking got a knife out. Shit. He shouted in my face. I realised I was being robbed and I turned my pockets out and shook my head. He stared at me then punched me in the face and I went down. They started kicking me and I curled up into a ball and used my arms to protect my face. The kicks kept coming, pounding against my arms, legs, stomach and I couldn't keep track of where the pain was. Then I felt a foot strike the top of my head and went a bit woozy, my body still getting kicked; the pain was duller now, not specific, just a general pain. Then it stopped. I waited a few minutes, then uncurled and looked around me. They were gone. I stood up; I was hurting but I could walk. I think I was in shock or something; the only thing I could think was that I probably needed to get off the beach as soon as possible. Once I got off the beach, I crossed the road and went back to the hotel and straight up to my room.

I looked at myself in the mirror. I had a cut on my face where I'd been hit and a red patch that had already begun to swell. Otherwise, I seemed to have protected my face from being kicked. I took my clothes off. I had a few red marks on my thighs and torso. I'd never been beaten up before. I went to bed.

I woke up in agony. Every part of my body hurt. I tried to sit up a few times but a sharp pain in my left side stopped me. On the fifth attempt I managed to haul myself out of bed and into the bathroom. I looked at myself in the mirror. Bloody hell. There were bruises all over my body. And I was purple in some places. The swelling had got worse on my face but bloody hell my body was in a really bad way. I didn't feel too bad about it though. I mean physically I did but I wasn't suffering from 'trauma', not that I was aware of. I kind of liked being covered in bruises. It was a bit of an effort moving about though. And washing my hair was tough; I couldn't get my arms above chest height.

At breakfast, a few people looked twice at me. I was able to eat more than yesterday and I even hobbled over to the buffet and got myself seconds. For some reason, having been beaten up, I felt more ready to go out into the city and face whatever there was to face. I nibbled on my watermelon until only the skin was left, then went up to my room to brush my teeth and went out.

I found the sun cream pretty quickly this morning and slapped a load on my face and on the back of my neck. That was the end of my good luck though. I decided to have a go at the buses so I waited at a bus stop and got on the first one that came along. I paid the woman collecting the money and that was all fine, then looked up to see who I was sharing the bus with. There were a couple of young guys about half way down and they triggered my memory of last night and I had to get a hold of my nerves and I sat down at the front of the bus. But the longer I stayed on the bus the tenser I got and people got on and off and I had no idea where I was and after about forty minutes I lost my nerve and got off the bus. From then, it took me six and a half hours to get back to the hotel. No sign of Leticia.

I nearly snapped at my friend at reception but recovered myself just in time. He commented on the swelling on my face and I signalled that I'd bumped into something and he looked worried for a moment, then shrugged and chuckled. Then he said, 'You have a message, sir.' It was from the guy I vaguely knew.

Hey, Sam

I know where you can find the little madam. I'll drop by
the hotel at seven and we can go there together.
Cheers,

G

G as in? Was this a new thing, signing with your initial?
It's ridiculous. What time is it? Shit, nearly half six already. I
rushed up to my room and got ready. I'd calmed down a bit
by the time I went down to meet him ('G') but still, the day
had taken its toll and I felt ready to bristle at any small thing.
I took a deep breath and stepped out of the lift.

He was sitting in the lobby, reading the paper. He looked
up, saw me and put his paper down. 'Alright, Sam, how's . . .
Christ, what happened to your face?'

I was going to tell him the bumped into something story
but I thought, sod it. 'I got beaten up. On the beach last
night.'

'Shit, Sam. How come you were on the beach?'

'I couldn't sleep,' I said. 'I fancied a walk.'

'You don't want to be going on the beach in the dark.'

'Yeah, I know.'

'Learned the hard way, eh? Never mind, you've got me to
look after you now. Come on, we're losing drinking time.'

We left the hotel and got into a taxi.

The guy I vaguely knew talked and talked and talked, in the
taxi and then in the bar, and we both drank a fair few beers.
I hadn't eaten all day and the alcohol went to my head a bit
and I phased in and out of what he was saying, which ranged
from television shows to his mother to 'mates who never

keep in touch.' 'It bothers me, Sam. If you can't keep in touch, what kind of friend are you, eh?' He said this with a sort of baffled frustration. 'How hard is it to keep in touch?' he asked. I shrugged and looked away. He knew I didn't have the answer; nobody had the answer. It was one of life's tragedies. He was quiet for the next ten minutes. Most of the time though I listened to him chatter on and felt calmer, just listening (and not even doing that sometimes, switching off, but he'd still be talking when I tuned in again) and drinking, the steady stream of his voice and alcohol allowing me to forget the irritation from earlier in the day.

Every so often though, he'd say something that gave me an unpleasant feeling inside, sometimes it would be about his conquests, 'she stuck her tongue up my arse and had a right good poke around, she'd do anything she would', and that was more embarrassing than anything else but sometimes it would be something more: 'they were keeping them in cages, this was when London sent me over there, have a look at what we'd be getting. I saw one of them and Christ, I mean *Christ*. You know what I mean? I say to the guy out there, "you keep something as beautiful as that caged up?" He thought I was upset or something, got all defensive. "No, no, no," I tell him. "I just think she needs some air. I think I'd best test her out." The guy was so relieved, bursts into laughter. She was only young but I'll tell you what, did she know how to suck. And she had the tightest little cunt, I really had to squeeze myself in there. Not half as tight as her arsehole though.' He gave me a wry smile and I had no idea how to respond. Then he went back to what's on TV. Later he said, 'These third world blokes, they really knock them about. I don't know, face too messed up, it's a bit . . . I mean I've seen them bashed up in London too but . . . It's in their culture though, isn't it?'

'Uh, yeah . . . Have you, have you ever worked for Ted?'

He looked at me, finished his drink, looked at me again. 'Ted? No. I almost made it though. Got an invite to the barbecue didn't I? But then this burger thing and I learn Ted's not even top dog anymore. Doesn't matter. I'm well positioned now. New blokes at the top know who I am.'

'So who is the new bloke? You know, the new top guy if it isn't Ted.'

He looked at me for a moment, then chuckled. 'Top secret, Sam, mate. These guys like to put layers in, insulate themselves. Come on, drink up. I'll take you to see your girl.'

As we were leaving he said, 'Remind me to give you a couple of those burgers. I've got some at my hotel. Beautiful they are. Even if you just do them in the oven.'

I fell asleep in the cab and when I woke up the guy I vaguely knew was paying the driver.

'Oh alright, Sam. Had a good sleep?'

'Yeah.' I felt a bit groggy and not as drunk as I'd been before I left the bar, but when we got out of the cab and the fresh air hit me, I felt drunk again. The place looked pretty seedy. I didn't even realise it was open to the public until we were going in. And we were inland; I looked both ways down the road and couldn't see the sea.

'Ready?'

'Yeah.'

As we went in the doorman handed me a card which I put in my pocket. The place was dingy inside. It was a bar rather than a nightclub like last night; much smaller, although the odd few people were dancing. There were quite a few single men dotted about talking to women who, it was pretty clear from what they were wearing, were prostitutes.

'Drink?'

I nodded.

The guy I vaguely knew ordered us a couple of beers. The place felt sort of like a cave. The music was really grungy, not like the banging party music last night.

'See anything you like?'

'Is this where she works?'

'Yeah. This is it. Not bad, eh? I was here last night. No complaints. There's my girl.' He waved at one of the girls and she waved back and gave him a big smile.

I said, 'So whereabouts is she then?'

'What, your girl? Can't see her at the minute. Could be she's gone upstairs. Be patient, mate. Relax.'

I closed my eyes and my head started spinning, but I sort of savoured the sensation, the rest of my body relaxing, swaying with the music.

The guy I vaguely knew tapped me on the shoulder. 'There she is. That's her, right?'

I opened my eyes. Yep, it was her. She was standing with some guy. She kissed his cheek and off he went.

The guy I vaguely knew shouted over to her. 'Hey. Hey.' She looked over at us, smiled, waved, and walked over.

'Sam,' she giggled. 'You no wear pyjamas.'

'What's this about pyjamas, Sam?'

'Nothing, nothing.'

There was a pause. The girl was smiling at me.

The guy I vaguely knew said, 'Aren't you going to introduce me?'

'Uh, yeah. Yeah, OK. This is, well I met her when I got here and, and . . .' I didn't know either of their names!

'He's had a bit to drink,' The guy I vaguely knew told the girl.

She smiled at me. 'How you find me, Sam? Rio is very enormous.'

'I just, luck I suppose.'

'Luck,' the guy said.

She was still smiling at me.

Another girl came over. 'Hi.'

'What have we got here then?' the guy said. 'How about a dance?'

The girls nodded; the guy took the hand of the girl from my room. 'Do you mind, Sam?'

I shook my head, caught the girl's eye; she stuck out her bottom lip. They went off to the dance floor. I was left with the other one.

'We dance?' she said.

'OK.'

It wasn't really dancing music though. We did some slow, 'sexy' dancing at first; she'd draw away from me and cup her breasts in her hands or turn around and stick her bum out and slap it. Then she stood really close to me and slid down my body into a crouching position, then slid back up my body and put her nose in my hair and then moved her nose down my cheek and neck, pressed her pelvis right into mine. Then she started kissing my neck, and I looked over at the guy I vaguely knew, and he had one hand under the jaw of the girl from my room, holding her head in place, and he was kissing her hard on the mouth, and I felt something growing inside me, burning, a sort of rage, and then I felt lips on my mouth and I kissed them, still looking at the other two. The guy I vaguely knew said, 'Hey, Sam. What say we take these bitches upstairs?' I didn't say anything. Then we took the girls upstairs.

My girl was really loud. I had this sickness in my stomach as I pounded away at her and I was in a bit of a panic and she was underneath me, screaming, and I kept going, my breath short, and my mind drifted away. I had an image of being curled up with Leticia, we were in no definable location, a black backdrop, curled up, and I ran my nose down her neck and she giggled, and my body strained with desire to hold her and make her giggle and I winced. I couldn't feel my legs any more, but I kept moving my hips automatically and I was sobbing now. I looked over the other side of the room and saw the guy I vaguely knew and the girl from my room. He was holding her leg right up in the air, high and forced back, it looked painful, and fucking her, his hand round her neck. The burning sensation inside me worked its way up my body, squeezed up my throat and I grunted then let out a cry. My face was twisted up and my whole body was shaking. He raised his hand and slapped her breasts. Then he moved his knee forward and dug it in her stomach and grasped her throat tighter. I was shaking uncontrollably and I let out a scream and jumped up. I ran over to the guy I vaguely knew and pulled him off of the bed and he fell to the floor. He was about to get up when I smashed him in the face and he fell back. Then I pinned him down with my knees and hit him again. And again. I don't know how many times I hit him but every time I did it was really satisfying and I only stopped when I was too tired to keep going. His face was a bloody mess but he moaned and groaned. I stood up and looked at the girls who looked back at me with blank expressions. My heart started beating fast and panic gripped me and I grabbed my clothes, put them on as fast as I could, falling over when I tried to get into my trousers, and then I left.

I had no idea where I was. I was really in a state. I couldn't control my breathing and was staggering through the dark streets and thought that if I could just find my way back to the sea . . . But I felt like every turn I took led me deeper into the city. My hand was starting to hurt. I think I've broken my wrist. There weren't many people about and I had no idea where I was and I remembered my beating on the beach, and what about the fact that I'm even in Brazil to start with?, and everything piled on me all at once, smothered me, so I couldn't function anymore, I couldn't walk, my body was shaking too much, and I fell back against the wall, shaking, unable to think clearly, everything coming at me in fragments, a sense of dread hanging over me, and I screamed out 'LETICIA! LETICIA!!!' and slid down the wall, and crawled along the floor, gasping for breath, my body tingling. And then I stopped, I couldn't drag myself any further. I rested my head on the concrete and fell asleep.

I blinked my eyes open. Daylight. I remembered everything immediately. Oh God. I bent my wrist and it felt OK. But then I clenched my fist then spread my fingers out and it was really painful. I sat up. God, it stinks; there was a really pungent smell of urine. I stood up and smelt myself. It didn't seem to have got on me although I did smell a bit tangy. I was in a long road. Nobody else was about but the road seemed to lead into some sort of square. I wandered towards it.

I found a theatre offering tours and almost went in because the tour guide standing outside looked so friendly but I knew my legs wouldn't be able to stand a tour so I went into a café and had breakfast. I had cake for breakfast and sat there listening to the sound of voices echoing under the high ceiling the place had. I thought back to last night and more than any particular event, remembered a feeling, a desire. And, sitting there eating my cake the desire was evoked again and a vacuum formed in my stomach. This is unbearable. Impossible.

I have to find her. How? Just look for her. She loves Rio. Ted said she loves Rio. She's bound to be out and about. You can find her. If you cover a lot of ground, you can find her. I stood up. I felt revitalised. I had an energy about me. Purpose. I set off on my search.

The streets were becoming crowded with shoppers and people going about their daily business. I started off my search in positive mood, with great hope. I would eye every face in the crowd and each one that wasn't hers I could strike off the list. One less person to search amongst. And I kept seeing women who I thought might be her and my heart would leap. And sometimes the woman would be quite far away and I would move through the crowds, closing in on her, my heart pounding and ready for joy to flow through me as I got closer and still it might be her. But eventually I would reach a distance where I could see it wasn't her. And that was disappointing. Of course it was. But I recovered pretty quickly. There were plenty of other women in Rio. For some reason the large number of women in Rio seemed to be a positive thing. And I continued my search, some women candidates for a split second, others for longer. And I walked up and down the streets, occasionally going into shops that I thought she might like, but always keeping an eye on the street, in case she walked past. After a while, I got hungry and stopped for an ice cream and sat outside and watched the people, sifted them, homing in on black women first, then black women of the right age. And the sun beat down on my head. This was the hottest day so far. If this is winter, what is summer going to be like? If this heat wave keeps up, half the world will be scorched.

By late afternoon the sun had gone in and there were thick clouds again. My energy and hopefulness faded with the light. Fewer people seemed to look like Leticia, and those who did looked like her for only half as long. But I kept on walking the streets. It was as if I was afraid to stop my search. What other options did I have? Then the skies opened up. It was a real storm, and I was immediately soaked in warm, heavy ran. I kept going for I don't know how long and my hair was matted to my face and the rain blurred my vision and the crowds thinned out and people put their umbrellas up and it was difficult to see their faces. But still I kept going. What else can I do? What else can I do? It began to get dark and the rain pounded against my head and I floated back to the hotel and into the lobby and sat down. The air conditioning was on and my teeth chattered and I shivered. I swelled with self-pity. What am I supposed to do? Sobs worked their way up my throat. Then an idea took me over. I went up to reception and my friend commented on how wet I was and I forced a smile. I dialled the number. It rang and rang and rang but nobody answered. Shit. I punched the wall. She's probably asleep. Fuck it. I dialled again. Come on. No answer. I dialled again.

'Hello?'

I couldn't speak.

'He*llo*?'

'Alice?'

She didn't say anything.

'Alice I'm, I'm soaked. It's been raining and . . .' Tears strangled me.

She didn't say anything.

'I . . . Hopefully I'll be back soon. I've been out all day. I . . .'

'Doug's looking for you.'

'. . . Doug?' It took me a moment to remember who he was.

'Yeah. He keeps, like, coming round. Finally I let him in just to get him to shut up. I told him you left without saying anything.'

'I would have done. I just . . . I just . . .' I burst into audible tears. 'Alice. Alice, I'll be home soon. I've been trying to find her. I've . . .'

'Yeah, listen, I have to go. You woke me up.'

'Alice, please.' I sobbed down the phone. '*Please*.' I didn't know exactly what I wanted from her but I kept saying '*please*' and sobbing. Eventually, I stopped. 'Alice? Alice?'

She hung up. My eyes swelled with fresh tears. I looked over at my friend at reception. He was staring at me, not sure what to make of it all. I looked at him, almost said '*please*' but started sobbing again and turned and walked towards the lift and went to my room.

I stayed under the covers for hours, never asleep, frozen in a state of distress. When I did poke my head out from under the covers, it was dark outside. I took a sip of water from the glass on my bedside table and stood up. My body ached and was still covered in bruises; I pressed one of the bruises until it made me wince. I looked out into the night. What now? Do I have enough money for a flight back to London? Who's paying for the hotel? What does it matter who's paying? Ted, Tre, what does it matter? I could go home. But Leticia's here. Leticia's here. I can't leave. What then? I could go back and see the girl. How do I know where the club is though? I have no idea where it was. I sighed and looked out the window. Then I remembered, the doorman, he handed me a card. I rushed over to my trousers and pulled the pocket inside out. The card fell out. I'll just give it to a taxi driver. He'll take me there. I brushed my teeth, got dressed, and went downstairs.

Towards the end of the cab ride, I started getting tense about how the girl might react to seeing me again. I'd gone pretty crazy last night. Still, I shrugged it off. It would be OK. She works in a brothel. She'll be used to fights. I paid the taxi driver and walked to the door. The doorman gave me a hard look. He said something in Portuguese. I shrugged. He said something else in Portuguese. I nodded and tried to walk in but he put his arm out and blocked my way. I looked at him and he stared back at me. Then, still blocking my way with his arm, he called inside the club. Then he turned back and stared at me. What's going on? I was pretty anxious to get in.

A man came out of the club. He spoke to the doorman in Portuguese then looked at me. 'You English?'

'Yeah.'

'You here last night?'

'Yeah.'

'You back now. You must like, huh?'

'Yeah.'

'I owner here. This place *mine*, man.' He was pretty intense. His head bobbed about when he spoke.

'It's nice,' I said.

'Yeah,' he said. 'We don't like trouble here, huh?' He looked at me as though he wanted an answer.

'. . .'

'You trouble. You make trouble here.'

'I didn't mean to. I just needed to . . .'

He punched me in the stomach and I felt all the wind go out of me and bent over double.

'Hold him up.'

The doorman came and pinned my arms behind me. The owner was standing in front of me. I felt really exposed.

'You like beating up my customers, huh?'

'It's not . . .'

'Huh? What you say, man?' He feigned a punch and I flinched and he burst into laughter. 'You got balls though, man. I cannot be*lieve* you come back, huh? You try to insult me, huh? That it, man?'

'No.'

'No?'

'No.'

He shrugged then punched me in the stomach again. While I was gasping for breath, I had a realisation.

'Wait . . .' I caught my breath. 'Wait.'

'Wait for what, man?' He punched me again.

I felt sick and waited until I'd got my breath back properly before I spoke. The idea of getting hit again made me feel like throwing up. 'You own this place?'

'Yeah. I own it and you fuck it up. That how this work, huh?'

'Do you know, do you know a guy called Ted?'

The name obviously meant something to him; his whole demeanour changed. 'What you say, man?' He tried to recover his menace but he was distracted now. He looked nervous.

'Ted. I was sent here by Ted. Do you, do you work for him?'

'Who the fuck are you?'

'I'm, I'm a friend.'

He stared at me, then he signalled for the doorman to let go of me. He shouted at the doorman who went inside. He stepped closer to me; I could feel his breath on my face. 'What you want, man? You don't look like no friend of Ted.'

'He sent me over here to look for someone.'

'Yeah? Who?'

'His daughter. Leticia.'

He didn't say anything for a moment. 'He think I can help?'

'Yeah.'

He backed away from me and started pacing. Then he turned to me. 'Where you staying?'

I told him the name of my hotel.

'OK, listen, man. I meet you there. Tomorrow. Twelve o clock. You be there, man.'

'OK.'

'Now get lost.' He looked up and down the street then went back into the club.

I wandered away, in no particular direction, I just started wandering. My whole body was aching. There were no taxis around though. It was just back street after back street. I yawned. I was completely shattered, I found a doorway and sat down. I yawned again. My eyelids were heavy. I fell asleep.

The sun was coming up. I checked my watch; it was half six. Less than six hours to get back to the hotel. He knew where she was. You could tell. He knew where she was. I started running. But bloody hell did my body hurt.

I was back in time for breakfast. I couldn't eat anything though. I was so excited I couldn't sit still and I was in the lobby and waiting by ten to ten. The next two hours and ten minutes were almost impossible to get through. A slight bit of interest came when the Americans checked out. Two of them looked as though they'd been beaten up and they all seemed pretty annoyed and argued about some tax they shouldn't have been charged. Apart from that though, there was nothing to do or see and it was agony. I even started wondering what if he means twelve midnight?, but at noon exactly, the brothel owner came through the door. He was pretty on edge and kept looking around. He saw me and came and sat down opposite me.

'This dangerous, man.'

'Sorry.'

'Fuck you, sorry. What this bullshit have to do with me, huh?' He looked around again. He was really nervous.

'Ted said you'd know something. Or you'd know someone who knew something.'

He spoke in Portuguese and smashed his fists down on the table, then muttered something under his breath. 'You got a room here, man?'

'Yeah.'

'We talk there. I not talking in no fucking lobby.'

'Yeah,' I said. 'Yeah, sure. Let's go.'

We stood up. We took a few steps. Then there was a BANG right in my ear and wet spots landed on my face and the brothel owner dropped to the floor with a bullet hole in his head. People were screaming. Somebody tugged at my arm. I turned and saw a guy with a gun pointed at me and then he led me out of the hotel and bundled me into the back of a car.

The windows were blacked out and I was screened off from the front of the car by a glass partition. My ears were still ringing from the sound of the gunshot and when I wiped my face I got blood on my fingers. I thought about my friend at reception and wondered what he'd made of this. Where were they taking me? Were they going to kill me? It had all happened so quickly. I sat back and waited.

The car stopped. Nothing happened for a moment, then the glass partition came down and the guy in the passenger seat turned around. He handed me an envelope.

'Tre sends his regards.'

I took the envelope.

He pointed the gun at me. 'You get out now.'

I got out and the car drove off. People were walking back and forth with luggage carts. Taxis were coming and going. I was at the airport. I opened the envelope. Inside was a ticket for London Heathrow, my passport, and a letter. The letter read:

> Sam,
>
> Ta for the help. Hows Ted feel now? Fuck loses another dickhead. We tight? I might use you again pal.
>
> T
>
> p.s. Taped a reward to the bottom of the page. Knock you out like that. Nobody wants to be awake on an eleven hour flight.

I put the letter back in the envelope and went into the airport.

On the plane, I took Tre's pill. And he was right. Next thing I knew I was waking up in Madrid. Four and a half hours later, I arrived in Heathrow.

Alice Asks Me To Kill Her

I didn't have any money for the train but I managed to get home without the ticket inspectors catching me. It was just gone ten in the morning when I got back to my building. The sky was blue and the sun was hot but, I don't know, it seemed a bit chillier than before I'd left. Maybe it was just the effect of the sleeping pills; they must have been quite strong because I felt queasy and generally not right at all, sort of off balance.

My building looked different somehow. I don't know why, it's sometimes like that when you've been away for a while. I went in. It was completely silent. It was a Tuesday I suppose. People would be at work. I started up the stairs.

Sixty seven stairs. Bloody hell. When I reached the top I was huffing and puffing and my legs had nothing left to give. It must be those sleeping pills. They've really knocked me off kilter. I rung on the doorbell. Alice was probably asleep but I didn't have a key so that was that. I should have given a key to my neighbour. I'll have to arrange that. Swap spare keys. Alice didn't answer. I tried again but still no answer. I sat down, back against the wall and yawned. Bloody hell, I'm whacked. I fell asleep.

I woke up zonked. The remnants of the sleeping pills were still with me. My neighbour was coming out of his flat. He turned around and saw me.

'Oh, alright, Sam? Haven't seen you around for a while. Did you forget your key?'

'Yeah . . . Yeah. It's alright, I'm expecting my . . . I'm expecting someone home soon.'

'We should do a key swap. Avoid this sort of thing.'

'Yeah, good idea.'

There was a pause.

'Listen, Sam. I just wanted to say, about the funeral. Thanks so much for coming. It meant such a lot to me.'

'That's OK.'

His eyes glazed over and he smiled. Then he snapped out of it. 'Oh, I meant to say. A guy knocked on my door yesterday, asked if I knew where you were.'

'Really?'

'Yeah, yeah. I said I hadn't seen you for a few days.'

'Right . . . Oh, that'll be Doug. Yeah, thanks, I know about that.'

'No. No. Doug wasn't his name. He gave me his name . . . Ted, that was it.'

'Ted?'

'Yep. Ted. That's the one. Great guy.' He smiled as if in recollection of the meeting.

Ted in my building. Wow.

'OK, so I best be off. Bus to catch. We'll arrange something though. Swap keys.'

'Yeah,' I said. 'Yeah, definitely.' And then my neighbour was off. I checked my watch. It was half two. I was really thirsty. I have to get into the flat. Even if I wake Alice up I have to get in. I got to my feet. My thirst suddenly seemed desperate and took me over. I hammered on the door. 'Alice! Alice, it's Sam. Let me in!' My mouth was frothy and I couldn't stand it anymore. 'Alice!' After a few minutes of hammering and calling Alice's name, the door swung open. Alice was sitting there in her wheelchair, staring at me. There were crusty sores on her face and her hair was thinner. Shit. She's dying.

'So you decided to come back, huh?'

'Sorry about the knocking and shouting. I, I'm really thirsty.'

'Uh huh.' She turned the chair and wheeled herself into the flat.

I went in, closed the door behind me.

'I'll get you some water.' She went into the kitchen and got a glass out.

'Thanks,' I looked around the flat; it was pretty much the same. Alice was running the tap. I glanced at her. She looks so ill. I can't just let her die here. I mean, I'd be charged with criminal negligence.

She came in with the water, stopped in front of me.

'Thanks,' I said.

She threw the water in my face.

I didn't know what to do; she was staring at me. She tilted her chair one way then the other. Please, not this. But then strain started to show on her face. She couldn't get it rocking. She stopped, breathing deeply.

'Are you OK?'

She looked up at me, smiled at first but then she said, 'Fuck you, Sam.' Then her voice took on a kind of screeching panic. 'FUCK *YOU*!' She turned the chair and wheeled herself into the bedroom and slammed the door.

Shit. I was frazzled. I slumped down in the armchair, my body twitching all over. What do I do? She's dying. Doug wants to kill me, I can't phone him. Celina? Maybe I should just phone an ambulance. God my mouth is dry. I went and got a drink. She can't stay here. It's wrong. I have to think of something. I poured myself another glass of water and drank it in one go. The phone went. I approached it carefully.

'Hello?'

'Sam, hi! How are you?'

It took me a moment, then I realised it was Angela. 'Hi, Angela.'

'So you don't sound too bad. Are you coming back to work soon?'

'To work?'

'Yeah. You were sick, right? Your niece phoned in for you. But you sound better now.'

Niece? 'Yeah. Yeah, I'm OK.'

'Great. It's boring as usual around here. They moved me to the other end of the office and then you got sick so the old desk is empty. It's sort of sad if you think about it.'

'Yeah.' I chuckled.

'You sound tired.'

'I'm OK.'

'So when you coming back?'

'Tomorrow. I should be back tomorrow.'

'Great. Maybe we'll have lunch, yeah?'

'Yeah, sure.'

'Great. I'd better go. Hit the targets.'

'Yeah. See you.'

'Bye.' She hung up.

I wandered over to the window. My view in Rio was nicer. I looked out at the car park and everything felt sort of drab. After all, Leticia was in Rio and I was in London. In London and back to work. And Alice would be dead soon. Back to work and back to normal. I suppose Doug might try to kill me. I didn't feel like he would though, not at that moment I didn't. Leticia's in a different hemisphere. I felt a crippling sense of nothingness, fell forward and had to use the window to steady myself.

'Sam. Sam.' It was Alice.

'Yeah?' I felt too weak to move.

There was a pause, then 'Sam.'

I backed away from the window, steadied myself, and headed for the bedroom. The room was dark but not pitch black, light filtering its way through the curtain. Alice was lying on the bed, her head propped up by a pillow. I let the bedroom door swing shut behind me, and just stood there; neither of us said anything for a couple of moments. Then she started crying. My eyes stung; it was all too much. I nearly left but instead lied down in bed and took her in my arms and she cried into my chest.

After a while I said, 'You need to see a doctor.'

'I've seen doctors.'

'Just in case. If there's anything they can do . . .'

'I've seen doctors. There's nothing they can do.' And she put her hand on the back of my neck and gripped hard as if she'd float away if she let go and I waited with her until she fell asleep.

I sat in front of the TV flicking the channels. So Alice must have told work I was ill. That was nice of her. I started twitching. My toes curled and my legs buzzed and I sprang out of my seat and stared at the TV. The picture made no sense to me. I scrolled through the channels. Nothing made any sense. I picked up the TV and threw it against the wall and the plug flew out of the socket and nearly hit me in the eye. I stood over the TV. When I smashed up the flat I'd been unable to smash the screen but now I knew what I'd do. I went into the bathroom and came back with the mop, then held it above my head and brought the handle down as hard as I could on the screen. It didn't smash. I tried again; didn't work. And again. The screen chipped and a little crack appeared. I tried taking swings at the screen, not with the end of the handle, just swung at it from side to side. Didn't work. Finally, I punched the screen. Ah *shit*. I backed away, hopped on the spot. It was the same hand I'd hurt when I beat up the guy I vaguely knew. I know what I'll do, I thought, as the pain resolved itself into a dull ache, I'll go and buy a hammer. I left the flat.

I found myself a good one. A good, sturdy hammer. Maybe I should get some goggles too. Just in case the glass flies all over the place. I went and found some plastic goggles. I felt pretty energized; I was really looking forward to smashing the TV screen in. The only thing that was distracting me, my hand was really throbbing.

I was about half way home when the throbbing just became too much. I didn't know what to do with myself. Shit, I'm going to have to go to hospital.

I was in the hospital for seven hours. In the waiting room, where I spent six of those hours, a feeling of panic grew inside me. She's not in London. She's not in London. If she's not in London, WHAT IS THE POINT? And I huffed and puffed and wriggled in my seat and pushed my feet backward and forward on the floor. I could go back to Rio? Not until Alice is dead. Do I even have the money to get there? How much money is there in my account?

By the time I finally signed out (my hand in strapping) my enthusiasm for smashing the TV screen in had dissipated. Just as I was about to leave, I remembered DCI Campbell and asked if they had a Mr. Riley Campbell admitted. They told me that he had died three days ago.

It was dark outside. Of course it was, it was nearly midnight. I got a cab home.

I got out of the cab and watched it drive away. Then, just as I was about to turn towards my building, I saw a figure standing at the other end of the car park. The car park was lit up but he was standing in the shadows and I couldn't make him out. But he was completely still, facing me. Doug? I turned and headed for the building. Just before I went in, I looked back. He was gone.

When I entered my flat, Alice was sitting at the computer.

She didn't look at me. 'What did you do to the TV?'

'I chucked it against the wall.'

'You did, huh?'

'Yeah.' I went and sat down in the armchair, put my bag from the DIY store on the table in front of me.

'I guess that explains why it doesn't work.'

'Hmm.' I looked at the back of her head. 'What are you doing on there?'

'Surfing.'

'What're you looking for?'

'Entertainment. You know, I kind of relied on that TV.'

'Yeah. Sorry.'

'The internet is so fucking boring.' She turned around and looked at me. She was a beautiful girl, she really was, I could see that now even with her face bony and drawn and covered with crusted over sores. I smiled.

'You have a double chin.'

'No I don't,' I said.

'Yes you do. I can see it.'

'It's just where I'm resting my jaw on my collarbone.'

There was a pause. Then she saw the bag from the DIY shop. 'Sam, were you going to, like, fix the TV?'

'No.'

She wheeled herself closer. 'That's so hilarious. I mean, the

TV will never work again if you get anywhere near it with a bunch of tools, but still.'

'I can fix things.'

'No you can't.'

I felt sort of resentful even though I knew she was right. Still, it was nice talking like this.

She pulled the hammer and goggles out of the bag. She stared at them. 'I don't understand.'

'Never mind.'

'What were you going to do with these, Sam?'

'I was, I was going to smash the screen in. I can't be bothered now though.'

'Right.' She put the hammer and goggles down. 'What happened to your hand?'

'I punched the television. And my hand was already hurt. I got into a fight in Brazil.'

There was a pause. She put the goggles on. 'How do I look?'

I laughed; she looked funny. There was warmth between us, there really was, but it was tinged with sadness somehow.

'Can I try? Smashing the TV?'

I said, 'Is it definitely broken?'

'Yeah.'

I shrugged.

She picked up the hammer and went over to the TV and raised the hammer above the TV and brought it down and smashed it through the screen.

'Was it satisfying?'

'Yeah. I guess. Like, I don't think the goggles were necessary.'

'I didn't know what would happen with the glass.'

'Of course you didn't. You don't have a mind for that stuff.'

She wheeled herself back over and took off the goggles. 'Are you going to get a new TV?'

'If you'd like.'

'I would.'

'OK then.'

We sat there quietly for a while, then I said, 'I was thinking, I mean, you said Doug came round and everything, I mean, don't you think your parents should see more of you?'

'No.'

'Have you even spoken to Celina since you moved in here?'

'What, you want Celina to come round so you can fuck her again?'

'No –'

'She's *ancient*, Sam.'

'I was more thinking of you could go back there, to stay. I mean, you know, they're your parents. They should be there at the end.'

She stared at me and I had to look away.

'You are so fucking pathetic.'

'I'm just trying to do the right thing.'

'Fuck you.'

'Alice.'

'Fuck. You.'

We were quiet for a while. The atmosphere was pretty unpleasant.

'What were you doing in Brazil anyway?'

'Nothing. It doesn't matter.'

'Was it a holiday or what?'

'. . . No.'

'You don't, I mean *please* tell me you didn't go there to look for Leticia.'

'No.'

'Why were you there then?'

'Ted wanted me to go but . . . It doesn't matter.'

'Ted?'

'Yeah.'

'You're as bad as Doug and Celina. Everything has to be about *Ted*. It makes me feel sick. Can't you even live your own life? It's disgusting. You can't face up to anything. And then going, like, thousands of miles because you fell in love with a *photo*. Don't you think that's completely pathetic. Huh?'

'Just leave it.'

'Why can't you just *deal* with things? Huh? You know what would be great for both of us? If you killed me. If you actually, like, took some real action.'

I didn't say anything.

'Well?'

'No, I'm not killing you.'

'Look at me, Sam. Look at my face. Do you have any idea how much pain I'm in? And I have these nightmares that just, like, I can't move after them. I'm literally petrified. So don't make out you're doing this out of kindness or something.'

'It's ridiculous,' I said. 'I'm obviously not going to kill you.'

'Why not? Huh? Do it with this hammer. Smash me in the skull. One, maybe two swings.'

'Stop this OK, Alice. It's just, it's ridiculous.'

'What, and going to another hemisphere to search for some girl you don't even know *isn't* ridiculous?'

'I didn't do that.'

'Sam, do you love Leticia?'

I didn't say anything.

'Huh? Do you *love* her?'

'Stop it.'

'You are so pathetic.' She paused. 'Some fucking photo. There are loads of, like, girls you can actually get to know out there.'

'Yeah.'

She laughed. 'She's rude too. When you tell her, "Oh, Leticia, I saw your photo and I'm so in love" she'll laugh right in your face and call you a weirdo.'

'You don't know what you're talking about.'

'No?'

'No.'

'So you don't love Leticia then?'

'Just drop it, please.' I couldn't take this much more.

'Loser.'

'Shut up, Alice.'

'Or what? Huh?'

I didn't answer. My whole body was tensed up.

'Go on. Smash my skull in with the hammer. Go on.' She tried to put the hammer in my hand and I shifted back in my chair. 'Please, Sam. It's, like, the nicest thing you could possibly do. I have new sores come up every day. I have this one sore on my vagina that when I urinate it stings so much I can only squeeze out a few drops. Do you want to see it? I'll let you spread my legs so you can see it.'

I felt as if my body was about to go off into a spasm and I burst out of my seat.

'Where are you going?'

'To bed.'

'Are you going to kill me?'

I started to go.

'Answer me!'

'No! I can't, can I?'

'You don't have to use the hammer. You can do something

211

else. Hold my head under water. Or I'll get in the bath and you can drop a toaster in.'

'You can do that yourself.'

'What, you want me to go through this myself?'

'No–'

'Have some fucking guts, Sam, and smash my fucking skull in.'

'I'm going to bed.' I started off to bed.

'You're pathetic, Sam. Leticia would hate you anyway. You are a complete fucking loser. Huh? Some *photo*. I hate you. I FUCKING HATE YOU.' I closed the door behind me. 'You fucking loser! LOSER!!!'

I collapsed on the bed and hid my head under the pillow.

I Get Bundled Into A Van

I held my breath as I went from the bathroom through to the front door, eyes straight ahead. But I'm pretty sure Alice was asleep anyway. I'd decided that I really had to give Doug and Celina the chance to see her before she dies. The only trouble was, Doug might still want to kill me which made me not want to initiate contact. I walked down the stairs. I was feeling tender and bruised from last night's altercation with Alice. Some of the things she'd said were true. It *was* only a photo. And maybe Leticia *would* hate me. But I'd never thought it would be easy with Leticia. I'd have to present the best side of myself. And what if I *had* only seen her in a photo? I mean, I'd forgotten the photo now. It wasn't the photo anymore. It was something else. Alice was completely wrong. I tingled as I realised that finding Leticia was the right thing to do. And if I find her . . . If I find her . . . My heart soared and for a moment I didn't feel so delicate. I walked outside. The sky was blue but the sun wasn't as bright as it had been, or it was but today was a little chillier and a gentle breeze moved the leaves on the trees.

A white van pulled out of a parking space a little way ahead of me and stopped, the engine still running. I slowed my pace, halted. I looked in the driver side window but the sun was reflecting off it and I couldn't see the driver. Then the van backed out all the way and drove off. It must be

Doug. I should phone the police really. I don't want to get him in trouble though, I've done enough bad things to him already. I walked to the bus stop.

Nothing much changes at work. Everybody was chatting and typing and wandering around with files. I walked in with all this activity going on around me, separate from it, unnoticed, and took my seat. I stared at my computer screen for a moment then moved the mouse around and the log in screen faded in. I stretched my feet out in front of me, tried to muster the energy to type in my user name.

'Sam.'

I looked up and saw my boss. 'Hi.' I sat up straight.

'Feeling better?'

'Yes. Thank you.'

'Hmm.' She looked at me. I sensed that she mistrusted me. She gave me a sheet of paper. 'These are the minutes from the team meeting yesterday. If you're on data entry you'll need to have a look at the new targets. They've been revised upwards.' She checked her planner. 'Yep. You're on data entry this week. For the rest of this week.'

'OK. Great.'

She gave me a look then left. She'd been pretty short with me before Brazil. Maybe she was holding a grudge because I gave her the finger. Oh well. I took a look at the new targets. Shit, they really have been revised upwards. I logged in and got going.

For an hour or so I was faster than I'd ever been. The new targets were tough but I enjoyed the challenge. And the task, repetitive as it was, as a test of my concentration and endurance, had its appeal. It was like work had been before the barbecue when I would set myself targets throughout the day and the hours would pass. And I would always feel, admittedly very faint, pride if I left the office having achieved high statistics.

Angela arrived and my concentration was thrown. I expected her to come and sit next to me but then she took a seat at the front of the office and I remembered that she'd been told to move seat; I was a 'bad influence.' I wanted to go over and talk to her straight away. I'll let her get settled first though. I turned back to my work but I was restless and fidgety now. I entered two file numbers but my fingers throbbed and I sat back and took a breather. In the five minutes that followed, I entered two digits of a seven digit number. I just couldn't enter the whole number; it seemed like too much effort. I jumped out of my chair and went over to see Angela.

'Angela, hi.'

'Oh, hi, Sam!' She gave me a big smile and went to get up (maybe to hug me?) but stayed where she was. It was great seeing her again and I wished she had hugged me. That would have been lovely. We started chatting and as usual the conversation flowed freely and easily and I felt relaxed and happy. Then my boss came up to us.

'Is there something you need over here, Sam?'

'Huh?' I felt sort of resentful that she'd interrupted mine and Angela's conversation.

'Only you've been over here for quite a while.'

'I was just saying hello.'

'A long hello.' She smiled.

This was a bit much. I felt like sticking my finger up at her again.

She turned to Angela. 'Angela, I need you to go down to the storeroom today. There's some files down there that need sorting out. I suspect you'll be down there all day so take what you need.'

'Will she get a lunch break?' I asked.

My boss looked at me. 'What was that, Sam?'

'A lunch break,' I said. 'Angela and I usually have lunch together.'

'Well I'd forget about that today. They're on a tight time-table down there. Angela, you'll have to take lunch when you can, OK?'

Angela nodded.

'Sam, I hope you're hitting those targets.' My boss smiled at me, turned and left.

I was feeling pretty agitated. How dare she? She's got Angela, a woman, a *mother*, moving files all day long. I should take some action. It's like Alice was saying. She was pretty mean about it but some of the things she'd said had struck a nerve. She was wrong about Leticia, but the rest of it. Take some action. Have some guts. I glanced at my boss who was now standing over the other side of the office. 'Bitch,' I said under my breath.

'Huh?'

I turned to Angela. 'Oh. Nothing. It's just . . . Never mind.'

Angela smiled and shrugged. 'I know but what can you do.'

I stared at my boss who was laughing with one of the other managers. I was irritated, I really was.

The rest of the day was tough. Hour by hour I'd just about keep up with the targets. I'd get behind in the first twenty minutes, then have to catch up. Then the first twenty minutes became the first thirty minutes. Then the first thirty minutes became the first forty minutes. I missed my target in the last hour. And I was sitting there thinking, How dare she? And taking it out on Angela. It's ridiculous. Holding a grudge like that. I hope Angela's OK. At two minutes to five I hadn't hit my target but I didn't care (my fingers were physically incapable of hitting any more keys) and I logged out and rushed out of the office, the file still open on my desk.

I came out of the lift at reception and Angela came out of the one opposite me. We smiled at each other. 'This is a coincidence,' I said. 'Are you off home?'

'Yep.'

'So how was it down there?' We walked out of the building. It was a nice day but there was a breeze that made my shirt flutter. We walked through the car park, in between the parked cars.

'OK. I hurt my back though.'

'I can't believe she sent you down there.'

Angela shrugged.

'I think we should do something,' I said.

'Like what?'

'I don't know. Report her for bullying in the workplace or something.'

'Don't be silly.'

'No, something else. I don't know, something more pro-active.'

'We could kidnap her?' Angela chuckled.

I smiled. She was a lovely person and I was very pleased to have her as my friend. 'We should have dinner again,' I said.

'That would be nice. No cuffs this time though.'

'No,' I said. And I was just about to make a joke when something grabbed me by the throat and jaw and pulled me up off my feet, the tendons in my neck feeling as though they were about to tear, and then my back hit a hard surface and I wasn't outside anymore. I heard Angela screaming, then a door slammed and an engine started and I was on the move, or the vehicle I was in was on the move. I lifted my head up and my neck really hurt. I winced. I was in a van. A white van? 'Doug?' Somebody pulled me up by the hair and the tendons in my neck strained and I cried out. I was shoved into a sitting position, propped up against the sliding door. There were two figures in the back of the van. One of them came and squatted down in front of me.

'Who the fuck is Doug?' It was Tre.

I didn't know what to say.

'Nice work in Rio. You've done a good job there, bruv. Just sweeping up now. Getting rid of the last few wankers still working for Ted.'

I didn't know what to say.

'I've told you nice job, bruv. You ain't going to fucking thank me for the praise I've given you?'

'Thank you.'

'You're welcome, cunt. And you would be very welcome. Only thing is, you've gone and done something I can't let pass. You've gone and given one of my blokes a good beating. True, bloke's a cunt. But he's still my bloke. What am I supposed to do about that, bruv?'

'I don't –'

'He was going to bring me back a burger too. I'm hungry now. I don't like being hungry. You listen to my tummy careful enough, you can hear it rumble. Here, move your ear closer, have a listen.'

I moved my ear closer, not that close though, my neck hurt too much. Tre punched me in the ear. 'He's helped you out. He's listened to you and he's gone and found your girl and that's how you've led us to our target. You've worked together. And this is how you repay him? Smash his face in. He's still in hospital, bruv. You've made a right mess. He might need a reconstruction. Terrible. Now granted, as soon as he got back to

London I'd have shot him myself. I don't like the bloke. I've got no time for him. He's a cunt. But still, that's my business.

I was clutching my ear. I wondered would Tre torture me? He seemed like the sort of person who might.

He grabbed me by the shoulders and pinned me to the van door, staring at me. I had an acute sense of how vicious he was capable of being.

He said, 'You've got to love it, don't you? Ted's gone and arranged this trip for you, find that bitch Leticia, bitch he calls his daughter. I've swooped in there. Scratch that, *we've* swooped in there, bruv. You and me. We've swooped in there and BAM, we've turned the tables. Love it. I fucking love it. Do you love it?'

'. . . Yeah.'

'What?'

'. . . I . . .'

'You what?'

'I . . . love it.'

He burst into laughter. 'You're a funny fuck. Except when you're knocking my bloke about. You're less funny then. But you are funny. A fucking hoot. Not a funny as Ted though. He's funnier. And you want to know the most fucking hilarious thing of all? She ain't even in Rio.'

'She's not?'

'Nope.'

'Where is she?'

'If I knew that I'd be there now, dragging her out by her pretty little head. Word is though, she's in London. Ted's been looking for her as long as I have. He ain't going to find her though. He's out of men and resources. I'm staring him in the fucking eyeballs and I'm holding a Royal Flush. And he ain't got nothing left. 'Cause he's a cunt.' He stared at me. 'You're mates with Ted, right?'

Johns*

'Uh . . . I, I know him.'

'I'll tell you what, I'll let you off. Forget that you've beaten up something that belongs to me. I'm prepared to wipe the slate clean. Ain't that good of me, bruv? Course it is. I'm a good bloke. All you have to do in return, you have to go tell Ted about your adventures in Rio. Especially tell him about how his bloke was shot to shit. And give him a message from me. Tell him I'll be getting to him soon. Can you do that? If I let you go, can you do that?'

'Yeah.'

'Repeat the message. The message you've got for Ted. Repeat it.'

I repeated the message.

'Good.' He shouted at the driver. 'Stop the fucking van, will you?'

While the van was coming to a stop, Tre stared right at me. I was pretty uncomfortable but too scared to look away. The van stopped. Tre grabbed me, pulled me towards the back of the van, opened the door, and chucked me out.

I hit a concrete surface and laid there until I heard the van pull away. I looked up at the clear blue sky. Leticia's in London. Cars were whooshing past. I stood up. I was on the hard shoulder. At least he hadn't dumped me in the middle of the motorway. I started walking the way I thought we'd come.

I was pretty tired when I got back. I'd really been beaten and thrown around recently. And then the long walk home. And the sixty seven stairs didn't help. I put my key in the lock and opened the door. Alice was sitting in her wheelchair staring at me. Had she been waiting for me? I really wish she wouldn't do that.

'Hi,' I said.

She came at me in the wheelchair. It took a moment for me to realise she was charging me, and by the time I did, it was too late to move out of the way. The chair smashed into my legs, knocking me back into the door.

'For God's sake, Alice –'

She reversed a few feet, then came at me again, smashed into my legs. She backed away. I tried to move, but I was hurting all over and too slow and she smashed into me again.

'Alice!' I looked at her but she had a hard expression of barely contained anger on her face. I turned around and tried the handle and opened the door a little way but she smashed into my legs and I fell into the door and the door closed again. Then she smashed into my legs again. Then, as soon as she started to back away, I turned the handle and escaped the flat and closed the door and now, standing outside the flat, I heard her smash into the other side of the door. I stood there, my legs were wobbly and beaten up. I couldn't face going in there again. I went and knocked on my neighbour's door. He opened up.

'Oh hello, Sam. How you doing?'

'Yeah . . . OK. Do you mind if I come in for a bit?'

'Absolutely, absolutely. Be my guest.'

I went in.

My neighbour gave me coffee and cake and we talked about this and that. He did most of the talking. He was one of those people, you could just switch off and relax while he talked. I suppose some people might find him boring, but I found his voice soothing and I let my mind wander as he talked on, never saying anything that made me feel uncomfortable, or was abrasive, or even remotely controversial. In fact, I can hardly remember a single thing he spoke about. I was sitting there with the significance of the fact that Leticia's

In London becoming clearer and clearer to me. Leticia's in London, I'm in London. I can find her. I need to give Tre's message to Ted soon otherwise Tre will come and kill me before I find her. Leticia's in London. I can find her. I could feel hope flowing back into my body again. After a few hours, I thanked my neighbour very much, promised to have him round to my flat next time, and left.

I turned my key as quietly as I could and crept into the flat. The lights were off and the curtains were shut and Alice was sitting in her wheelchair, not facing me this time. I tip toed past her, pretty pleased with myself for how light of foot I'd been. Then, just as I was walking into the kitchen, she came at me; I darted out of the way and the wheelchair smacked into the kitchen cupboard. I ran into my room and closed the door behind me and stood with my back to the door. She rammed the door a few more times, then all went quiet. About ten minutes later, I crept into bed. I lay there, tense for a while, eye on the door, wondering would she kill me in my sleep? She doesn't seem stable right now. She's a nineteen year old who knows she's dying, anything could be going on in her head. But then my fear faded and I remembered that Leticia Is In London and lay there drifting into sleep imagining wonderful scenarios where we would meet and laugh and smile . . .

I Talk With Doug About Alice

Stepping out of my building (the sun warm, blue sky, a bit of a breeze) I thought I saw someone stood watching me. Then he moved behind the bushes. I don't know if I imagined it, I had plenty of reason to get paranoid lately. Anyway, I dismissed it from my mind and set off for the bus. I felt a bit dirty today. I'd been afraid of waking Alice, so I hadn't shaved or brushed my teeth, I'd just put my clothes on in my bedroom and hurried out, treading as lightly as I could. Thankfully, Alice was asleep. This is silly though, I hate feeling grubby. I particularly hate not brushing my teeth. My breath must smell bad. Did I brush them last night either? I also realised, walking to the bus stop, that I really needed the toilet.

I bought some mints on the way to work and when I got there I went to the toilet and splashed my face with water, but it wasn't very satisfactory. I really needed to do something about Alice. And, after all, she should spend her last few weeks (days?) with her family. I know how much it would mean to them. They're such a loving family. And what about her little brother? I felt a pang and resolved to do something about it, I didn't know what, but something.

As soon as I stepped into the office, Angela, who sat close to the door now, accosted me. 'Sam, are you OK?'

'Yeah, I'm fine.'

'What happened last night?' She was holding onto my arm. 'I called the police but of course they were useless weren't they.'

'It was, it was a really stupid prank.'

'I was beside myself.'

'Sorry.'

'I was so scared.' A tear rolled down her cheek.

I felt protective of her and wiped the tear away and smiled at her.

'Would you two come with me please?' It was my boss. She didn't seem happy. We followed her to her office.

In her office, we were alerted to a number of 'home truths.' Among them were that turning up when we felt like it, going for extended lunches, chatting all day, petting in the office, and 'adopting an aloof attitude' were detrimental to productivity and sound working relationships. We were 'strongly advised' to stay away from each other since we clearly inspired the worst in one another. If we wanted to 'pet' socially then fine, but it's inappropriate in the workplace. Her (my boss's) husband worked in the building and they (my boss and her husband) were always professional with one another during work hours. 'Sam, you didn't hit your target yesterday. This has to stop. And I really detect, particularly in you, an unhealthy attitude to work and work colleagues. Don't think you're above it all. This is the job you're employed to do. So do it.' And then she turned to Angela and spoke to her as though she were a little child 'You've always been a reliable worker, Angela. Don't get distracted. The last thing you want to be is his partner in crime. Don't sink with him.' She paused after all that. Then she said 'you two had better get off to work then. You're behind already today.'

I had decided that enough was enough, particularly with

the implication that I was leading Angela astray, so I said. 'Is this because I gave you the finger?'

'What?'

'Is that why you're doing this? Because I gave you the finger? Because I don't think it's very fair on Angela if you are.'

'I don't know what you're talking about.' I went to say something but she put her hand out. 'And if I were you I'd stop talking right now.' She paused. 'Otherwise I'll have to think about inviting you to a disciplinary meeting.'

I looked at her. She looked back, then picked up her pen and started writing. 'Off you go then. We've all got work to do.'

And then we left. Angela hurried straight back to her desk with a quick 'see you later.' I was twitching with indignation. She's still denying it. How can she deny it? How can she look right at me and deny it? It's ridiculous. I went and sat at my desk and started the day in an agitated state which made it pretty difficult to fill in data fields. After an hour, I was already behind target. Then the agitation started to fade as Leticia came back into my mind. That she was in London. I thought of all the places we could meet and all the places we could go and laughed out loud. I'd floated off, not really aware of my physical surroundings anymore. I imagined having a picnic with her in St. James' Park, and she'd take a bite of an apple and then she'd pass it to me and I'd take a bite from where she took a bite. And when we'd finished eating we would lie back looking at the clear blue sky and holding hands, not saying anything, just with each other. Feelings of warmth and joy came over me and intensified with the realisation that, it's possible, it could happen, she's in London, and the idea of it all really coming true, of *really* being with her, in the flesh, was so intense in it's joy that I burst out into a fit of laughter. Then I slowly came round to my surroundings again, to my keyboard, my monitor. My fingers were tingling and I still had a smile on my face. She's in London. I can find her. Then I realised, she's in London and I'm not trying to find her. Right now I'm not trying to find her. She's out there and I'm in here. I started getting fidgety. I kept looking out the window. I need to get out there. I'll have a wander around tonight. Get a map of London out. See which areas I need to cover. The next few hours were merciless in the way that they crawled by. I burst out of the building at lunchtime, but when I got out there into the car park and was about to walk across to the shopping centre, I stopped short. For some reason, I couldn't do it, my legs were buzzing too much. I couldn't do anything. I didn't even want a cigarette. I rushed back into the building.

I don't know how I got through the afternoon. I spent it in a frazzled state. I didn't touch my keyboard. I just sat there, tensed up, twitching, in a kind of trance. Five o' clock came. I left the building.

I got outside and the fresh air hit me. What now? Go home or start searching straight away? I'd been in such a state all afternoon that I hadn't devised a strategy.

'Hello, Sam.'

I looked over at where the voice was coming from, and saw Doug, leaning against a car. I thought about running away, certainly a big part of me felt that it was the prudent thing to do, but for some reason I didn't.

'Fancy a lift home?'

I nodded and got in the car. Doug turned the engine on and we drove off. We sat there in silence. There was a lot of traffic, rush hour and all the rest of it, but Doug seemed to be driving in the right direction for my flat.

After about ten minutes he said, 'So where did you get to then?'

'Brazil.'

He glanced at me. 'Brazil? Fancy a holiday did you, Sam?'

'No. Ted wanted me to go there.'

'Ted?' He'd been pretty relaxed so far, or acting like he was, but mention of Ted's name changed that.

'Yeah. But it wasn't Ted who sent me there. Another guy turned up.' I told him a short version of what had happened at Ted's house and in Rio.

Doug was quiet for a while. Then he said, 'Tre. I've heard of him. Never met him.' The traffic was starting to thin out but Doug was still driving in the direction of my flat.

'Why did you pick me up?' I said.

'What, you mean what am I planning on doing to you?'

'Yeah.'

'I don't know.' He was quiet for a while. 'Before all the rest of it happened, did you get a chance to talk to him about me and Celina? You know, like we discussed.'

'No.' I was going to give him an excuse, it all happened so fast and so on. But that wasn't true. I'd had a chance to bring up Doug and Celina but I hadn't. I don't know why, I just hadn't.

'I think Alice should move back in with you,' I said. 'She should be with her family.'

'She'll come home?'

'Well, not willingly.'

Doug parked up outside my building. 'You can't make her come back, Sam.'

'I could put something in her food. Drug her and we could put her in a car or something.'

'She'd never forgive any of us.'

'Then you should come around with Celina. I'll go out or something.'

'You're a good bloke, Sam. I'll be in touch about that.' He started crying but quickly wiped away the tears with his sleeve and cleared his throat.

I said, 'I'm seeing Ted again. I could tell him about you and Celina.'

He smiled, didn't say anything. Then we reached my building and he stopped the car.

'Bye,' I said, but he didn't answer or look at me so I got out and walked across the car park to my building.

I let myself in. Alice was in her wheelchair, asleep. I went to the toilet, then came out into the kitchen, toasted some crumpets, spread butter and jam on them and went and sat down in the front room. I'd start the search off tonight, take a map with me and cross off the streets (I'd have to search all the streets twice of course, once in the day, once at night). It was really quiet. I really need a new TV. All I could hear was the sound of me chewing crumpets. I listened hard. I couldn't even hear Alice breathing. I would have thought she might have woken up when the toaster popped. I got nervous, stood up and went over to her wheelchair. She was still. Her lips were slightly parted, her head cocked to one side. I leant over and listened for her breathing. Nothing. I couldn't feel her breath on my ear either. My heart started beating fast. I wet the back of my hand and put it in front of her mouth; I couldn't feel anything. I took her pulse. She didn't have one. Her heart had stopped beating. She was dead.

Doug and Celina Come Round

I didn't know what arrangements you make when you're dealing with a dead body, but I phoned the hospital and they came and took Alice away. They asked who I was and I said I was a friend and they asked me who her relatives were and I gave them Doug and Celina's details. Then they left. The flat felt very quiet. I was living alone again. I checked my watch; quarter past eight, and wondered did I have enough time to go out and start my search for Leticia? I paced up and down, looked out the window at the setting sun. It's too late to go out tonight. Start out properly tomorrow. I went and sat in my chair but there wasn't even a TV to watch and trying to read anything was impossible, and within ten minutes I was squirming in my skin and I leapt out of the chair and left the flat to go and search for Leticia.

It was getting dark by the time I got to London Bridge station. I got my map out and headed off. The idea of crossing off the streets was a good one because even though I hadn't seen Leticia, I was still able to cross bits of the map and I felt a sense of achievement in that. I didn't expect to find her tonight (it would be nice though) but the important thing was that she was in London, and however many times I had to comb the city, I'd find her. I felt good. I had purpose. I strode along, keeping my eye out. After a while though, I started to think about Alice, and then I realised I hadn't been keeping an eye out for Leticia and I had to go back to where I last remembered being alert. When I got there, I stopped and sat down in a shop door. Alice is gone. I felt a wave of self-pity, a need to be comforted. And my flat would be empty. A chill went through me at the idea of going back there. I couldn't face it. If I was going to avoid going back to that flat on my own, I had to find Leticia tonight. I stood up and continued my search.

Three hours later I was starting to get tired. I yawned as I struck another street off my map. A group of people piled out of a pub, a few young black women amongst them, and my heart leapt and I studied their faces but nope, not her. I looked at my watch. I'd missed the last tube home and I didn't really like buses. I yawned again. It was a warm night and I don't mind sleeping outside. After all, I'd done it in Rio. I found a doorway and curled up and went to sleep.

A bleep, bleep, bleep sound penetrated my dreams and I woke up and heard 'This vehicle is reversing. This vehicle is reversing. This vehicle is reversing.' I realised that it was parking up right alongside the pub whose door I was sleeping in and I got up and walked away.

I felt pretty low when I got to work. And my nose was bunged up. Angela wasn't in yet and I went in and sat down at my desk. I stared at my computer screen. I had no energy, just a shitty sadness inside me. I couldn't possibly do any work. Shit, I feel terrible. My eyes swelled and my nose stung and I could feel myself starting to panic and I closed my eyes and tried to calm down. I have to get out of here, I have to get out of here. Get some fresh air. And then what? There's nobody at my flat. My heart was pounding and my head was woozy. Then I heard a voice, only faintly at first, but then more clearly. My boss was standing by my desk. I looked at her, realised that my eyes were moist.

She said, 'Is there something wrong?'

'No.' I could feel the panic rising up inside me again, tried to steady myself.

She cast her eyes sideways, a 'give me strength' sort of look.

'We need to have a chat' – my heart started racing – 'It's about your targets' – and it wasn't just sadness, disorientation, panic I felt anymore, there was something else – 'I looked at the statistics for yesterday' – something bubbling underneath it all – 'As far as I can tell, Sam, it doesn't seem that you did any work all afternoon. Now I don't know how you'd like to account for that, or exactly how you think I should respond but –' 'AAAAAARGH!' I smashed my fists down on the desk. She stopped talking, stood there staring at me. Everything was quiet, still. She went to say something and I slammed my fists down again. She looked away, smiled a nervous smile, then looked worried. I looked around; everyone was quiet and still. There were a few whispers. I grinned. I stood up, walked past my boss and towards the door. The whispers grew a bit louder. I turned around and said to my boss, 'You see this?' I gave her the finger and left the office.

As I descended in the lift, a feeling came over me that I couldn't quite identify but it made my whole body tingle, right out to my fingers and toes. I left the lift and the building and burst out into the fresh air and felt . . . elated. I felt incredible, capable of anything. I burst into a fit of laughter and fell to the ground and had to drag myself, still laughing, away from where a car might come and run me over. I didn't stop laughing for a long time and when I stopped my sides and face ached and my throat felt stretched and strained. The smokers didn't know what to make of me. I got to my feet, chuckled at the smokers, and then I was off.

I walked aimlessly for a while, a long way past the bus stop, still chuckling occasionally, hiccupping, slowly calming down. I felt good about what I'd done. It felt right. I was wasting my time in that shitty job and I went out the right way. I hiccupped. Yeah, it was fantastic really. She can't deny it now. The whole office saw me give her the finger. The only thing is not seeing Angela again. I can always phone her . . . Fantastic. I chuckled. Then hiccupped. Slowly however, my pleasure at what I'd done was overtaken by the question, what do I do now? I can't go home, the flat is empty. Go and search for Leticia then. It's still early, you can get a whole day in. But I don't want to be alone. I really wanted some company, to talk to someone. Maybe my neighbour would be interested. It would be great to have him along. We could search London together, have a chat. He doesn't seem to have a job. Or any friends. Or, judging by the funeral, any family who he talks to. He might be up for it. I had a good feeling about the idea. An extra pair of eyes too. He'd need a photo though. I could just give him a general description. But it would be better with a photo. Ted would give me a photo. He wanted me to find her in Brazil. If he knew she was in London, he'd want me to look for her in London too. Maybe Ted will even search with me. It might be dangerous for him though, walking around in the open. And it would be a lot of pressure, having Ted for company all day. Pressure to impress. That walk we had was nice though. On the night of the barbecue. But that was just a short trot. I decided that I would be more relaxed, and in charge of the search, with my neighbour.

One thing was clear to me: my next destination should be Ted's house. After all, both Doug and Tre had given me a message to deliver to him. And either might kill me if I didn't. I set about making my way there.

I got a bit nervous as I closed in on Ted's house. After all, I'd inadvertently got one of his 'men' killed in Rio. I could hardly be blamed for that though. Still, with all that's going on he might be in a pretty foul mood. If I lost a daughter like Leticia . . . What is it all about? This tug of war over her. Was Ted like Tre when he was younger? No. Ted has manners. He knows how to conduct himself. He has respect for people. I arrived at his house and walked up to the door. Something seemed different, I couldn't put my finger on what. I rang the doorbell. No answer. I rang again. No answer. I knocked. No answer. I stepped back from the door and saw what was different. All the windows had been blacked out. What's going on? I saw that the door that led down the side of the house was open. I went over. 'Hello? Hello?' No answer. I went down the side of the house and came out in the back garden. It was empty. Of people and clutter. A sense of nostalgia came over me. The noise and people from the barbecue filled up the garden for a moment. What a wonderful day. I smiled.

The windows at the back of the house were blacked out too. So were the double doors that lead out to the patio. What was going on? I heard a noise in the bushes and jumped. It must be a bird or a squirrel or something. More rustling in the bushes; I jumped again, then hurried back down the side of the house and walked away.

Did somebody die in there? Maybe. Or maybe Ted took his family and went into hiding. It does seem like Tre's out to get him. What if he's found Leticia? Tre said she was in London, what if Ted's found her and he's left the city with

Leticia? I went cold. My neighbour said Ted came round. Maybe it was to tell me he was leaving. Maybe he knew Leticia was in London all along and used Rio to wrong foot Tre. They could be anywhere in the world. No. No. NO. 'NO!' I waved my fist around, a shudder went through me, and I sat on a garden wall and tried to recover.

After about half an hour my legs felt tender and shaky, but I was able to walk again. This is all assumptions. You're making assumptions. Tre will come and find you again. And he'll know where Ted is. Then you'll find out. Until then just, just keep searching. She might be in London. She might very well be in London. Just keep looking. In my trancelike state I'd walked all the way home without really noticing. I decided to go in, have a quick shower, change clothes, and go out and look for Leticia. I could get my toothbrush too. That way I'd have it with me if I had to stay out all night. I imagined having bad breath for my first meeting with Leticia. It was not something that I wanted to happen.

As I rounded the corner, ready to take on the final nine of the sixty seven stairs, I saw Doug and Celina sitting outside my flat. I stopped. They saw me. They stood up.

'Hello, Sam,' Doug said.

Celina glanced at me. She looked like she'd been crying.

'Hi,' I said.

'Alright with you if we come in.' Doug said.

'Yeah,' I said. 'Yeah, sure.' I stepped in between them (there was no other way to the door) and opened the door and we all went in.

We all just stood there for a moment. 'Do you want any-thing?' I said. 'I can get you a drink or something.'

Celina said, 'This is where she was living.'

I didn't know if I should respond.

'We'll have some water,' Doug said. 'Would you like some water, darling?'

Celina didn't reply.

'Two glasses of water please, mate.'

I nodded and went into the kitchen. I took my time, tried to think clearly. Why are they here? Does Doug still want to kill me? Would he really bring Celina along for the 'hit'? I drank a glass of water myself, then took their glasses out to them. They were sitting down on my settee. Doug had his hand on Celina's knee. Her face was red and blotchy. She looked like a broken woman. So broken it was as though she were dead and I felt like that was that for her.

I handed them their water (in Celina's case she didn't take it and I just put it on the floor next to her) and sat down.

'Just in case you were wondering,' Doug said. 'We were told about Alice. We've been making funeral arrangements this morning.'

'I'm sorry about everything,' I said.

He nodded.

There was a pause, then Celina started crying. Doug tried to take her by the shoulders but she pushed him away and the tears flowed, and she bent double, her head between her knees, sobbing. I caught Doug's eye and he seemed to communicate something to me, but I couldn't tell what. What an emotional man. He felt things deeply, he really did.

Finally, Celina stopped crying. Her face was dark red. She, too, caught my eye, and all I could see was hatred. Perhaps I deserved it. I didn't know anymore.

Doug sighed.

I thought maybe I should say something but I didn't know what it should be.

Then Doug said, 'We are in a tremendous amount of pain, Sam. We've not been right for a few years to be honest.

But you know all about that. But now, with Alice dying. I mean, we're just . . . And I'm a family man. I've got a son. And you see what's happened. And now our daughter is dead. Didn't even die in our home. Clearly I've failed some-where along the line. Clearly I've been a fucking idiot. Otherwise I wouldn't have dropped the ball so many times and my family wouldn't be in pieces.' He paused. 'But I did ask you for a favour, Sam. A favour that could have really helped me out. A favour that, if you'd done it, could have made all the difference to be honest. You didn't do us that favour. For whatever reason, it was never the right time, whatever, it doesn't matter, that favour wasn't done. You met with Ted on a couple of occasions and, like I say, who cares about the reason, it's immaterial, but you met with him and as far as I know you never even mentioned us. I'm not sure why you didn't because you gave the impression of being a decent, reliable bloke and we thought we could count on you. But you didn't. And so the problem that's been with us for two years, admittedly one of our own making, that problem has persisted. It has persisted and gnawed at our family at the very hardest of times, Sam. With our daughter dying. A couple of weeks ago, you came along and we thought we'd found our solution. Couldn't believe our luck. But since that time, you have brought infidelity into our relationship, mine and Celina's. And you have taken our daughter away from us in her final two weeks. And on one of those weeks you were where? Where were you?'

'Brazil.'

'In fucking Brazil. Now Celina, she was unhappy when I told her I'd threatened to kill you. Celina likes to deny cer-tain things. But I am the man that I am. And I'm capable of pulling the trigger even if she pretends that I'm not. She realises that. And us, we've come round here today, we've come round here with this.' He pulled out a gun. 'And I think she wants to pull the trigger herself.'

I looked at the gun. It didn't seem real somehow.

'I've not got a lot of love left for you, Sam,' Doug said.

'Sorry,' I said.

'Yeah but sorry doesn't explain things. Namely, it doesn't explain why you've fucked my life up even more than it already was.' He paused. 'It wasn't a big thing, Sam. Not for you. It was a fucking massive thing for us though.'

'I suppose I never . . .'

'Yeah?'

'I suppose I never really, I mean I never really understood.'

'What the fuck does that mean? All I wanted, put a good word in for us. How hard is that?'

I felt under pressure. I knew what I meant though. 'I mean, it was such a small thing that . . . it sort of . . . I mean, it got lost in everything else. I didn't really understand how . . . I mean, put a good word in . . . It had no . . . result. Ted would have just nodded or something and that would have been that. And, and you seemed so grateful but I never, I never really understood what I could do for you. I mean, put in a good word, OK. But how would that help? Even if you did get to meet up with Ted again. I didn't understand why it meant so much to you.' Yes, that was about it. That was right. It felt good to have got it out.

Doug just stared at me. Then Celina said, 'Tell him.'

'Eh?'

'Tell him,' Celina said. 'If he doesn't understand, tell him.'

Doug sighed.

Celina said, 'Tell him, you fucking idiot.'

Doug looked at her, then at me. 'OK,' he said. 'OK, fine.

It's probably for the best.' He paused. 'South America. We're sitting around, me, Celina, Ted and his wife and . . . To understand this you have to be clear about the kind of relationship Celina and I have. Used to have. All I care about is my family. We love each other. I was never any good at anything other than loving my family. To be honest, that's why I retired. Never had the aptitude for it. Or the stomach. Anyway, the four of us are sitting around, I don't know who suggested it . . . Well, tell a lie, it was me that suggested it, but I was fucking joking. It was a fucking joke. Then the whole thing escalates. Sort of geeing each other on. "What, you can't handle it?" "We can handle it!" "Oh, so the wife's not good enough for you?" All that. Banter. We're old friends us four. Our families. We really used to rely on each other. Ted's a man, I don't know, you've seen how people act around him. You've seen it. You know. He's got that pull. You know what I mean. We used to love seeing him and his wife. Became part of our life. Got so we really looked forward to it. Marked our visits on the calendar and all the rest of it. Week built up to them. This was in the early days. And when the four of us, we became friends, you know, proper good friends, what that done for us you'll never know. It just felt great. That friendship it just, it gave us something extra. A glow when you wake up in the morning. All great. Anyway, this banter's flying about. It gets out of hand. Whatever. And then, I don't know, it became a real thing. You know, swap wives. And we did. We did. Weren't so bad right after we done it but it poisoned everything. Ted started cutting ties, we're not invited round there so much. And, slowly, we're ostracized, cut off. We're on our own. On our own with this thing that's happened. And we just feel even now, I mean you've seen the holiday photos, we just feel that if we could look past this partner swapping thing, we could get things back on track. You know, get back to how things were with Ted and his lot. And me and Celina wouldn't be cut off. You know, alone. And I could save my family. Because so far I've failed. I've fucking failed.' He looked down at the floor.

My first thought was that Alice was right. It wasn't about Ted. They should sort things out on their own. Alice was right about a lot of things. Not everything, but a lot of things. Maybe things become clearer if you know that you're approaching death.

Celina said, 'Give me the gun.'

'Eh?'

'I said give me the fucking gun.'

'I don't think that's a good idea, love.'

'Give. Me. The. Gun.'

'Why do you want it?'

'Maybe I want to shoot you.' She stared at him.

He loosened his grip on the gun, allowed her to pull it out of his hand.

She looked at me. 'You ruined my life, Sam. Well, this idiot ruined my life. You made it worse. You took my daughter from me. You tricked me into sucking your disgusting cock. I feel absolutely sick when I think about that. I wanted you to know that. And to say fuck you. And fuck you, too, Doug. Fuck you both.' She put the gun in her mouth and pulled the trigger. Click. She pulled the trigger again. Click. Again, again. Click, click. She kept pulling the trigger but the gun didn't fire. She turned to Doug. She was shaking. 'Why isn't it loaded?'

'I thought you might try and shoot yourself. Or Sam.'

'So what?'

He just looked at her.

'SO WHAT?' She went for him; he managed to put his hands up but she kept smacking him with the gun. Eventually, he grabbed her wrists and got the gun from her. She tried to bite him but he grabbed her head and held it close to him; at first she wriggled, then she just cried into his body, shaking with tears.

I just sat there. The air was thick with grief, and I was in a heightened emotional state, tingling all over.

Doug looked at me. 'Give it one last go, mate. You've seen what a state we're in. You can do that for us. Now that you know, you can do that for us.'

Celina was still crying and Doug looked at me, a tear rolling down his cheek.

'I would,' I said. 'I don't know where Ted is though. I went over to his house. His windows are all blacked out.'

'He's gone then. That's that. He's gone.' Doug stared at the floor for a while, then he stood up and Celina flopped full length on the settee, still crying, but not so loudly.

'Shit.' Doug looked right at me. 'Shit.' Doug looked right at me. 'Shit! How many chances did you fucking need?' He came at me and grabbed me in a headlock and pulled me to the floor. Then he got to his knees and raised his fist above me. The way Doug looked, I thought he'd punch me until I was dead, but then his face crumpled into an expression of grief and his knees collapsed from under him and he lay on the floor, sobbing. And Celina was still on the settee. And I was on the floor too. All of us prostrate. It was like we'd been though a bombing attack together or something. I felt a sense of camaraderie in our grief, and I cried for Alice and felt like they were keeping me company doing the same. Then Doug got up. He just stood there for a while before Celina sat up then stood up herself. I sat on the floor looking at them.

'Ted came to see me,' I said.

'When?' Doug asked.

'A few days ago.'

'His house was blacked up?'

'Yeah.'

'He's gone.'

And then, moving as though their bodies were broken, they left the flat. It took me some while to recover.

I didn't feel like company anymore when I went out to search for Leticia. It would be a solitary search. I took a rucksack with me with a change of clothes and a toothbrush in it. I left the map behind. There was no point being methodical. Crossing off streets. I would just go wherever, follow my instinct. I would keep looking until I found her. That is what I would do.

In The Alley

I walked through the streets in a trance, eyes wide open. I stared into the crowds, scanned the faces. And it got dark and if my legs were tired I wasn't aware of it and I just kept walking. I just kept walking. Eventually I sat down and watched the people going past and I became choked up with emotion. It was just, it was all too much. I fell asleep. When I woke up my mind was filled with fragmented thoughts, I couldn't connect anything. Nothing made sense. I was confused and my eyes were wide open and every face felt like a threat, twisted, contorted in my mind's eye, and the faces surrounded me, mouths open, teeth, tongues, nostrils, and I was aware of a pounding, pounding, POUNDING in my chest but I kept my eyes on the faces, knew that I had to look at every one (For what? For *what?*) and I kept walking and my insides bled with panic and frustration. Then I stopped walking. It was dark and cold (Didn't it used to be hot?) and my chest swelled and I closed my eyes and remembered, first Alice (she's dead), then Leticia. She's in London. I smiled. She's in London. I laughed so much my chest hurt.

My body was making itself heard. My legs were stiff and my stomach was sick and gnawing at me. My mouth felt horrible and I breathed on my hand and my breath was hot and thick. I sneezed. The sun was bright but it was really quite chilly

242

out. I checked my watch. Six thirty in the morning. I feel like shit. I have to get some food. And some toothpaste. I should look in places she's likely to go. I really felt rotten. I hauled myself up and my body creaked and I ached all over. I started walking, checking the faces, but I seemed to have developed an aversion to people's faces. (Why? I couldn't remember). Each face made me feel a sort of nauseous pang. But I had to. I had to look. Just in case.

I found a sandwich shop. Nothing looked particularly appetizing but I had to eat so I got them to make me a cheese sandwich and bought a bottle of water and left. I took a bite of my sandwich and realised that eating would not be an easy task. My jaw ached and felt half numb and it was a struggle to swallow. I nibbled on the sandwich as I wandered. Eventually the faces became too much for me and I found a little square and sat down on a bench under a tree and forced myself to eat. It was quiet at first, but then people started walking past and I made myself look at them and the nauseous pangs started up again. I got up, left the rest of my sandwich on the bench, and started walking. I needed a break but there were faces everywhere and I didn't know how to get away from them. So I kept walking, and it seemed as though the streets were getting busier, but I kept looking, swallowing the nauseous pangs, feeling sicker but getting used to the sickness. Although I was aware that I was not well and kept sneezing and my body shivered. But I still scanned the faces. Looking. Looking . . .

'Come with me.' Somebody grabbed my arm and pulled me off the street and into an alley. Then he was behind me, digging something into my back. 'Keep walking.' I walked down the alley then he nudged me rightwards, into another alley. I saw an overturned bin. There was a smell of urine in the air. He let go of me.

'Alright, Sam.'

It took a second, then I realised I was looking at Ted.

'Sorry for all the cloak and dagger bollocks. I've got to watch myself.'

'That's OK.'

Ted looked agitated, nervous.

'I went looking for you, mate. You was still in Brazil I presume.'

'Yeah. I went round your house.' I hesitated. 'The windows were blacked out.'

'Absolutely.' He looked at me as if expecting something.

I didn't know what to say.

He grabbed me and shook me hard. 'Tell me then!'

'I don't understand . . .'

'You went to Rio, mate. You was there. Not like I planned it but you was there.'

'Yeah.'

'What did you fucking find out then? For fuck's sake, this is like pulling teeth.'

'I don't know . . . Nothing really. I mean, about what?'

He pushed me against the wall, pinned his arm against my throat. 'WHERE IS SHE?'

'I don't know.'

He dug his arm into my throat.

'I . . . don't . . . know . . .'

He stared at me, his arm still tight against me, then backed away.

I caught my breath. 'She wasn't there. She's in London.'

'London?'

I told him about what had happened in Rio, and what Tre had told me to tell him. He listened with a stony expression on his face; it was difficult to read him.

Then he said, 'She ain't in London.'

'Huh?'

'The one place she ain't is London. I've been following you, Sam, mate. What the fuck you playing at, wandering around the streets day and night?'

'I was looking for her.'

'You're a young bloke. Live your life.' He looked right into my eyes. 'You're alright, you. I knew you was.'

I didn't know how to respond but I knew that he meant it and felt profoundly moved.

He turned and paced the width of the alley and back again. 'Fucking Tre. This is what you get. If I weren't winding things down, Tre wouldn't fuck with me like this. I'll tell you something, you never get out.'

There was a pause, then I said, 'How do you know she's not in London?'

'Eh? Oh, how do I know? You've seen her photo, Sam. What colour is she?'

'Black.'

'What colour am I?'

'White.'

'You think she's my daughter?'

I shrugged.

'Of course she fucking ain't. She was in a shipment. Shipment meant for Tre. I took her didn't I? I took her for myself.'

'Why?'

He looked at me. 'I don't know. Why you looking for her? Something about her. I don't know.'

We were quiet for a while. Then there was a noise. Ted pulled a gun out and pointed it down the end of the alley. 'Fuck.' He rubbed his face with his hands.

'So how do you know she's not in London?'

'She's from Sierra Leone. That's where she's gone. Find her

family. I told her the truth a couple of years back. We was in South America. Worst fucking holiday I've ever had. She didn't take it well. Finding out what I was. And off she went. Find her family. Except she ain't in Sierra Leone is she? I've had it combed. So has fucking Tre.'

'So where is she?'

'I don't fucking know!'

There was a pause. Then I said, 'So why did you send me to Rio?'

'Contact gave me a tip off. Said he'd seen her at that idiot's club. The one what got shot. And she always loved Rio. She fucking loved it she did.' He paused. 'Maybe Tre set the whole thing up. Right from the start. Fuck knows, mate.'

I hesitated. 'So she could be anywhere?'

'That's about the size of it, yeah.' He looked at me. 'I love her, mate.' He paused. 'You though. You need to sort yourself out.'

'Listen, Ted. I met a guy called Doug at your barbecue, do you know who I mean?'

Before Ted could answer, there was a BANG and he fell to the floor, holding his leg, a red patch spreading on his trousers. I heard voices at the end of the alley.

I said, 'Ted, are you alright?'

'Not really.'

I heard a laugh that I recognised. Tre. He was walking towards us with two other guys; one of them was Ben. Tre was holding a shotgun.

'You two cunts are fucking geniuses,' he said. 'I've followed this one, what's your name?'

'Sam.'

'I've followed Sam. And Ted's followed Sam. So Sam's led me straight to Ted.' He went over to Ted, put one foot either side of him. 'Do you know where she is?'

'What do you think?'

Tre stepped on the wound on Ted's leg. 'Yes or no?'

Ted winced. 'No.'

'Cheers. That's what I thought. Listen, Ted, mate. I understand there's this opinion going around, I don't have no respect and all that bollocks. And that worries me. It's not an adequate reflection of my character. I respect you, bruv. What you've made of yourself. So I ain't going to torture you or nothing. I ain't even going to dust you up. I want that noted. I'm going to treat you with respect.'

'Cheers.'

Tre pointed the gun at Ted's head and blew his brains out all over the concrete. Tre stood there for a moment, then he said to Ben. 'That's going to happen to me one day you know.'

'. . . Yeah.'

'You fucking dickhead.' Tre shot Ben in the chest then, before the third guy could react, Tre shot him in the throat and the third guy went down bleeding all over the place.

Then Tre turned to me. I was petrified. He smiled at me, then hugged me. He said into my ear. 'I don't need her no more. I mean I want her, but fuck it, I don't need her. You find her, you enjoy her, yeah?' He released me, backed away. He indicated the three dead bodies. 'This'll happen to me one day.' Then he broke into a jog and at the end of the alley he jumped into a white van and the white van screeched away.

A few seconds later, I ran down the alley in the opposite direction and emerged on a crowded street.

I Think I'm Being Followed

At a pay phone I made an anonymous call to the police about the three bodies in the alleyway. I would have been more responsible, given my name and details, but I knew they'd never catch Tre and I had to go home and pack.

The flat felt strange after a few days on the street. And still and quiet. It didn't matter though. I was just packing a few things and leaving. I'd have to widen my search. I'd go to Sierra Leone first. It might be that Leticia and her family were in hiding or in another country when Tre and Ted were searching over there and now they've gone back again. After all, she didn't need to hide anymore. Ted was dead and Tre had deferred to me. Anyway, Sierra Leone was a good place to start. And maybe somebody there would know something.

Now I was sitting in my living room zipping up my suitcase. I'd packed some clothes and a wash bag and that was it. On the way back to my flat I'd checked my balance and I actually had £5,800 which was a very pleasant surprise. I'd thought I only had a few hundred pounds but £5,800, while not a huge amount, would be enough to get one of those round the world plane tickets and keep me going for quite a while in developing countries at least. And, I don't know, I could earn some money teaching English or something.

Hopefully I'll find her before I run out of money though. Right, well, I'm packed. I'd checked with the airport and the next flight out to Sierra Leone was half eleven in the morning. The time right now was three in the afternoon. What to do until then? I could go to the airport right now? Go and say goodbye to my neighbour? But I didn't feel like talking. I was fidgety, tense. Go out for a run? No. I got out of my chair and paced back and forth. She's not in London. She's not in London and I can't get a flight out of London for absolutely hours (unless I change my destination?) Shit! I went and looked out the window. An hour or so ago it had looked a little bit grey for the first time since I could remember, but now the sky was blue again and the sun was bright. I love summer, I thought. It really invites you into it. Out into the world. I started to feel cooped up in my flat. I needed to get out there. I realised that I was pressing my nose against the window. I really do need to get out there. What's the point? She's not in London. Who says so though? Ted said it was the last place she'd be. That's because he assumed she doesn't want him to find her. Maybe she's found her family and she's come back here. Leticia would forgive Ted. She wouldn't hold a grudge forever. It's possible that she's back but she was hiding out, waiting for the Tre/Ted thing to blow over. Tre thought she was in London. And if she is in London, now she'll be able to come out of hiding. I should go and look. Before I go halfway across the world I should have one last look in London. Yes. Good. I felt energised. I grabbed my keys and was about to go. Then I realised, I haven't showered and these clothes are old. If I meet her, I want to make a good impression. I pulled my wash bag and my favourite pair of jeans and my favourite T shirt out of my suitcase and went into the bathroom.

Twenty minutes later, I came out, feeling fresh and raring

to go. I was excited. I felt like something exciting might happen.

I walked up and down the streets with new hope, my eyes darting around, my heart jumping when I saw someone who might be her. I had no idea what she looked like anymore, but I knew I'd know when I saw her. The hours wore on and the sky clouded over and it started to rain and the streets thinned out and people's faces were obscured by umbrellas. I started searching in pubs and restaurants and shops; a few people, particularly in restaurants when I got too close to their table, gave me looks and raised objections and called me names but I was pretty much oblivious to it. I just kept searching and darkness fell and I went on, through the streets, pushing through bars, one thing on my mind: Find Leticia. And I sorted through the faces with painful concentration. My head hurt but it was as though my eyes were pinned open. Find Leticia. Find Leticia. That single thought was like a brick wall blocking off any other thoughts or feelings. Sometimes I tried to get past it, find Leticia, but it was no good. I kept walking. In and out of bars. Up and down streets. Find Leticia. Find Leticia. FIND LETICIA and my head was pounding and my hands were shaking. Then something else crept up on me, a feeling of apprehension. Then I realised. Someone is following me. I glanced behind me, then sped up. Who is it? I've upset loads of people lately. I felt certain that whoever it was wanted to do something terrible to me. I went into a bar and ordered a drink and sat down and my nerves calmed a little. I looked around. Lots of people. You're safe here. But then my heart started to beat faster and my legs started jigging. I was terrified. I burst out of my seat and left the bar. Outside, I had to concentrate hard not to break into a run. Then I saw a queue for a nightclub and joined the queue, leaned against the wall and closed my eyes, then I heard 'hurry up, mate,' and moved along and paid £15 and went in.

The music was pounding and bodies were everywhere and I walked up some steps and saw neon lights flashing and smoke machines puffing out smoke and looked across the dance floor and I saw her. She looked straight at me. Then the smoke machine puffed out another cloud of smoke and the smoke cleared and she was gone. I rushed onto the dance floor, pushed my way through and angry faces appeared in the corner of my eye and I got to the other side and saw the women's toilets straight ahead of me and ran in and shouted 'Leticia!' and a bouncer came and pulled me out. I stood there and my eyes darted around but the place was too crowded and I knew she was in the toilets and I went back in and hammered on the cubicle doors and the bouncer came and pulled me out and kept hold of me and shoved me out the back door and I tripped over and lay there on the road. I stood up. I was in a quiet little back street. She's in there. I tried the door I'd just been thrown out of but it didn't open from the outside. She's in there. It hit me, how close she was. Wait for her out the front. She has to come out eventually. It's the only thing you can do.

I was about to turn and go when I saw a figure walking up the road. I just stood there and the figure walked closer and then she came out of the shadows. It was her. We both stopped walking. I looked into her eyes. Her lips curled into a tiny smile. We just stood there; I didn't know what to say or do. Then something came over me. A sense of calm, a sort of serenity. You're OK, Sam. You're OK. And I felt OK, I really did. I offered her my hand.

'Hi, I'm Sam.'

Acknowledgements

My parents for their love, support and encouragement; Tim Taylor for his spirit of abandon in the face of danger; Ivy Johns (Nanny) for always believing in me; Simon Petherick for his faith in this novel; and my editor Anthony Nott, who understands my writing and has helped to make it better.

The
Beautiful
Group